Praise for *T*

About the author

Isabella rediscovered her love of writing fiction during two happy years working on and completing her MA in Professional Writing.

The setting for the *Janie Juke* mystery series is based on the area where Isabella was born and lived most of her life. When she thinks of Tamarisk Bay she pictures her birthplace in St Leonards-on-sea, East Sussex and its surroundings.

Aside from her love of words, Isabel has a love of all things caravan-like. She has enjoyed several years travelling in the UK and abroad and in recent times has been running a small campsite in West Sussex, with her husband.

Her faithful companion, Scottish terrier Hamish, is never far from her side.

Find out more about Isabella, her published books, as well as her forthcoming titles at:
www.isabellamuir.com
and follow Isabella on Twitter: **@SussexMysteries**

By the same author

**LOST PROPERTY
THE INVISIBLE CASE
IVORY VELLUM: A COLLECTION OF SHORT
STORIES**

THE TAPESTRY BAG

A JANIE JUKE MYSTERY

By Isabella Muir

Isabella Muir

Published in Great Britain
By Outset Publishing Ltd

Second edition published June 2018
First edition published October 2017

ISBN:1-872889-12-3
ISBN-978-1-872889-12-2

www.isabellamuir.com

Cover photo: by Danis Lou on Unsplash
Cover design: by Christoffer Petersen

On a summer's evening in 1969, in a quiet seaside town in Sussex, Janie Juke hears something that will turn her life upside down…

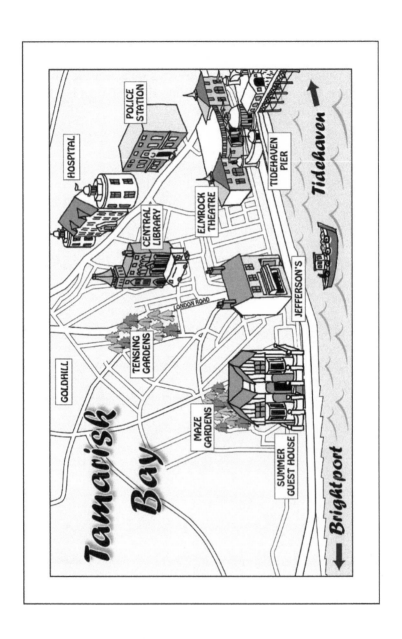

Chapter 1

There had been times when I hardly thought that Poirot
appreciated me at my true worth. 'Yes,' he continued,
staring at me thoughtfully, 'you will be invaluable.'
The Mysterious Affair at Styles - Agatha Christie

It was the last item on the news. As the newsreader
spoke Zara's name we both stopped breathing for a few
seconds. It was a moment and then it was gone. Perhaps
we'd imagined it, as now the weatherman was standing in
front of a map of the British Isles, pointing and waving
his hands, telling us a bitter wind would arrive from the
north-east.

The news report had given us so little and yet it
changed the intensity in the room. Minutes ago we were
relaxing after an ordinary day. Now it was as though a
magnetic force had entered the room, drawing us to that
snippet of news. We were both caught in our own
thoughts. Mine were for Zara. Did the report mean she
was still alive? I prayed that it did. My head was bent and
my gaze focused on my knees. In truth I was seeing
nothing, just the images that had been repeating in my
mind since the day Zara disappeared. We'd made a
connection as adults that was so much more than our
schoolday friendship and her disappearance left not a gap,
but a chasm.

I flinched as Greg put his hand on my leg.

'It's good there's news, Janie,' he said.

'Perhaps not,' I said. Both of us knew the
implications.

It would be pointless now trying to sleep. The
television was still on, the black and white images

1

flickering, but we had turned away.

'Tea?' I said, needing to focus on something to fill the void.

'Hot milk maybe.' We moved into the kitchen and Greg stood, shuffling his feet, watching me pour the milk into the small saucepan and light the gas.

'There's nothing we can do, you know that don't you?' he said.

I didn't answer.

'Don't get angry with me, I'm just saying.'

'What are you saying? You know as well as me the police have lost interest. We did more to try to find her than they did.' Opening the fridge, I took out butter and cheese, although I wanted nothing to eat. 'Do you want a sandwich?'

'No, do you?'

'I need to do something, I can't just sit around here.'

'There's nothing you or anyone else can do right now. The police have it in hand. If they didn't then it wouldn't have been on the news, would it?'

'We both know our local constabulary does not exactly have Zara high up on their list of missing persons.'

The manner of Joel's death was a shock to us all, but for Zara it was as though her world had ended the day a police officer explained to her, as gently as possible, that her boyfriend had been killed in a hit and run accident.

She was in my thoughts every day, even though Greg had persuaded me to give up on our search for her. Since the day Zara went missing I was determined not to believe what many others did; that she'd had enough. More than one person suggested that a year of grief may have been as much as her body and soul could bear.

I'd left the spare room just as it was the day she

disappeared. I regularly aired and dusted in there, foolishly imagining one day she would walk back into our lives and everything would be right again.

'Early start tomorrow?' I asked Greg, just for the want of hearing a voice that might dull the sounds in my head.

'Same as usual,' he said and we sipped our hot milk in silence.

The newsreader's words were on a repeat loop in my mind, '*There has been a new development in the police case regarding Zara Carpenter, the young woman who went missing three months ago in the seaside resort of Tamarisk Bay.*'

I had to force myself not to grab my coat and march down to the police station, demanding to know more about this 'new development'. I went back into the sitting room where the television was still entertaining two empty chairs. A late-night news programme had started and the presenter was reporting on the latest events in Vietnam; thousands of young men dead.

'What are you doing? Don't watch, it'll only depress you.' Greg stood at the doorway and held out his hand. 'Turn the stupid thing off and come to bed.'

'I remember now why I avoid the news. I'll come in a minute.'

I turned the television off and put our mugs in the sink. I heard Greg use the bathroom, brush his teeth and then pad through to our bedroom. I climbed the stairs purposefully, pleased to be moving, hoping any action might distract me from my thoughts. Instead of going into our bedroom, I opened the door opposite and walked into the spare room. I smoothed down the bedspread and plumped up the pillows. The curtains were open, letting the light from the lamppost across the road shine onto the simple wooden furniture. A room

3

that had offered my friend a comfortable sanctuary now felt bare and empty.

I had looked through the chest of drawers many times since she left, wishing I would find something that she had left behind, a clue to where she had gone and why. Now I opened each drawer again, the emptiness mirroring a hollow sensation I couldn't shake off. Running my fingers over the empty spaces, I tried to picture Zara starting a new life somewhere. But the image was as vague as an early morning fret, blocking out the sun and chilling the air.

Greg was already asleep by the time I got into bed. I wished for the instant switch he seemed to have, to go from waking to sleep, with no tossing and turning in between. I took a book from my bedside table. I was half-way through it, but now I couldn't even recall the storyline. I read a few lines and then read them again. The letters jumbled up in front of me and for the first time in my life the words were just ink marks on the page.

It was Zara's face I saw when I closed my eyes much later that night. Zara who had come back into my life unexpectedly, only to leave again in such strange circumstances.

Chapter 2

Surely her face grew a little paler as she answered: 'Yes'.
The Mysterious Affair at Styles - Agatha Christie

I first met Zara when she joined our school in the fourth year. We were inseparable for those last eighteen months of our schooldays, meeting up at weekends and hanging around coffee bars and record shops. Shortly after she finished school she moved away with her family. We wrote to each other for a while, but soon the letters dried up and we lost touch. Then, nearly six years later, I was strolling through the town centre and noticed something familiar about the person I was following. Seeing her back view made me pause as I ran through a mental checklist. The willowy figure ahead of me reminded me of someone. It was only when she paused to glance in a bookshop window and I saw her profile, that everything fell into place.

'Zara,' I called out. I walked towards her and put my hand on her shoulder. She turned and for a moment I couldn't tell if she was choosing to ignore me, or if it was just that her memory wasn't as sharp as mine. Then her face transformed into a beaming smile and she held her arms out to me.

'Janie,' she said and we embraced. We strolled arm in arm as we caught up on the last few years. I told her how our English teacher, Mrs Frobisher, had got me a job looking after the mobile library van. She laughed when I reminded her how we used to joke about Mrs Frobisher's hairy chin, while in truth we both wished she could have been our grandmother. She asked about dad's physiotherapy practice and told me how she had fond memories of Charlie, dad's German Shepherd. I flashed my wedding ring at her and told her about Greg. She said how thrilled she was for me.

Later when I was at home, recounting my chance encounter to Greg, I realised she'd said little about her life. I'd been so busy chatting away, I hadn't even asked her why she'd moved back. I didn't even know then whether she had moved back, or if she was only passing through.

We arranged to meet the next day for lunch and a proper catch up, so when I arrived at the café I was armed with all the right questions. I was taken by surprise to find Zara was not alone. As I approached the table she stood up.

'Janie, meet Joel,' she said. She blushed as I went to hug her and sat down next to Joel, taking his hand in hers.

Joel's chiselled looks made me wonder if he was a male model. His hair was neatly styled, his perfect teeth shining white, in contrast to his bronzed skin.

'Pleased to meet you,' I said and shook his hand, feeling rather stupid about my formal greeting.

'Joel's a photographer,' Zara said.

'I thought there was something familiar about you, but I couldn't put my finger on it,' I said to him. 'You've held exhibitions at the Elmrock Theatre, haven't you? Quite a talent by all accounts.'

'Did you have a chance to visit? They've promised me another slot, maybe next year,' he said, with enthusiasm.

'I didn't go, but I saw the reviews in the *Observer*. You've got a star there, Zara.'

She beamed and couldn't have looked prouder if she had been chosen for the front cover of *Vogue*. They were the perfect match. A beautiful couple. Zara's olive skin and almond-shaped eyes had always been the envy of all her classmates. At school her thick dark hair was cut into a chic bob, but now it flowed loosely over her shoulders and down her back.

She explained she'd recently moved back into the area from Brighton.

'How did you two meet?' I asked.

She told me how she wandered into Joel's photographic studio to hand in a roll of film and came out with an invitation for a date.

'My lucky day,' Joel said. He told me Zara had moved into his flat over the studio and was looking around for work.

'What kind of work?' I asked her. 'What were you doing in Brighton?'

'Zara wants to change the world,' Joel said.

It was inevitable that the relationship Zara and I had as adults felt different to our earlier friendship. We were no longer a couple of schoolgirls fascinated with the pop and fashion scene. The intriguing side of Zara, that had been there in its embryonic form when we were fifteen, had developed. Now when we met I would chat away, while she listened intently, probing me with questions. When I mentioned dad and how busy he was with patients, she'd ask me which type of patients he preferred, ones with physical ailments only, or ones who benefitted from his counselling.

'He just chats to them, it's not really counselling,' I explained.

'He gives them time, someone to relate to; we all need that,' she said.

She asked me how dad felt about the war.

'He was just a boy when he joined up. He never talks about it,' I said.

'So many young men killed, a whole generation.'

'They had no choice though. Hitler was mad, he had to be stopped.'

'All fighting is mad,' she said.

Our conversations didn't just help me view the world differently - it was more than that. It was as though she was looked outside the confines of her own life and it fascinated me. She questioned everything, always trying to establish the reasons for actions and showing concern for the potential consequences. Looking at the world through Zara's eyes I could imagine layers of meaning I had never considered.

The times we spent together were limited. It was natural she'd want to spend her weekends with Joel, after all, they were in the early throes of their relationship. Occasionally we met up as a foursome, but the men soon got bored as they had little in common, which meant Zara and I had to work hard to keep the conversation flowing. Greg loved his football, but it appeared that Joel wasn't interested in any sport. He'd introduced Zara to art galleries and museums, which was Greg's idea of the worst possible tedium.

So, Zara and I met up on our own, although Joel tended to be the main topic of conversation. She was enthralled by him and it was easy to understand why. He'd taken over the photographic studio a couple of years earlier and made a huge success of it. She explained that he was self-taught, even though his dad had had more than a passing interest in photography. Having met Joel, I started to watch out for his name among the photo credits in the local paper. He'd built up an impressive

8

reputation as a wedding photographer. His style was quite distinctive. Rather than the traditional approach, with the happy couple posing in front of the church door, he wasn't afraid to try out something new. One of his trademark shots was a head and shoulders of a bride, looking in a mirror at her groom, who was looking over her shoulder. Clever.

When it was just Zara and me, and the weather permitted, we walked along the seafront and chatted, stopping en route at one of the new coffee bars that had opened at the bottom of London Road. My favourite was *Jefferson's*. Richie, the chap who ran it, was really into his music and he installed a juke box. Zara and I took turns to choose a record, pleading with Richie to turn the volume up loud, which must have delighted the poor couple who lived in the flat above.

Sometimes we met in town and wandered around clothes shops, window shopping, drooling over everything we coveted, but couldn't afford. Mary Quant's designs had filtered down from London, with local boutiques offering decent copies, but without the label. Even copies were outside our budget. We spent hours browsing through fashion magazines featuring Twiggy, with her big eyes, close cropped hair and boyish figure. Zara dared me to get my long dark hair cut and coloured, but I would never have been brave enough. Instead we used to practise posing like Twiggy, in front of shop mirrors, ignoring the dubious glares from the shop assistants.

During our schooldays we'd jigged around to Elvis and Adam Faith, but now we had new favourites. We still loved our music and had followed the meteoritic rise of the Beatles, dreaming about the day when we could hear them live. Like thousands of other fans we were mortified over the rumours that they might disband and frustrated that we couldn't have been in London for their impromptu live session on the roof of the Apple building. We found a record shop in King's Road with booths where you could listen to the record of your choice, without having to buy it. We got to be regulars, so the chap running the shop would have Beatles' singles lined up for us as soon as we came in.

It was easy enough for me to get a few spare hours in the week to meet her. Dad remembered her from when she used to be a regular visitor at our house during that last year of school.

'It's great you've met up again,' he said, when I told him. 'What's she been up to all these years?'

I tried to raise the topic a few times with Zara, asking her what type of work she was looking for, what she'd been doing in Brighton.

'You should work in fashion, you'd be brilliant,' I told her. 'You could start off in one of the boutiques in town, learn all there is to know. Imagine all those beautiful window displays you could create.'

'It's a thought,' was all she said. I wondered how she was managing for money. I guessed Joel was helping her out. He was certainly doing well enough and from everything Zara had told me, he seemed to be a generous sort.

'She'll find something when she's ready,' Greg said, when I raised the subject one evening over dinner. 'Perhaps her parents are subbing her.'

'I doubt it. She never mentions them. I might ask her, see what she says.'

'Don't interfere. She won't thank you for it in the end.

Enjoy her company and let her find her own way. If she's not worried about money, then accept she's okay.'

'Mm, maybe.'

The next time I saw her I did my usual and ignored Greg's advice.

'So, how are your parents?' I asked her. 'Are they well?'

'They've moved back to France. We don't keep in touch.'

'Oh, that's a shame.' Digging any further felt like prying, but I couldn't stop myself. 'I know it's none of my business, but you don't appear to be too anxious to get a job? Are you okay for money?' As I said the words I felt as though I'd overstepped the mark. Greg was right, it was none of my business.

'I've got an interview at the new boutique in Queen's Road. It's tomorrow, you can help me choose what to wear, if you like?'

'Yes, I'd love to,' I said. I wondered if she would have told me if I hadn't asked. Perhaps I'd have walked in one day and found her behind the shop counter.

It was the first time she'd invited me into their flat. She popped her head into the studio where Joel was serving a customer. 'Is it okay if I take Janie upstairs? She's going to help me choose something for the interview.'

'Good idea. Apologies in advance for the mess, we have too much fun to bother about housework, don't we, gorgeous?' he said, winking at Zara. 'Go for something sexy, that's bound to get you the job. That little black number, the one I bought you last week, it makes you look real cute.'

'He's smitten, isn't he?' I said, following her up the narrow staircase.

'I can't believe how lucky I am to have found him, Janie, he's everything I could wish for. Generous, kind, clever, he could have anyone.'

'From where I'm standing, I would say he's lucky too. You're a well-matched pair. Now, what's all this about a mess?'

I don't know what I expected to see as we walked into the flat. Perhaps I'd imagined tasteful black and white prints covering the walls, psychedelic colours, modern, minimal furniture. Instead there was nothing groovy about the two small rooms, nothing to reflect the talented photographer and his fashion-conscious girlfriend. The living room had a corner kitchenette with two gas rings and a small sink, filled with dirty cups and a couple of pans. I couldn't tell if the cupboard doors were supposed to be pale yellow, or if they were discoloured with smoke and grease. A small two-seater sofa was pushed up against one wall with a patchwork blanket thrown over it, which partly hid its stained and threadbare arms. There was a little folded table, which I guessed they used for mealtimes and two wooden chairs, positioned beside a half-empty bookshelf.

'Cup of tea?' Zara asked me, as she poured herself a glass of water.

'Er, no, you're okay. Shall we go through your wardrobe then? Find you the perfect outfit?'

I followed her into the bedroom. The curtains were pulled closed, making the room dark and airless. Once she opened them it made little difference to the murky light and musty smell. The bed was flanked by two old-fashioned wardrobes, and on one side was a small chair, with what appeared to be several pairs of Joel's trousers and various shirts thrown across it.

'This is mine,' she said, revealing a half-empty wardrobe. She slid the hangers across the rail. 'There's this black dress that Joel got me, or if not, how about this black one, the neckline might be better for an interview? Or this grey one? What do you think?'

Zara's knowledge of French fashion intrigued all of us in our clique of school friends. She could even make the school uniform appear chic. Knowing she had a French mother created a romantic air about her and her subdued nature only added to the mystery. The girls at school joked that Zara could wear a paper bag and still be stylish and her beauty hadn't faded, but it seemed her confidence had. She could carry off the boldest of pinks, the most startling yellow, but now it was as though she wanted to blend into the background with blacks and greys.

'Try this?' I suggested, handing her a black dress with white edging around the neck. 'What jewellery do you have? I can just see it, with loads of bright coloured beads and big, bold earrings. You can borrow some of mine, if you like?'

She ferreted around in one of the chest of drawers and by the time we'd finished she looked stunning.

'Take a look at yourself, you'll walk into the job, no problem. Remember to smile.' When we were inside the flat there was an uncertainty about Zara, she was no longer the girl who jigged around to Sgt Pepper and posed like Twiggy. My laughing, colourful friend had become monochrome.

She got the job in the Q boutique and life appeared to be taking an upward turn for Zara, but just a short time later her world fell apart.

Chapter 3

'The moment has come,' said Poirot thoughtfully, 'and I do not know what to do. For, see you, it is a big stake for which I play. No-one but I, Hercule Poirot, would attempt it!'
The Mysterious Affair at Styles - Agatha Christie

It was pure chance that resulted in me hearing about Joel's accident within hours of it happening. I'd arranged to meet Zara that morning. She was going to help me choose an outfit for a wedding Greg and I had been invited to. I wasn't even sure I wanted to go, but it was the daughter of one of Greg's regular customers who was getting wed. Greg was looking forward to it and I felt an obligation. Coincidentally, Joel was to be the wedding photographer.

Zara was the perfect person to clothes shop with. I told her I was completely in her hands, as long as the outfit was within my budget. The budget, of course, presented the ultimate challenge as it needed to stretch to a bag and shoes, but at least I didn't need a hat.

We'd agreed to meet at the café on the Pier at 11am. There was no sign of Zara when I arrived. I got myself an orange juice and sat at one of the tables by the window so I could spot her arriving. After half an hour she was still not in evidence, so I paid for my drink and left. What little I knew of Zara's nature made me doubt she would have forgotten me, or let me down by not turning up. Without any other means of contacting her, I decided to call round to the flat. Perhaps she'd been laid low with a bug of some kind.

The entrance to Joel's flat was to the side of the shop, down a passageway and up an iron staircase. As I approached, I spotted a police car parked in the street, a little way from the studio. Two policemen were sitting in the front, deep in conversation and a policewoman was just getting into the back.

I climbed the staircase and knocked rather timidly at first, half worried Zara might be asleep. When there was no response I knocked a little louder and a few seconds later the door opened. As soon as I saw her I realised something was dreadfully wrong. She was wearing a cotton wrap, pulled clumsily around her, covering what I imagined were her nightclothes. She had bare feet and her hair hung unbrushed across her face. She was so far removed from the immaculately presented Zara I was used to seeing that I gasped. She said nothing, but stood back from the door, allowing me to enter the dimly lit hallway.

'Bless you, Zara, you don't look well at all. I'm so sorry, I've got you out of bed, haven't I? It was just when you didn't turn up…' I paused, wondering whether in her poorly state she had forgotten we were going to meet. 'You were going to help me choose some clothes for that silly wedding. But hey, it really doesn't matter at all. Get yourself back to bed and I'll make you a hot drink.'

She remained motionless in front of me. It was as though she hadn't heard a word I'd said and was barely aware of me standing there. I took her hand and, as gently as I could, I led her towards the bedroom. She followed me, unquestioning and once we were in the room I put my hand on her shoulder and eased her down to sit on the bed. A bed that strangely was still made, neat and tidy.

It was difficult to know whether to leave her to go to the kitchen, or if it was better to forget the drink and persuade her to get into bed. I decided on the latter. Pulling back the bedcover I gestured to her to lay down. At that point she started to scream. The sound was chilling, as though some part of her was breaking. I clasped my arms around her tightly and held her close to me, not knowing what else to do. I expected a banging on the door at any moment, a neighbour wondering who was being murdered. After a few seconds she stopped as suddenly as she'd started.

She was sitting beside me now and I sensed she felt a little calmer. And then she spoke.

'Joel is dead,' she said, in a voice devoid of emotion. Then she laid on the bed and pulled the covers over her. 'I need to sleep now,' she said. 'Stay with me.' It was a statement, not a question.

I stayed, of course, stroking her head, trying to ease her into a restful slumber. As I watched her, a hundred questions tumbled around in my mind. Had she taken a drug of some kind? Friends of friends had been experimenting with LSD. Tales of hallucinations and weird trips were bandied about when Greg and I were down the pub. Yet I couldn't imagine Zara being stupid enough to try anything so dangerous.

She had a dark side to her, thoughts she would never share with me. Occasionally a shadow would pass across her eyes and she would lose attention for a while. It was that secret side of Zara that had always intrigued me, if I was honest. I'd never known anyone quite like her. All my other schoolfriends were much like me, interested in the fun side of life, but clueless when it came to anything important like politics or world affairs. Zara was different. She got into a row once about the Cuba crisis. I came home from school and had to search for Cuba on an atlas. But politics was one thing; I still couldn't see her dabbling with hard drugs.

Zara fell into a fitful sleep for an hour or so. I sat in a wicker chair beside the bed, watching her as she twisted and turned. A few times she called out in her sleep, but her words were incomprehensible and as I stroked her head she settled again. When she woke she looked surprised to see me sitting beside her.

'Janie,' she said. 'I've been asleep.' It was as if she wanted to apologise for dozing off.

'Let me get you a hot drink. Stay in bed, I'll bring it to you.'

She settled back down, with her head on the pillow.

'The police,' she said, pausing, as though completing a sentence was beyond her.

'Ssh, try to rest. We don't need to talk now. I'll stay with you.'

She nodded and closed her eyes again. Greg wouldn't be worried about me for several hours. He knew well enough that a shopping trip with Zara would last a while.

It was late afternoon before she finally repeated the words of the police officer. She didn't add to them, just said them starkly, like lines in a play she hadn't rehearsed. All she'd been told was that Joel had been killed in a car accident and the driver hadn't reported the crash. A hit and run. A phrase that runs off the tongue and takes no account of the devastation that follows in its wake.

As she dozed again I moved quietly around the room and gathered a few things for her. There was a tapestry bag stuffed into the bottom of her wardrobe. I pulled it out and put it on the chair. Then I just needed to choose some outfits from among the skirts and dresses we'd looked at together only a few weeks before. One of the doors of Joel's wardrobe was partly open and as I tugged at the wooden handle it came off in my hand. I tried to push it back in place, but giving up, I left it on the bedside table.

I checked the cupboard in the kitchenette for any food that might need using up, or throwing away, but apart from a few tins and two packets of cream crackers, that was it. The little fridge was bare as well, just half a pint of milk and some dried-up cheese. I poured the milk down the sink and threw away the cheese, gathering the rubbish bag together and putting it next to the front door, so I could take it with me when we left.

As I straightened the cushions on the settee, I noticed something stuffed down the back of the seat. I pushed my hand down and retrieved a small diary. Determined not to breach her privacy, I left the diary unopened and put it into the top of the bag.

Once I had all I thought she might need, I scanned the room again to see if I had forgotten anything. At that point I remembered her makeup. I hadn't come across anything in the bedroom drawers, so I guessed she must have kept it all in the bathroom cabinet. Her makeup store was minimal; just one lipstick, a powder compact and mascara and a couple of eyeshadows. When Zara and I had become reacquainted, the heavily made-up trends of our teenage years had been replaced with a bare-faced look. She could carry it off better than most; the merest hint of mascara and a pale lipstick did nothing to detract from her beauty.

Once Zara woke I helped her to wash and dress. She was childlike in her movements. I asked her to hold out her arms as I slid a tee-shirt over her head. Ferreting through the pile of trousers laying over the back of the chair I chose a black cotton pair, which looked more like Zara's than Joel's. She followed me meekly around the flat while I checked everything was switched off. I wrote a note cancelling the milk, rolled it up and popped it inside one of the milk bottles, before putting it outside the front door. I told her simply she was coming to stay at my house for as long as she wanted and I wouldn't take any argument. She said nothing, but her acquiescence was evident from her manner.

Greg opened the door to us when we got back to my house. He grinned, ready to launch into some teasing comment about how much we'd bought, how much I'd spent. Before he said anything, I shook my head and motioned to the bag I'd packed for Zara while she slept. As we walked through our little hallway I whispered to him, 'Put the kettle on? I'm just taking Zara upstairs.' He raised an eyebrow as a silent question. I shook my head in answer and mouthed, 'Thank you'.

Once I'd settled her into our spare bedroom and persuaded her to rest, I went down to the kitchen to tell Greg about the bizarre events of the day. I had been in action mode, not allowing myself time to think about the tragedy. Now, recounting the news of Joel's death, it felt chillingly real. I could only imagine how it must be for Zara.

'She'll feel as though she's fallen into her worst nightmare,' I told Greg, as he held my hand. 'We're going to need to be strong for her to help her through. I'm sure she hasn't taken it in yet. Who knows how she'll be when it hits her. How can it have happened? Why would someone just leave him lying there?' I could feel my face flushing with rage.

'Calm down. I know it's dreadful, but these things happen. Maybe the driver didn't realise...'

'Are you crazy? You don't hit someone and not know it. More likely the driver was drunk, or speeding, or both.'

'Don't get mad at me, I'm just saying...'

'What? What are you saying? That it's just one of those things? A young man gets killed and no-one is accountable?'

It was at Greg's suggestion I walked down to the phone box at the end of our road and called the police. I told the duty officer that Zara was a friend and she'd been given some bad news but didn't feel able to talk about it. He gave me the bare bones, no more than the brief report that appeared on the television that evening.

Joel Stewart, 26-year-old photographer from Sussex, was knocked down by a vehicle today and did not survive his injuries. The driver did not stop to report the incident. Would anyone who might have information relating to the incident, please contact Tidehaven Police Station.

I told the police Zara would be staying with us, giving them our name and address. I waited for them to turn up that evening and tell us they had found the driver, that he had come into the police station full of guilt. I imagined how Zara might get some comfort that at least someone would be charged and made accountable for this thoughtless event that had ended Joel's life. I didn't expect what did happen, which was absolutely nothing.

Chapter 4

'Why did you not tell me? Why? Why?' He appeared to
be in an absolute frenzy.
'My dear Poirot,' I expostulated, 'I never thought it would
interest you. I didn't know it was of any importance.'
'Importance? It is of the first importance!'
The Mysterious Affair at Styles - Agatha Christie

Over the following weeks Zara spent much of her time
sitting in our kitchen, staring out of the little window that
overlooked the back yard. When she wasn't there she
would be in her bedroom, or at the kitchen table, with her
head down on her hands. The fundamental depth of her
grief was frightening to watch. Sometimes I came home
from food shopping to find her curled up on the sofa
with one of my jackets covering her, as if the thought of
wakefulness was too much to bear. Some people find
sleep itself a fearful thing after a trauma, bringing with it
dark dreams from which there is no escape, except to
wake up into the living nightmare. But for Zara it seemed
that sleep was her only solace. There was no medication
involved either, on prescription or out of a bottle.

   Each day Greg and I waited for her to go to bed in
the evening before we turned on the television, hoping
for more information about the accident. After the initial
news report there was little coverage.

   The local paper presented a double-page spread,
focusing on Joel's photography. Alongside the photos
they printed letters from grateful customers. The
editorial suggested he had the potential to be
internationally famous, such was the calibre of his work.

   For a couple of weeks there were articles about the

tragedy of hit-and-run accidents, sparking letters to the editor over the lack of speed restrictions. One letter-writer complained it was a foolhardy idea that young people should be allowed to drive, when they were all probably smoking pot and drinking alcohol. The assumption being made was that the driver was young and careless.

Joel's parents travelled down from Scotland as soon as they learned about the accident and made all the arrangements for the funeral. They tried to involve Zara, but she was in no fit state. After the short ceremony in the little chapel, his father stood beside the grave, looking as though his heart had broken and his mother wept, clinging onto her husband's arm. After the burial they walked across to shake Zara's hand. She had been standing with us on the opposite side of the grave. She bowed her head and said nothing.

I persuaded them to come back to our house afterwards, although they were concerned they would be putting us out. The few sandwiches I'd made were barely touched, neither were the beers that Greg had bought. We moved around each other in our little sitting room. I don't know which of us felt more awkward.

'You're a devoted friend to Zara, she'll really need your support,' Mr Stewart said. 'My son wrote to us, telling us about his new girlfriend. We had hoped the first time we met her it would have been in happier circumstances.'

'They were close,' I said. 'They hadn't been together long, but you could see how well matched they were.'

'No-one should have to bury their child,' Mr Stewart said and looked away.

'What will happen to his studio?' I asked, trying to ease

his discomfort by providing another focus.

'We'll stay to sort out the lease, clear the flat. If Zara wants to stay on there, then I'm sure something can be arranged.'

'I don't want to speak for her, but I've a feeling she won't want to go back there. Too many memories.'

A few of Joel's regular customers attended the funeral, as well as Petula, the girl who used to help out in the photographic studio on a Saturday. Mr Stewart thanked everyone for coming. Zara chose not to speak, she had barely spoken a word since the accident. I hoped things might be a little easier for her once the funeral was over.

The weeks passed and nothing much changed. She slept a lot and would often sit in front of the television with her eyes glazed, unaware when the test card came on. I tried to make sure she ate something each day, but she said she had little appetite.

I called into Q Boutique straight after the accident, telling them Zara wouldn't be in until further notice. As the time passed I accepted they wouldn't be able to keep her job open forever. When I attempted to talk to her about it she just shook her head. 'I can't think about that now,' was her stock reply to most things. She never asked or spoke about the accident. Of course, it made sense she was trying to push the memory away as much as she could.

Then, after she had been with us about six months, it was as though a switch had been clicked. She was now awake most of the day and night. Perhaps her body had squirreled away enough sleep and now she was feeding off the store. Some days when Greg had an extra early start for a customer, I would join him for his first cuppa.

We'd arrive in the kitchen to find Zara already there, sitting quietly, sipping her second, or third cup of coffee. When I returned from shopping, or from dad's, she would greet me at the door, as though she'd been hovering in the hallway for the whole time I'd been out. Greg and I usually gave in to yawns just after 10pm and we would leave her sitting on the sofa, looking bright-eyed, as though she'd just woken.

We still avoided the television news when she was around and would only glance at newspapers when we were out of the house, but we didn't really expect to hear any reports about Joel. It was unlikely now that the driver would suddenly turn up and admit to their crime. Nevertheless, we waited and hoped.

The months passed by and I could tell Greg was becoming increasingly irritated by her presence.

'Haven't we done enough for her now,' he whispered to me one evening, when she had gone up to her room.

'Do you want me to throw her out? Is that what you're suggesting?'

'No, I'm just saying. We're not helping her move on, at some point she needs to get a grip and sort her life out.'

'There speaks my considerate husband. Where do you think she can go? She's got no money, Joel's flat is no longer an option and she's lost her job.'

'She could go stay with her folks. I know the two of you have become close friends, but friendship should work both ways, shouldn't it? Seems to me she is taking advantage of your kindness.'

'You're all heart,' I said and made a point of turning my back on him.

The one-year anniversary of Joel's death fell on a Thursday and I was acutely aware of the importance of the day. Every day for a week beforehand I brought the subject up with Zara, as gently as I could.

'Um, would you like to go somewhere together next Thursday?' I asked her. She glanced at me quizzically, as though she didn't understand the question.

'Would you prefer to be on your own next Thursday, or would you like company?' was another tack.

Eventually I surmised she was planning her own commemoration and it was best to leave her to it.

As far I knew she'd never once been to the cemetery. I made several visits over the months following his death, it was an easy detour on my way back from dad's. Whenever I visited, mine were the only flowers and I found myself apologising to Joel.

'You're not forgotten, you know, it's just that it's too painful for her still,' I whispered, looking around furtively and praying no-one would think me crazy to be talking to a gravestone. 'By not visiting she can pretend you've gone on a trip and one day you'll come home.' I liked this idea myself in truth.

Greg had promised to finish work early that Thursday and dad was happy for me to take the afternoon off. After a few weeks of glorious weather, the forecasters said it was due to break, so Greg and I planned a walk together beside the river and a picnic. We sat on the banks of the river and talked about fishing. Neither of us had ever tried it and doubtless we never would, but on that day it seemed like the perfect pastime to while away a warm afternoon. When we returned from our river walk, I didn't immediately panic when Zara wasn't sitting downstairs, or even hovering in the hall.

'Looks as though Zara's gone out. That's positive isn't it? She could be visiting the cemetery after all.'

I rifled through cookery books, looking at fish recipes. We waited to cook supper until she returned. In the end, we had beans on toast.

By 8pm we were both anxious. I knocked on her bedroom door, half hoping she would be curled up, back in sleep mode. Having no response, I pushed open the door to gaze with dismay at an empty room. For the last year the tapestry bag I'd packed for her had sat on the chair by the window. It was as though by leaving it there she was reminding herself that our spare room would only ever be a temporary home for her. Now the chair was empty, as was the wardrobe and the chest of drawers.

'Is there a note?' Greg asked, having followed me into the bedroom.

'Not an obvious one. Where do you think she's gone?' The churning in my stomach had nothing to do with hunger.

After two days I was convinced she must have had an accident. I woke in a sweat from a series of nightmares involving various car crashes, with Zara's bloodied face staring up at me. I visited the local hospital, asking at reception if she'd been admitted, half dreading the reply.

'She's taken her bag, all her things,' I said, hoping Greg would appreciate the importance of my words. But his expression was blank.

'Don't you see, if she took all her belongings then it must mean she's okay. Someone doesn't pack a bag if they intend to end it all,' I said.

His impassive expression did nothing to allay my fears.

I hadn't told Greg that when I did another search of her room that first night I found a note. It was screwed up at the back of one of the drawers, as though she had written it and then thought better of it. All it said was: *'I can't do this anymore.'*

Late evening on the second day I contacted the police. Greg was less than enthusiastic about the idea.

'They'll say she's an adult,' he said, the exasperation evident in his voice, 'she can choose to go where she wants without telling anyone. We'll be done for wasting police time.'

The police were understanding, but said there was little they could do unless we feared suspicious circumstances. They suggested we do our own search, put up posters, speak to people who knew her. So we launched our own campaign. The local newspaper agreed to print a notice in their latest edition, with Zara's photo. We got some posters printed and put them up all around the town. One of the posters was pinned up inside the mobile library and I asked every customer who came in to study it.

'Are you sure you haven't seen her?' I said to each of them. A few of my regulars stopped coming in for their weekly library book exchange, fearing me pouncing on them as soon as they stepped in the door. I scanned each person who passed the library van, confident I would spot her strolling by.

The days and weeks passed and there was nothing, no leads. Zara had vanished. We turned the television on each night, hoping for some mention of her, dreading the news she'd been found hurt, or worse.

It was Greg who voiced what I'd been thinking since that first day. 'Maybe she'd just had enough,' he said one evening.

'Don't say it, I don't want to hear it.'

'Okay, but we may have to face it.'

'She never cried you know. I've never seen her cry.'

Now the television news has given us a glimmer of hope. There is a new lead. I pray it means my friend is alive and well.

Chapter 5

'Like a good detective story myself,' remarked Miss
Howard. 'Lots of nonsense written, though. Criminal
discovered in last Chapter. Every one dumbfounded.
Real crime – you'd know at once.'
The Mysterious Affair at Styles - Agatha Christie

Tuesdays and Thursdays are my days at dad's. My dad is
blind. I was five years old when a bus ran into him. He
was crossing the road to get me a doughnut. It had been
snowing, a light sprinkling that made the roads glisten.
Beautiful to gaze at, but treacherous to drive on or to
walk across. I watched the accident unfold and, like they
say about any tragic event, it happened in slow motion. If
I close my eyes I can feel the chill of the snowflakes and
hear the screech of the horn when the bus driver realised
too late what was going to happen. He retired on the
grounds of ill health after my dad's encounter with his
front wheels. The police said it was an unfortunate
accident, the weather was to blame, but that poor driver
blamed himself.

He visited dad in hospital several times. According to
the nurses, he'd sit beside dad's bed, rarely speaking.
Dad's eyes were all bandaged up, so he often didn't know
who was visiting him, particularly if they didn't say a
word. We never heard from the bus driver again after
dad came out of hospital. It's no surprise he didn't keep
in touch, but I think about him from time to time and
hope he's okay.

On the rare occasion I was allowed to visit my dad in
hospital I'd sing to him. Nursery rhymes mostly,
anything to make him smile. Sometimes the nurses

would join in. One afternoon we even got a few of the other patients on the ward joining in with *Oh, the Grand Old Duke of York*, until a doctor arrived to do his rounds and Matron told us all to hush up. I was certain the doctor would have enjoyed it as much as the rest of us, he looked like a cheery sort as far as I remember.

Dad's sister, Aunt Jessica, moved in to look after me at around the same time as mum moved out. When her strapping detective became a blind ex-policeman who needed a helping hand, mum decided that hand wouldn't be hers.

Once he was out of hospital it took dad ages to get used to moving around the house. He kept bumping into furniture, or fumbling for light switches. I never understood why he bothered with the light switch. I figured being blind meant you would be forever in the dark, regardless of the time of day or night. When I was old enough to understand, he explained how sometimes he could see vague shadows, different patterns of light and shade. He told me he wanted to carry on as he was before. If that meant switching on a light when he entered a room, then he'd jolly well do just that.

If I had to sum my dad up in one word, it would be 'determined'. For a while it was the three of us, Aunt Jessica, dad and me. Then Charlie came to stay. Charlie was the first of a series of beautiful German Shepherd dogs who have become dad's eyes. When Charlie the 1st came to live with us I thought he was just there for me to play with. He was nearly two years old and had learned how to be a proper guide dog, but once he was off shift he was ready to act like a puppy again. He and I would run around the garden together until we dropped from pleasurable exhaustion.

By the time Charlie the 1st was seven and I was ten, dad had applied to study physiotherapy. He'd mastered pretty much everything else about day-to-day living, with Charlie's help, and now it was time for him to discover a new career.

After the war dad had joined the police force. He was getting used to it all and from what he's told me he loved every minute; the organisation, the rules and the fact he was making a difference. After a couple of years as a bobby on the beat, watching out for children whose worse misdemeanours were scrumping, he was promoted to detective. It was temporary at first, giving him an opportunity to learn the ropes. But it wasn't to be.

It wasn't only his eyes that were damaged in the accident. His left leg had broken in two places. The physiotherapists performed wonders and that, together with dad's natural persistence, means he's barely got a limp now. So, his new career choice reflected his experience during those first weeks after his accident. He transferred all his visual skills into his fingers.

'The physiotherapy team helped me realise there was a difference between living a life or just existing,' he told me much later, when I was old enough to understand.

Aunt Jessica stayed with us for nine years. Then, on my fourteenth birthday she announced it was time for her to do some exploring. As far as I know she'd never fallen in love, in fact, I never found out what she was doing before she came to live with us. My dad and I owed her a huge debt; like the physiotherapy team she had made the difference between us having a life or just existing. Without her we would have even struggled to do the latter.

After she left we received regular postcards from all

over Europe. I read them out to dad, tracing her journey on the atlas. She travelled by train through France and Switzerland, into Italy and across to Greece. I envisaged her on her adventures, promising myself I'd do the same thing. As soon as I left school I'd be off. When it came to it that was the last thing on my mind. Right now I have no idea where Aunt Jessica is. When we last heard from her she wrote to tell us she planned to explore life in a commune.

I let myself in the front door and called out hello. Dad was chatting to Charlie, something about the promise of a walk later, when the rain stopped.

'Hi, how are things?' I said, as I headed for the kitchen and put the kettle on.

'You've heard the news?' he said, knowing I wouldn't want to bother with small talk when this was the single most important thing that had happened to us.

'Yes and I'm hoping you'll have some idea of what the police might be doing.'

'Princess, I know you have a high opinion of me and for that I am forever grateful. But a brief spell as a detective many years ago does not mean I have access to all things policing.'

'Point taken. I'm planning to go to the station, try to find out what the lead is, the report was vague.'

'You can try, but I'm not sure they'll tell you much.' Dad knew me well. Once I have an idea in my head there's not much anyone can say to change it. 'How about doing some work then? You are supposed to be my admin assistant, aren't you?'

On the two days I'm not looking after the mobile library, I call round to dad's and type up his patient notes.

Since he qualified he's been steadily busy and gained an excellent reputation locally. The doctors all know him and point patients in his direction. More often than not the forty-five minute physiotherapy session turns into an hour, as patients tell dad their latest worries about a child or grandchild, or ask his advice about a work problem. I told him he should charge them extra for counselling.

'Who's been in today then?' I said, picking up the appointment list and looking through the names, many of whom are familiar to me. 'Not Mrs Potts again. I'm certain that shoulder of hers is fixed now and she likes coming in for a chit-chat.'

'Her grandson has managed to get into Cambridge.'

'University?'

'Yes, how about that. She's so proud, she was barely through the door before she told me. She told me all about the entrance exam and how difficult it is and how Luther scored top marks. She's convinced he's going to change the world.'

'Next Nobel prize winner then? Not like your numbskull of a daughter?'

'That doesn't even deserve a reply. Did the library say yes to the new books you ordered?'

'They've approved the latest 007 and Alastair Mclean, but no to *The Valley of the Dolls*, and I can't imagine why. For now, anyway, but I'll keep on at them. All I'm waiting for is the new Agatha Christie, I've read everything on the crime shelves twice over.'

'My little bookworm. Come on, let's have a cuppa and then we'd better get on with some work.'

'Er, the thing is dad I can't stand tea anymore. I'm convinced they're putting something into the water. I've asked Greg to check our water supply. I've descaled the kettle, but nothing I do makes a difference. Greg told me to try another brand of tea. I've even bought a more expensive one. It's the smell of it, it turns my stomach.'

'Can't stand tea, eh? I remember your mother saying just the same thing.'

'Mum?' It was so rare for dad to mention her, he took me by surprise and I wasn't sure what to say next.

'I don't think there's anything wrong with the water, love, but maybe make an appointment with the doctor?'

'Is it some strange illness then, is that what you're trying to tell me, without much success?'

'I wouldn't call motherhood an illness, although it will play havoc with your body I'm sure. But in a nice way, I'm told.'

Since Zara's disappearance, Greg and I had slipped back into our own routine. Perhaps it was the undiscussed sadness of recent events, or the fact that we only had ourselves to think about, but whatever it was we found we were closer than ever. So, there it was. A visit to the doctor's confirmed it. The two of us would soon be three.

I waited until after supper to tell Greg. We'd cleared up and he'd been telling me about his day. He's been a window cleaner since he left school. Not the most intellectually demanding of jobs, but he and his workmates were doing something right because the work kept coming in, with recommendations and repeat business. They had a long list of regular customers and now and again were asked to do a posh manor house or suchlike, ready for a family party or special occasion. I had the feeling Greg would like a new challenge, but whenever I asked him he just told me he was lucky to be earning a reasonable living and what was the point because he didn't have any skills that would earn him a packet.

'So, the man came out and complained? Why didn't you tell him to do it himself if he's so fussy?' I said.

'Because he's the customer and he's always right. Besides, I'd been there two hours and I wanted to make sure he paid me.'

'You had to redo all the back windows? I'd have thrown the dirty water all over him. You have the patience of a saint.'

'Yes, I do. I married you, didn't I?' he said, pulling me close and moving his hand to tickle me around the middle.

'No, don't,' I said and held his hands in mine.

'Why? You love being tickled, go on, admit it.'

'Er, it's not that, it's just you won't only be tickling me.'

The expression on his face was better than words. It was a mixture of pride, exhilaration, awe and tenderness. He made me sit down on the sofa and put my feet up on the stool.

'What are you doing silly? I'm not ill, I'm expecting.'

'You are going to be a mum and I'm going to be a dad.'

'Um, that's pretty much the size of it, yes. Is that okay?'

'Is it okay? It's just about the best present you could have given me. I'd say, yes, okay covers it pretty well.'

We spent the rest of the evening laying on the sofa together, listening to *All I see is you* on repeat and for those few hours Zara was furthest from our minds. All we thought about was the new life nestling between us.

Chapter 6

'My dear Poirot,' I said coldly, 'it is not for me to dictate to you. You have a right to your own opinion, just as I have to mine.'
The Mysterious Affair at Styles - Agatha Christie

The next day was Friday, so I'd have the opportunity to visit the police station as soon as I finished my shift in the library van. I didn't plan to be a librarian, but the job seemed to acquire me. I'd always been a bookworm and was one of those rare and annoying pupils who asked for extra homework, especially from Mrs Frobisher, our English teacher. After her retirement Phyllis Frobisher gravitated to running the mobile library van and I was one of her regulars.

Books had connected dad and I, ever since his accident. Once I was old enough to make sense of the words on the page I would read aloud to him; it was our special time. My school playtimes were spent lingering in the corner of the playground out of the wind, immersed in my storybook world. Most of the teachers would clap their hands and tell me to get up and run around, but Phyllis would leave me be. Perhaps I was a reminder of her younger self. Now and then I challenged her with a word I'd just discovered, try to put her on the spot for a definition. She always came up trumps, but I could tell she loved the intellectual banter.

Once I left school I made a weekly visit to the library van and enjoyed Phyllis' recommendations. We'd chat about books and Phyllis would guide me to anything about the sea, which was dad's passion; boats, fishes, even submarines. On alternate weeks I got to choose. Dad was patient with me as we worked our way through all the Agatha Christie's. We'd reach the halfway mark in one of her stories and he'd ask me to identify the culprit and gradually I learned to spot the clues she had dropped in.

A couple of years after I left school, Phyllis had a heart attack. The van didn't pull up into Milburn Avenue for its usual Monday afternoon slot. It wasn't on Rockwell Crescent on Wednesday either. By Friday I was concerned and called into the main library to be told Phyllis was in hospital. For a few days she wasn't up to visitors, but then, instead of making my regular visit to the library van, I visited the hospital. She'd been in hospital for three weeks when she told me, just as I was leaving, 'I won't be able to do it anymore.'

'The library?'

'Yes, the doctors say I have to take it easy, at least for a few months.'

'You'll be back on your feet in no time, I bet,' I said, sounding more optimistic than I was feeling.

'No, I don't think I will.'

'Who's going to help me choose my books?'

'You are.'

'What do you mean?'

'You love books as much as I do and besides helping your dad out, well you've not found your place yet, have you?'

'I'll admit I have been drifting a bit, but a librarian? Are you being serious?'

'You'll make the perfect stand in. I'll be back soon enough, but in the meantime I'll call in when I can and between us we'll make an indomitable team.'

'Won't they say I'm too young?'

'No, they'll be delighted with my recommendation.

Trust me, it'll save them the trouble of interviewing. I'll speak to Jonathan Phillpot, he's head of library services and I'll let you know what he says.'

And that was it. Phyllis kept her word and I started two weeks later. I'd taken copious notes as I sat beside her hospital bed, while she explained the routine to me. There was nothing to be daunted about, I told myself; it was a short-term fill-in and Phyllis would soon be back at the helm. A few weeks turned into a few months and it became clear that from now on Phyllis's visits to the van would be as a customer only. I had become the new librarian.

Fridays were often busy days in the mobile library. Even though dad and Greg teased me for being scatty and disorganised at home, the library was my domain, with everything ordered and neat. The central library liked to know how many customers came in each day. I suppose it was their way of making sure we were providing the best possible service. I kept a list of the numbers of browsers and borrowers. Over the months a pattern emerged and I enjoyed working out likely reasons for the varied customer attendance.

Mondays were usually quiet, with a few browsers, but not many borrowers and I had a theory which I explained to dad, only to have him laugh at me.

'I reckon people have more time over the weekend. So, they almost finish their library book, then on Monday night they relish the final chapter. What? Why are you laughing? It's what you and I have always done,' I told him. 'You used to ask me to leave the last few pages so we could mull over what we'd read and savour the ending.'

'And you think there are other crazy folk out there like us?' My dad had a strong sense of the ridiculous.

Of course, it could just as easily have been because Monday was washing day.

But Fridays were my days for tidying, double-checking all the shelves, updating any paperwork and looking over the new order list I had to prepare each month. As a mobile library, we were encouraged to ask customers what books they would like to see added to our selection. The new titles might be brought in from the main library, or they might be ordered, provided the budget allowed.

I knew all my regulars and had become familiar with their reading habits. Some would be waiting anxiously for the next Agatha Christie (me included), others borrowing thrillers for their husbands. Then there were the young mums who worked their way through the children's books, gradually moving from picture books to Enid Blyton, as the little ones grew.

During the quiet periods I made time to read, and now, with my new state of impending motherhood I fancied doing some research. The reference section was only small, but I found a textbook that gave me just enough information about the little person who was growing inside me, without frightening me witless about the birth. I was deep in the middle of the chapter about how the tiny fingernails grow around the twelfth week, when someone came in. My regulars usually preferred to browse uninterrupted, but I hadn't seen this chap before, so I thought he might be grateful for a guiding hand.

'Good morning, if you need any help just ask,' I said. 'Fiction is all down that side, it's grouped though, so hopefully you'll have no trouble finding what you're looking for. What will it be? Science fiction, thrillers, crime?'

He smiled and nodded, but didn't respond, so I guessed he was a quiet type who liked to be left to his own devices. I kept the van quite warm, mainly because I was always freezing, even in mid-summer. When customers came in with their heavy overcoats, they often found it a bit stuffy so I cleared an area next to the door where there were a couple of coat hooks. Despite it being July, the weather had turned. The day had started with milky sunshine, which soon turned to rain clouds, pushed across the sky by an easterly wind. Phyllis Frobisher's favourite phrase for such a day, was '*too bright, too early*'.

The man wore a dark grey gaberdine mac, with a red, silk cravat wrapped around his neck and a smart, grey Trilby, which he removed as soon as he entered the van. He was around my dad's age, so mid to late-forties, but there was something about him that seemed out of place for our little town.

He moved slowly around, browsing through all the fiction sections, before moving on to the reference area. Finally, he pulled out a book on the Second World War. I was aware I'd been watching him a little too closely, so I glanced down at my baby book and tried to concentrate. At that point he started coughing, not just a tickly or throaty type of cough, but one that appeared difficult to stop.

'Are you okay there? Would you like to sit down, have a drink of water?' I said.

'Thank you, no,' he said, in between the rasping and wheezing that had now overtaken the coughing.

He put the book back and was supporting himself with one hand on the bookshelf.

'It's no trouble. I'm so sorry, it's really stuffy in here. I'll open the door, let some fresh air in,' I said.

'Thank you, but I must be going,' he said and with that he put his hat back on and left, leaving the door slightly ajar. It was only when I went over to close the door properly that I noticed something had fallen out of his hat. It was a small ticket, which when I looked at it more closely, turned out to be a left luggage ticket. I stepped outside the van to work out which way he'd gone, hoping to at least call after him, but he was nowhere to be seen.

At the end of the day I drove the van back to its overnight parking space and locked it up. It felt daunting walking into the police station, as though I was guilty of something. I took a deep breath, stood up straight, trying to make my five feet five inches stretch to several inches taller and used the firmest tone I could with the desk sergeant.

'Good evening. I'd like to speak to the officer in charge of the Zara Carpenter case.' I hadn't exactly prepared my opening gambit and as I said it I realised she may no longer even warrant an 'officer in charge'. Zara was an adult and she'd decided to move out of our house. It was hardly a case for Poirot.

Since she'd disappeared I'd called into the police station every few weeks, but never got beyond the desk sergeant. I'd ask if there was any news, he'd say no and that would be that. Now they had a lead and my hopes were raised.

'I'm Zara Carpenter's friend, Janie Juke,' I said, knowing as I spoke that I was likely to be given short shrift. I was shown into a small room, with just one desk and two chairs. There were no windows and the light bulb swung over the desk, reminding me of a scene from a gangster movie. It was intriguing to imagine how many criminals had been in this room, how heinous their crimes might have been. I hovered for a few moments, wondering which side of the desk to sit at and then the door opened and in walked a detective sergeant.

'Good morning, Miss,' he said.

'Janie Juke, Mrs.'

'How can I help you? I'm Detective Sergeant Frank Bright.'

'It's the Zara Carpenter case. I heard on the news you've had a new lead.' I paused, not knowing how much to say.

'Sorry, Miss, but you are? That is, what exactly is your connection to Miss Carpenter?'

'I'm her friend. She was living with me, with us, when she went missing. We were interviewed at the time. Another detective, I don't remember his name.'

'Ah, yes, of course. I do recall your name now, from the case notes.'

He was testing me, as though he knew all along.

'So, the new lead?' Pregnancy had not only altered my taste buds, but now whenever I got anxious or overexcited I was treated to an attack of hiccups. They were about to kick in, which would be a distraction I could do without. 'Could I have a drink of water?'

He nodded, left the room for a moment and came back with a rather grubby glass, half-full of water. I took a sip and thanked him.

'You were going to tell me about the new lead?' I said, hopeful that, as well as the water, he had returned with a more helpful demeanour.

'We can't share that information with anyone apart from Miss Carpenter's family.'

'And have you?'

'Have we what?' He was being as unhelpful as it was possible to be.

'Have you shared the information with her family?'

'Now that's not any of your business, Miss, is it?'

When he entered the room he'd brought an ashtray with him. He leaned back in his chair and took a packet of cigarettes out of his jacket pocket. He offered the packet to me. Shaking my head, I prayed he wouldn't light one himself. The smell of cigarette smoke had always made me queasy, but now in my relatively new state of motherhood, I found it made me want to throw up. Not the way to get into Detective Sergeant Bright's good books, which is where I wanted to be, as it was only then I was likely to be given the information I hoped for. He put the cigarette packet down on the table, pushed his chair away from the desk and stood up.

'Well, Miss, if that's all. I'll show you out.'

'But you haven't told me anything,' I said, trying to keep the indignation I felt from being evident in my tone.

'That's right, Miss. Like I said, you're not family. If you should hear anything from Miss Carpenter, you'll be sure to let us know?'

'You know she's still alive and well then? You can tell me that at least? If that's the case, you're likely to see her before me. After all, you're the one with the new lead.'

Stupid, I thought to myself, as soon as I was outside the police station. Dad would have told me off for trying to be clever with my sarcastic remarks. *This will not endear you to Detective Sergeant Bright*, I mused. But what was done was done and I resolved to keep a tighter rein on my

43

opinions in the future, particularly when it came to my dealings with the police department.

I left the station none the wiser and wondered what my next move should be.

Chapter 7

'No, *mon ami*, I am not in my second childhood! I steady
my nerves, that is all.'
The Mysterious Affair at Styles - Agatha Christie

It's a long while since Greg and I went dancing. Before
Zara came to live with us we'd go most Saturday nights.
Greg is a superb dancer, with natural rhythm, in fact
that's how we met. I'd been to one of the smaller
nightclubs a couple of times before I was officially of age,
piling on the makeup and offering the bouncer on the
door my sweetest smile. I know that at least half of the
girls dancing around me were under age, I recognised
them from school. As far as dad was concerned I was at
a friend's house and I always made sure I was home by
11pm. I'm sure he knew the truth, but I like to think he
trusted me enough not to make it an issue.

Once I was allowed to dance the night away, that was
exactly what I planned to do. My eighteenth birthday fell
on a Saturday, which made it all the more perfect and I
couldn't wait to buy my first legal drink. I declined dad's
offer of a party, which probably came as a relief to him.
A dozen or so teenage girls singing along to loud music
and getting tipsy must have been his idea of a nightmare.
Particularly as he couldn't see what was going on and how
many drinks were being spilt all over the carpet.

So, on my birthday I started to get ready about five
hours before leaving the house. There were finger and
toenails to be carefully painted, my outfit needed ironing
and then it was time to treat myself to a long, hot bath,
rich with scented bubbles. Thanks to a suggestion from
Zara, when we were at school together, I'd taken to

wearing a headband to keep back my mass of unruly hair. I had one in just about every colour. The wages from my Saturday job at a local newsagents went into a pot, labelled 'Birthday'. The week before the big day, I took the stash of notes out, stuffed them in my purse and explored the shops. I bought the most fashionable dress I could afford. It was a bright yellow shift dress, with an emerald green ribbon tied under the bust and around the sleeve edges. I found a yellow and green scarf in the same shop, which I tied around my hair, instead of a band. By the time I was ready to leave I checked my reflection in the mirror and was pleased with the result.

'You'll do,' I whispered to myself and hadn't noticed that dad was behind me.

'I can imagine just how beautiful you look, princess,' he said, which made me want to cry.

'Don't say another word, or you'll make me mess up my makeup.'

'Ah, well, we can't have that, can we? I'm so proud of you, you're a young woman now and you have your whole life ahead of you.'

'Scary thought.'

'Why scary?'

'I don't even know what I want to do with my life.'

'All in good time, for now enjoy each day, especially today.'

'I might not be home by 11pm.'

'I'm expecting nothing less, in fact I'll be listening out about 2.30am for you falling up the stairs.'

'I'll take my shoes off and try not to wake you.'

'I won't be asleep.'

'I love you.'

'Ditto. Now off you go and have a wild time. Is that

what they say, nowadays?'

'Probably not, but I get your drift.'
A few of my friends surprised me by telling the DJ it was my birthday and requesting my favourite record. We danced to one Beatles track after another. *I want to hold your hand*, *She loves you* and every other song he played and I barely had time to drink the vodka and orange I'd proudly bought.

Greg was standing with a girl, over to the side of the dance floor. If I had to describe my ideal bloke, Greg was it. Slightly taller than me, sandy coloured hair that fell casually across his forehead and just long enough to catch the collar of his shirt. There was a quiet confidence about him. I'd glanced his way a couple of times, but then tried not to, because he was clearly taken. So, when the slow dances came on at the end of the evening and he walked towards me, I wished I'd been faster at disappearing into the toilets.

'Do you want to dance?' he said.

'Um, won't your girlfriend mind?' I nodded my head in the direction of the girl, who oddly was now dancing with someone else.

'No, she's not my girlfriend, she's my sister.'
'Oh.'

'So, do you want to dance?'

My mouth was dry and it seemed that my voice had completely disappeared. So I nodded and he took my hand. He led me to the dance floor and while Cilla's *Anyone who had a heart* was playing in the background we discovered we both loved dogs, dancing and music. The last record played, the lights came up and I noticed his eyes were the deepest colour of chocolate. I was smitten.

'Can I walk you home?' he asked, as I went off to the

cloakroom to get my jacket.

'What about your sister?'

'Becca's okay, she's teamed up with Paul, he's a mate, so I trust him to see her home safely.'

'It's quite a walk, I could grab a taxi?'

'Save your money. Anyway, I like walking.'

And that was that. I introduced him to dad a couple of weeks later and some of my happiest times were listening to the two of them chatting together. Dad had been a keen Brighton football fan since he was a lad and now, although he couldn't watch the game, he kept up with their progress every week. Greg went to most of the home matches and would come round the house afterwards and give dad a kick by kick account of the whole game.

On our six-month anniversary Greg proposed and I thought he was joking.

'I'm not old enough to get married,' I told him, attempting to hide my joy and failing miserably.

'Okay if I ask you again then?'

I didn't need to answer. The kiss, which must have lasted at least two minutes, would have told him all he needed to know. He asked me twice more, once on my nineteenth birthday and finally on my twentieth I couldn't wait any longer. Each time he asked me he'd approached my dad first, which was funny and old-fashioned, but lovely too. Apparently, dad did his usual teasing and reassured Greg he'd be delighted to get rid of me, but I could tell he was thrilled with the thought of a son-in-law, who would always be more like a son.

We went back to Aquarius to celebrate our engagement and had the spotlight on us, as we danced to The Supremes telling us *You can't hurry love.*

48

Since Zara had moved in dancing had taken a back seat. She was in a dark place and the thought of me dressing up in my favourite mini skirt, with newly lacquered nails, seemed cruel and unfeeling.

But when Greg came home from work on Friday, I told him I had an idea.

'Why don't we go dancing tomorrow night? We haven't been for ages and it's time we brushed up our moves while I'm still able,' I said.

'You sure? You'll be okay?'

'I'm just pregnant, not ill.'

'If you think it'll be alright,' he said, laying a hand on my stomach.

'I've been reading about our new little person. Right about now it looks exactly like a kidney bean. Who would have thought it? How can a little bean be giving me so much trouble already? Turned me off tea, given me hiccups, stopped me from enjoying my lie-in at weekends. You, little bean, have a lot to answer for,' I said and poked my stomach.

'Don't do that, it'll hear you.'

'I don't think it will have ears yet.'

'Well, it will definitely feel you, prodding it like that. Besides I don't like calling our child an 'it'. It doesn't sound right.'

'Our little bean then, that's what we'll call it, okay? Sorry little Bean, I won't poke you again. In return, give me a break in the morning and let me lie in?'

'I've missed this,' he said, taking my hand and swinging me around. Aquarius was the perfect place to twist and shout. The atmosphere was buzzing and the music loud enough to blast away my worries, at least for a few hours.

49

'Me too, and you're still the best dancer on the dance floor.'

'Well, thank you, Mrs Juke. You're not bad yourself, especially for a mum to be.'

We danced and laughed and relaxed, but as midnight approached I felt weary.

'Not quite the party girl I used to be.'

'Yeah, well, you're not a teenager anymore either.'

'Will you still love me when I'm old, wrinkled and grumbly?'

'You might be grumbly before you're old.'

'Charming, what happened to my chivalrous husband?'

'He's gone to the toilet.'

'Seriously though, will you?'

'What's got into you? Of course, why wouldn't I?'

'Do you reckon Zara and Joel would have married eventually?'

'Weren't we supposed to be having a Zara-free night?'

'It's hard not to think about her, Greg, I wish I understood why she left. I just want to know she's okay.'

We sat for a while and people watched.

'See if you can guess who'll end up together, let's matchmake,' I said.

'Pretty, blonde-haired girl by the bar, the one with the long legs and the lad with the Beatles haircut. He's been watching her all night.'

'Sounds like you might have noticed her too, Mr Juke, and you a married man.'

'You asked me to guess. Anyway, me appreciating beauty is a compliment to you, means I've got excellent taste.'

'You got out of that one nicely.'

Our conversation was interrupted by a tall lad who

50

approached our table.

'Hello, you're Zara's friend, aren't you? Janie, isn't it?'

'Hi, sorry, I don't think we've met?' I asked him.

'Owen Mowbray,' he said, leaning over our table.

'This is my husband Greg,' I said, nodding towards Greg. 'So, you know Zara?'

'Yes, but I haven't seen her for ages, how's she doing?'

Greg and I looked at each other, before Greg replied, 'Not sure to be honest, we haven't seen her for a while ourselves.'

'Do you mind my asking how you know her?' I said. 'To tell you the truth we're worried about her, so anything you can tell us might help.'

'I met her on a protest march. It was a couple of years ago. We kept in touch for a while but then I moved away and I'm just back visiting my parents. I was thinking it would be fun to look her up, but you say she's not around at the moment?'

'Take a seat, it's a long story.'

We explained about Joel's accident and Zara's disappearance, skirting over the detail. He listened and said little.

'Do you think she's okay?' he said, when I'd finished speaking. 'Maybe she's gone away to get herself together?'

'We don't know, but yes, probably something like that. By the way, how did you know I'm Zara's friend, how did you know my name?'

'She showed me a photo of you both, when we were on the march. I'm good with faces and names, plus the headband you're wearing, it caught my eye. You were wearing one in the photo.'

I didn't respond as I was trying to recall the photo, but

51

then he said, 'Well, it's nice to meet you.' And with that he shook Greg's hand and walked off.

'Well, that was weird,' I said, as we went to the cloakroom to pick up our coats.

'Why weird?'

'I don't know, it's strange he should turn up like that. How come Zara never mentioned him if they were such great friends?'

'You read too many crime novels, they feed your already over-active imagination. Come on, home for you and young Bean.'

Greg was asleep before I'd even got undressed, leaving me to toss and turn and try to work out why I felt disconcerted about Owen Mowbray.

Chapter 8

'You are annoyed, is it not so?' he asked anxiously, as we walked through the park.
'Not at all,' I said coldly.
The Mysterious Affair at Styles - Agatha Christie

The next morning Greg was up before me. I could tell he was upset about something from the way he was throwing himself around the kitchen, slamming the kettle down on the gas and banging the cutlery drawer shut.

'You okay?' I asked him.

'Not really, no.'

'Too late last night? Didn't you sleep well?'

'It's not that, I'm just worried.'

'About what? Is it work?'

'No, it's you if you want to know.'

'What have I done? I thought we had a fun time, we should do it again, not leave it so long next time.'

I took my drink upstairs and got dressed, but when I returned to the kitchen Greg was still looking annoyed.

'What is it about her?' he said.

'Who?'

'Who do you think? Zara.'

'How do you mean?'

'Why do you feel so responsible?'

'She's our friend, isn't she? Where's all this come from? It was only when that Owen fellow turned up last night that we even mentioned her.'

'The way I see it, you knew her at school, but not that well. Then you didn't see her for ages and suddenly she's living with us. We did all we could for her at a bad time in her life and then she decided to strike out on her own.

It's a good thing, isn't it? Perhaps she just felt strong enough to start again.'

'How do you know she's started again? She could be lying dead somewhere.'

'Being positive then, are we?'

'Why are you being so horrible? Why shouldn't I care?'

'Do you think she'd do the same for you, if you went missing?'

'Yes, I do, actually.'

'All I'm saying is you're too involved. We're too involved.'

'I'm going out,' I said and didn't wait for his reply.

Greg's words made me feel uncomfortable and I didn't know if it was because he was right or wrong. I wondered how much angrier he'd be if he discovered just how involved I planned to be. I hadn't intended to go out, so now I needed to give myself a destination. Dad would always be pleased to see me, but I wasn't in the mood to talk or listen, I just wanted to walk and think.

There were puddles everywhere and I felt like jumping up and down in them, as I did when I was little. I'd delight in making as big a splash as possible, even when I wasn't wearing wellies. Aunt Jessica rarely reprimanded me; I'm certain she would have liked to do exactly the same thing. Now I'm all grown up I can guess how she felt.

I walked down through the town towards Fortune Park. It was a long walk, but just what I needed to clear my head. The first part of the park was always busy at the weekend with young families and dog walkers. I chose a bench over to one side of the play area and watched as the children ran between the slide, swings and roundabout. At one point two little boys jostled together in their rush to grab one of the swings when a dainty, pig-tailed girl hopped off it.

Greg and I had never talked about whether we wanted a boy or a girl. I don't think either of us were bothered, although I could imagine Greg enjoying the banter with a son. Off they'd go to football, or have a kick about in the garden. If Bean turned out to be a girl would she be as close to Greg as I am to my dad? A wave of sadness hit me as I got to thinking that dad would never see my child's face. It would be another milestone we would bluster our way through.

My wedding day was the last significant event where dad and I both did a good job of pretending. I described every last detail of my wedding dress to him before he took my arm to walk me down the aisle. I don't know if it was harder for him or for me. He missed the sight of his only daughter being wed and I felt sad that I couldn't enjoy his expression of pride to see me all grown up.

Mum came to the wedding, but stood rigid in the front row, clearly embarrassed at the reality of me guiding dad towards the altar, when it should have been the other way round. Her false laugh tinkled constantly during the reception, as she made sure she mingled, carefully avoiding any meaningful discussions. Then, when I took dad out on to the dance floor half-way through the evening, it was more than she could bear and I watched her disappear into the toilets.

Later, before Greg and I left for our wedding night I waited for her to say something to me. I hoped for the words of wisdom I always imagined a mother would offer her daughter on her special day. Instead, all she managed was to squeeze my hand and say, 'Be happy', as though she was doubtful I would be.

We'd saved every penny we could and, with dad's help, we were able to put a deposit down on a little terraced house. We kept the wedding as low key as possible and rather than any grand honeymoon, we had two nights away in a country house hotel. When we got back mum had already departed, returning to wherever it was she had made her life.

So, there was me and dad and Greg and that had been perfect. But when Zara came back into my life I loved having the special girl-time we had together. Since leaving school I'd kept in touch with a few of the girls, but I didn't have much in common with any of them. It was different with Zara, she brought out a side of me I didn't know was there. Until my friendship with Zara, I did my best to be a helpful daughter and a loving wife, but she made me feel that being Janie Juke was just as important.

'I was thinking about Owen,' I said.

Our arguments never lasted long and by the time I got home we were both ready to kiss and make up.

'Is there something you want to tell me? Got your eye on him, have you?'

'Seriously, I was mulling over what he'd said, about how he recognised me.'

'Yeah, from a photo Zara showed him.'

'Don't you think it's weird though? The only photos Zara would have had were from our schooldays.'

'You haven't changed much. Possibly not so many teenage pimples.'

I went to poke him in the ribs, but he stood back just

56

in time.

'Well, it's quite a stretch, isn't it? He's seen a photo of a sixteen-year-old me and then he recognises me in a dimly lit nightclub?' I said.

'Stranger things have happened.'

'Maybe he's lying.'

'Why would he lie?'

'It could be that he's seen her more recently?'

'Enough now, otherwise we'll be arguing again and I'm fed up with the subject. Accept what he's told you and forget about it.'

'Sorry, you're probably right.'

But I wasn't going to forget about it. I needed to know for sure and wondered how I could arrange to bump into Owen Mowbray. I knew nothing about him, except that his parents lived locally and he was back to visit them. The chances were he had already returned to wherever he'd come from.

'There's a job going at the builders up Wiley Avenue,' Greg announced, as we sat down to supper on Monday night.

'You've got a job.'

'I know, but that's all it is. If I join the building trade I'll be able to learn.'

'Learn what?'

'I don't know, bricklaying or plumbing.'

'Is that what you want?'

'The money won't be much to begin with, but I'll hardly be giving up a career. Once I've learned the trade I'll be on a better wage and we can finally start paying your dad back.'

'He won't expect you to.'

'I know, but he's done so much for us, the deposit for this place, the car. And I bet he pays you more than the going rate for those two days you work for him.'

'You're not suggesting I'm not worth every penny, are you? Because you're in danger of having your dinner tipped over your head if you are.'

'I'm just saying I'd like to learn a trade. With bricklaying I could build us our own house.'

'We've got a house.'

'Aren't you supposed to support me, be pleased I'm ambitious?'

'Sorry, I'm being mean. Yes, it's a great idea. You would make a wonderful bricklayer and I'd love you to build us a house. Do you really fancy it then?'

'I'm going up there, just to ask, see what's on offer. Do you want to come?'

'Count me in, when are you going?'

'First thing tomorrow, builders start early. 7.30 okay with you? Then I can get to work straight after and I'll not be missed. If we go in the car I can drop you round your dad's if you like?'

Greg used our car to get to and from work and most of the time I walked to dad's or to pick up the library van. Occasionally I'd cheat and catch a bus, even though it was only two stops. It meant another five minutes in bed for me and after a restless night even five minutes made a difference.

Greg wasn't keen on me driving the mobile library around, which was hopefully more to do with his concern for me than envy. Greg had already passed his driving test by the time I met him. His dad had paid for his lessons and taken him out to practise in their Ford Cortina. Clearly my dad couldn't do the same for me and I vowed I'd never sit behind a steering wheel. Maybe it was the memory of dad's accident that coloured my view.

'Why drive when you can cycle? It's quieter, cheaper and more fun,' I told Greg when he quizzed me, soon after we'd got together.

'In the rain?'

'There's always the bus.'

'Are you scared?'

'Why should I be scared? As far as I can see there's nothing to it, although it helps if you have a car to start with.'

Soon after we were married Greg announced he'd be home a bit later than usual and that I should hold off from preparing supper.

'When will we eat then? If you're going to the pub I might as well eat on my own and leave yours in the oven.'

'I'm not going to the pub. Trust me and stop asking so many questions,' was all he said before he left for work.

Then, at around 6pm, when I was making myself a cuppa and contemplating whether to grab a quick snack, I heard a car horn blaring. The noise was loud and persistent and I wondered if there'd been an incident of some kind.

Once I was outside I discovered the culprit. Greg was standing proudly beside a pale blue Morris Minor, with the driver's door open and one hand on the horn.

'Enough,' I shouted, 'you'll have the law on us for disturbing the peace, or possibly car theft. What are you doing?'

'Showing you our new car. Fancy a drive?'

An hour later and I was ready to take back everything I'd said about cars.

'That was a blast. Is it really ours? Can we afford it?'

'Yes and yes. What's more I'm going to teach you to drive, starting tomorrow.'

'You're either brave or stupid.'

'I'll tell you which after your first lesson.'

I'm sure even Greg would agree I was a quick learner and once I'd passed my test, driving became one of my favourite pastimes. I guessed that dad had made a generous contribution to our car fund, telling Greg there was no hurry about paying it back. During the week Greg used the car to get to and from work, but at weekends if we went on a jaunt together then I tended to be the driver.

So, when Phyllis encouraged me to take on the library van, the driving aspect of the job was the least of my worries. Greg, on the other hand, always looked uncertain when he watched me practising my manoeuvres.

'Just remember, this is not our Morris Minor. Don't take any risks and watch out for buses.'

'I'm hoping the buses will watch out for me. Can I remind you who passed their test first time?'

I teased Greg when I found out he had taken three attempts to pass his test.

'You were just lucky,' he said, 'my examiner didn't like me, he was in a bad mood. All you had to do was flash your sweet smile and he was a pushover.'

Once I realised it was a sore subject with him I didn't mention it again.

Wiley Avenue is a short drive from our house and the entrance to the builder's was in between two detached houses. The yard was filled with bricks, sand, cement and various tools and equipment, but it was orderly, with everything neatly stacked and a large broom suitably placed by the door to the portacabin, which I guessed was the office. As we approached, a short, stocky man was loading a small truck with lengths of timber. Greg went over and helped the man lift one of the longest pieces and once it was on the truck he held out his hand.

'Hello, I'm Greg. Are you the owner?'

'That's me. Thanks for your help lad, much appreciated.'

'I heard there's a job going, is that right?'

'You've heard right. What's your trade lad?'

'I'm a window cleaner, but I'm keen to learn a real trade, bricklaying, plumbing. I'm a hard worker.'

'Bricklaying's a fine trade for a strong young lad like you. There's a lot to learn, if you don't mind starting at the bottom. Plenty of lifting and carrying, working outside in most weathers, although that's nothing new for you. Of course, with bricks you're making something permanent, whether it's a garden wall or a whole house. Job for life, that's what it is. Shame my son didn't recognise it.'

'What do I need to do to apply? Have you had much interest?'

'I'll get you a form, just jot down a few particulars and drop it back into me. I can see you're keen, always a good start. I pay a fair wage for a fair day's work. Three weeks holiday a year and I'll need you to work every other Saturday. So many youngsters think they're entitled to money for nothing, as long as they turn up. Well, Mowbray and Son believe in giving our best, that's why our customers come back to us. I've got a good team, they're all hard workers, but they like a laugh too, as long as it's only on their tea break.'

'Thanks, Mr Mowbray, I'd be grateful for the opportunity. This is my wife, Janie.'

'Not expecting me to give her a job as well, are you lad?' Mr Mowbray smiled and held out his hand to shake mine. 'Nice you've come along together though, not many wives would be bothered. 'Specially since it's an early start for us builders. Look after her well, I reckon you've got a treasure there. And don't expect her to make your sandwiches for you, either. I make my own, have done my whole working life.'

'Yes, I will, I do,' Greg said, looking slightly flustered.

'Truth is, Mrs Mowbray doesn't ever put enough butter in for me,' he said, winking at us both.

Greg was almost skipping on the way back to the bus stop.

'What a lovely man,' I said. 'He liked you, didn't he? He's in my good books already, telling you to make your own lunch. Shame he didn't suggest you do the ironing too.'

It didn't register at first, probably because I was still half asleep, but on the return journey it dawned on me. *Mowbray and Son*. Not that common a name, surely. For once fate was on my side, or the gods were looking favourably on me, or both.

Chapter 9

'Beware! Peril to the detective who says: 'It is so small –
it does not matter. It will not agree. I will forget it.' That
way lies confusion. Everything matters.'
The Mysterious Affair at Styles - Agatha Christie

After a few rainy days it appeared all my regulars had
spent their evenings reading, because on my next day in
the library they all turned up, bringing back their books
and wanting to choose new ones. There were so many
people in the van at one point that I was going to suggest
they formed an orderly queue. In the end, they merged
and shuffled around each other and everyone seemed
content.

I hadn't looked up when the last couple of people
came in, as I was busy working out the overdue library
fees for Mrs Candy, who was as sweet as her name
suggested and rarely managed to bring her books back on
time.

'Just three days over this time,' I told her, as she
handed me *Alice in Wonderland.* 'I expect you've been
reading it to your grandchildren? Did they love it?'

'What's that dear?' Mrs Candy's hearing was not what
it used to be.

'Three days,' I said, trying not to disturb the rest of my
customers.

'There's this one too,' she said, pulling out another
book from an inside pocket of her raincoat. 'I'd forgotten
I had it. Do you know, this was the first book I learned
to read.' She handed over a tattered copy of *The Wind in
the Willows.*

'This doesn't belong to the library, perhaps it's your own copy?' I said, pushing the book back at her.

'What's that dear?' My patience with my dad's blindness wasn't helping me cope with Mrs Candy and her hearing difficulties. While I was mulling over what to do or say next, a male customer approached the desk. I looked up and realised he was the same customer who had suffered a coughing fit when he was last in.

'Ah, Mr...? How can I help?'

'Write it down,' he said.

'I'm sorry?'

'Write down what you want her to understand. It'll be quicker and quieter in the long run.'

'Good idea.' He stood and watched me as I wrote a short note to Mrs Candy and handed it to her. While she read it, I turned back to the gentleman. 'I think you might have left something behind when you called in last time.'

'No, I don't think so.'

'Oh, right. It's just that I found a left luggage ticket and wondered if it might have been yours.'

'No, not mine. I'll take this, when you're ready,' he said, and handed over a Second World War history book by Winston Churchill, together with his library card.

'Certainly, Mr Furness. There you are,' I said, stamping the book and passing it back to him.

Mrs Candy had by now put her coins on the counter, picked up her copy of *The Wind in the Willows* and was walking towards the door.

'All alright?' I called out to her as she went to leave, before realising I was wasting my time.

I kept a cardboard box under the counter where I put any forgotten items hoping they will be reclaimed. Over time I had accumulated plenty of interesting objects. There were the inevitable umbrellas, which wouldn't fit into the box, but which I laid on the floor beside the counter. Since working in the van I had come across two single gloves, one woollen and one leather, a spectacle case, a hatpin and an antique cameo brooch. One of the oddest things to go into my lost property box was a sock. Understandable, possibly, if it had been a pair of socks, but this was a single pink ankle sock, adult size and recently worn. I longed for someone to come and reclaim it so I could discover how it had come to be left in the library without its matching pair. But they never did.

I pulled the box out from under the counter, glanced again at the luggage ticket and then tucked it inside an envelope for safekeeping and put it back into the box. It was odd that Mr Furness hadn't missed it, but perhaps I had read too many detective novels and was seeing mysteries around every corner.

'I'll drop that form in for you, if you like,' I told Greg later that day.

'Blimey, you're keen. I haven't even looked at it yet.'

'You only need to fill in your details, it won't be complicated. Strike while the iron's hot and all that jazz. I'm just saying, don't trust it to the post. I can pop it in before I go to dad's tomorrow.'

'I'm not doing it tonight. I need time to think about it.'

'About what? You want the job, don't you? Mr Mowbray seemed like a nice man and he'll teach you the trade. I should tell you, I've been designing our new house. Can we have two bathrooms?'

'You're crazy, remind me why I married you? Bean

will be all grown up before we ever get the money together to build a house. Two bathrooms means twice the hot water. Too expensive. My mum had to make do with washing me in the sink, yours probably did too.'

'Yes, well it's 1969 and times are a-changing. I've also got my eye on a twin tub, so make sure you get those bricks perfect and he might give you a bonus. Do you want some help with the form?'

I was still rehearsing my opening lines as I walked up to Mowbray's yard the next morning. Mr Mowbray was out the front loading his truck with tools and materials and when he saw me he raised his hand to wave.

'Morning, lass, another early start for you. How's that husband of yours? Any more thoughts about the job? He'll fit in well here, I'm sure of it.'

'Hello there. Thanks, yes. In fact, that's why I'm here. Greg's really keen, he's already completed the form you gave him.' I handed him the sealed envelope, which he stuffed into his jacket pocket.

'Mowbray and Son?' I pointed to the sign over the doorway to his makeshift office.

'It was supposed to be. I started the business straight after Owen was born. Thought it'd be grand for him working alongside his dad.'

'Doesn't he then? Work alongside you, I mean?'

'No, doesn't like to get his hands dirty. College lad, prefers books to bricks. Left home as soon as he could, rarely comes back.'

'That's a shame. You must miss him. You and Mrs Mowbray. Is it a long time since you last saw him?'

'Three months and we didn't hear a peep, not even a postcard. Then he turns up a few days ago just like that, no explanations. Says he needs to stay with us for a while. Seems he's lost his job. Won't even talk to his mother about it.'

'Kids, eh,' I said, feeling stupid, as Owen was about my age. Thankfully his father paid no attention to my inane and inappropriate comment.

'Well my dear, I can't keep rambling on, I need to get on site, the lads will be waiting for me. Make the most of this weather, you never know when it's going to change.'

I was wracking my brain to come up with a way to continue the conversation.

'Sounds like Owen is having a rough time, it can't be easy to come back when things haven't worked out as he'd hoped.'

'Needs a good talking to if you ask me. Not that anyone does.'

'Greg and I would be happy to meet him for a drink, if you think it might help?' I tried to avoid a pleading tone in my voice and kept my fingers firmly crossed behind my back as I spoke.

'That's kind lass. I'm not sure he needs to be out partying, mind you. Time for him to learn the meaning of a hard day's work.'

'Well, the offer's there.'

As he got into the front of his van I could see my chances vanishing.

'Um, where will we find him, if he did want to join us?' It was a long shot, but it paid off.

'23 Leighton Street, just round the back of the Dorsetshire Hotel, in the town centre. My wife's usually home, unless she's shopping. Owen will probably be asleep, it's all he's done since he got home.'

Greg was right, I was letting the situation get the better of me. I had no idea of the next step, or even if there should be one. There were no guarantees Owen would be prepared to talk to me and even if he did what was I going to say? He'd told us he hadn't seen Zara for a couple of years. If he'd seen Zara and I together more recently, why would he lie? The more I thought about it, the more convinced I was there was more to Owen Mowbray than was at first apparent.

Later that day I left dad a little earlier than usual. Today's patient's notes didn't take long to type up and I made the excuse I wanted to cook a special meal for Greg, which I still planned to do. But not before making an attempt at seeing Owen.

I found the house without difficulty, but was surprised to see a modest Edwardian terraced property. I had visions of some grand and imposing detached building that showed off the skills of Mowbray and Son. Perhaps there was less chance of my dream two-bathroom new build, after all.

Within seconds of ringing the bell, the door was opened by a buxom woman, her hair pulled back in a bun, with strands of it escaping and framing her flushed face.

'Sorry dear, I'm in the middle of baking,' she waved two floury hands at me, before wiping them down the front of her even flourier apron.

'Oh, I'm disturbing you. I do apologise. I'm Janie Juke. I was wondering if Owen was around?'

'Pleasure to meet you dear, friend of Owen are you? Well, that's lovely. We haven't met many of his friends. Come on in and I'll put the kettle on.' Her voice had a clear Welsh lilt to it.

She gestured to me to follow her down the narrow hallway into the little kitchen that sat at the back of the house. The kitchen table was covered with baking tins, some filled, others greased and waiting. Wonderful aromas of vanilla and mixed spice emanated from the oven where the next batch of cooking was underway.

'The jam tarts are still warm. You've come just in time, you'll have one with a cup of tea?'

'That's so kind, thank you. But I don't want to disturb you.'

'No trouble dear, have a seat. I can call Owen, he's just having a lie down. He's not been feeling too good, so he'll be pleased to see a friendly face.'

'If you're sure, but no tea for me, thanks. I'll try one of your delicious tarts, though, if that's okay?'

She left the kitchen and standing at the foot of the steep staircase, she shouted up, 'Owen, someone here to see you'.

There was no reply and no sound of movement from upstairs. I was beginning to wish I'd never come, then suddenly there he was at the back door.

'I was out the back, mum. Oh, Janie, hello. Sorry, I hadn't realised you...'

'Your mum has just kindly offered me one of her freshly baked jam tarts. I've struck lucky and arrived on the right day.'

'But how did you...?'

'It's a coincidence really. Greg is thinking of applying for a job at your dad's yard and one thing led to another. I didn't realise you were still in town.'

'No, well...'

'Owen is staying with us for a while,' his mother said, continuing to fill the rest of the baking tins.

'Great, well, I just dropped by. But if you fancy a night out, a drink or something some time,' I said.

'Yes, sounds good.'

'We live over near Maze Gardens, I'll jot our address down, shall I? We're in most nights, you're welcome to pop round whenever you're at a loose end.'

'I'll do that. It's kind of you, Janie, really.'

All I needed to worry about now was how to explain it to Greg, when or if Owen dropped by.

Chapter 10

'Will you repeat to us what you overheard of the quarrel?'
'I really do not remember hearing anything.'
'Do you mean to say you did not hear voices?'
'Oh, yes, I heard the voices, but I did not hear what they said.'
The Mysterious Affair at Styles - Agatha Christie

Although I was fit and well and Bean seemed quite happy, the doctor had recommended I attend the ante-natal clinic. With no mum to advise me and no friends who had recently had babies, the experience was a novelty for me and I was keen to do everything right. Greg was desperate to come to the clinic with me, but we'd been told it was strictly out of bounds for fathers. It was as though pregnancy and childbirth was a thing of secrecy and wonderment that only women should understand and, although men were needed to start the whole thing off, they certainly were not required at any stage after that.

Strangely, I was quite nervous when I turned up at the little side door, which opened into the maternity clinic. Briarsbank Maternity Home had recently opened, having been converted from an old chest hospital. The exterior of the maternity home was austere, but once inside it felt welcoming, with freshly painted walls and scrubbed linoleum floors. There were two wards, a delivery suite, and a large entrance area that was used for the ante-natal clinic. To avoid us mothers feeling too exposed they had divided the clinic area into curtained bays, which provided privacy during the all-important examinations.

Midwives ran the clinic, but there was always a doctor

on hand should he be needed. Mothers-to-be were discouraged from having their baby at home, which was the way it had always been and how it was for my mum and I guess her mum before her. I'd already picked up a leaflet from the doctor's surgery, detailing the equipment that was available now, as well as improved pain relief, which in my opinion was the best thing about all the recent medical advances.

Briarsbank was about a fifteen-minute walk from our house, and although I set off from home in time, I ended up rushing the last few yards for fear of being late. As I walked in I was breathless and I suppose a little flushed, partly from the rushing and partly from nerves. There were six other women already there, all seated in a line on a row of wooden chairs that reminded me of schooldays. I had visions of a stern midwife telling me to stand up straight and stop slouching. I was also acutely aware my shoes needed a polish and smiled to myself when I thought of Greg telling me how ridiculous I was being. The smell of antiseptic was all-pervasive and didn't help with my state of permanent queasiness.

Two of the women had toddlers who had no intention of being still or quiet. The children were chasing each other up and down past the row of chairs, until one of toddlers toppled over and started to cry. Then the other one let out a cry as well, perhaps coming out in sympathy with her new friend. The mothers appeared to be oblivious and just carried on chatting. Eventually, both children stopped crying and tottered back to their mothers. The thought of having to cope with a new baby, while still struggling to control a toddler, filled me with dread. I said a silent thank you to the heavens that there was just the one little Bean for me to consider.

None of the other mothers were familiar to me, so I sat down on one of the empty chairs and smiled at the freckle-faced girl sitting next to me.

'Hello, I'm Nikki,' she said. 'There's quite a wait. There doesn't appear to be much of a system, I think they may be short staffed.'

'Janie,' I said and smiled again.

'Your first?' Nikki said, nodding her head in the direction of my midriff.

'Yes. Yours?'

'Yes. Scary, isn't it? I'm fine with the idea of being pregnant and all that, but giving birth. The thought of a human being coming out of a hole the size of a milk bottle top fills me with dread. Sometimes I think I'd like to send it back, change my mind.' Despite her freckles her complexion was pale.

'The trickiest thing so far is that I have almost permanent hiccups,' I said.

'Really annoying, I bet?'

'And embarrassing. They come on every time I'm nervous or excited and then I'm hiccuping away and it doesn't matter how much water I drink they take forever to wear off. And drinking tea used to be one of my favourite things, but now just the smell of it makes me queasy. Have you gone off anything?' I asked her.

'Everything pretty much. I just look at toast now and I want to throw up. The only thing I can keep down without too much trouble is a plate of chips, with loads of salt and vinegar. Our house smells like a chip shop most of the time, but Frank doesn't seem to mind.'

As we waited to be called through by the midwife we continued chatting. I discovered Nikki had moved into the area from East Anglia. She didn't live far from me

73

and we arranged to walk back home together once the clinic was over.

'Frank and I have just moved into one of the new houses on the Goldhill Estate,' she told me as we walked. 'My husband got a transfer. He's a detective sergeant up at Tidehaven Station. It was promotion for him, so worth the move. It's been a lot of upheaval though, what with the baby on the way and all.'

It was difficult to imagine Nikki with Detective Sergeant Bright. He must have been at least ten years older than her, maybe on his second marriage? She was petite, birdlike almost, with a hopeful demeanour - bright in name and nature. DS Bright, on the other hand, was portly, with a jowly face and thinning hair and little that was hopeful about him. Perhaps detective work shattered your faith in people after a while, or it could be he was just a glass half-empty kind of person.

We chatted about our husbands, our babies and the traumas of house moves and while we spoke I started to formulate a plan.

'Did you want to meet up after next week's clinic?' I asked her, as we reached the end of the street where we were due to part. One of the midwives told us that each week there would be a talk or a demonstration and we were all welcome to attend.

'Yes, let's. We won't go anywhere for tea, though,' she said, remembering what I'd told her.

'Or toast,' I said.

The following week I made certain I arrived at the clinic early. I saved Nikki a seat beside me and waved when I spotted her arriving. There weren't as many mothers or children as on the previous occasion and one of the midwives was distributing leaflets about the benefits of bottle-feeding versus breast-feeding.

'I can't imagine why anyone would want to bottle-feed,' Nikki said, as she looked through the leaflet. 'It must be such a palaver with all the sterilising and what not. We've got all we need, right here,' she said, pushing her chest out and laughing.

'Do you reckon it hurts?' I said. 'It says in this leaflet that some people can get trouble with their ducts. Sounds nasty.'

'It's the natural thing to do, though. Our mums wouldn't have dreamt of using bottles, I bet.'

According to dad, my mum had been delighted when infant formula was widely available after the war, but I guessed this was not the time to mention it. I stuffed the leaflet in my pocket, having already decided that bottle-feeding would suit Bean and me very well.

Once the clinic was over we bought a couple of cans of drink and sat in Tensing Gardens for a while. Summer had returned and we were grateful for the shade offered by the umbrella of trees, which overhung one of the benches. The gardens were peaceful, with few people around, bar a few dog walkers. We chatted about impending motherhood and how we both promised ourselves it wouldn't change a thing.

'I mentioned to Frank I might get a little job once the baby is a bit older, when it's at school. He hit the roof. Sometimes I wonder if it's the police force that makes him the way he is, but then his father is old fashioned like that, would never let his mother go out to work. A woman's place is in the home and all that rot.'

'I know what you mean. Greg has visions of us having a mini football team, likes the idea of me as an earth

75

mother, but he can just dream on. He's not the one having to go through the birth, is he? Or the pregnancy.'

'And moods, I'm finding I'm so moody all the time. It's driving Frank mad. We end up arguing about the silliest of things. He loves to talk about his work, although he's not supposed to tell anyone a lot of it, not even me. I used to be interested, but now I just don't want to hear. It's all so depressing.'

I shuffled my feet around and finished my drink. 'Still it must be exciting when they get a breakthrough. I've always thought police work must be quite fun, well not fun exactly, but every day something new.' I kept my voice as level as possible.

'I should show a bit more interest, I know,' Nikki said. 'In fact, the other night I couldn't stop him talking he was so fired up - you might know something about the case, a local girl went missing.'

My heart started jumping in my chest and I breathed deeply to keep the hiccups at bay. 'Er, yes, I remember something about it. A while ago though, wasn't it?'

'Yes, apparently she disappeared after her boyfriend had been killed in a hit and run. So sad. Frank told me the man who was originally in charge of the case reckoned she must have decided to end it all, with the grief. A shock like that - you can just imagine.'

'Crikey,' I said, busying myself by kicking around some leaves that had gathered under the bench.

'But they've never found a body or heard any more from her. I'm sure if I was her I'd want to move out of the area. Too many reminders. But Frank doesn't want to hear my opinion. What do I know, I'm just a housewife.'

The picture that Nikki was painting of her husband

76

made me feel uncomfortable.

'Anyway, my Frank is looking after the case now. They said they needed some fresh eyes on it and what with him moving here and just being promoted. It's quite a responsibility, but he was dead chuffed.'

I flinched slightly at her unfortunate choice of words, but continued to avert my gaze, to make sure my face didn't give anything away.

'Well, he'd read all the case notes, said he couldn't come up with any new angles. Then out of the blue someone came into the police station. Turns out it's that Mr Peters.'

'Peters? I don't think I know him.'

'Well, I probably shouldn't say, but he's the chap who's just taken over the newsagent's on Waterstone Avenue.'

'You mean the one that closed down when the previous couple ran out of money?'

'I don't know about that, it was before my time.'

'Frank told you about it?'

'No, it was a coincidence really. I'd called into the station to give Frank his lunch, he'd left his sandwich box behind and I wasn't going to see all that food going to waste. There I was, waiting at the front desk, when a man walked in, stocky chap, in his fifties. Asked to speak to the detective in charge of the Zara Carpenter case. Then a week or so later I went into the paper shop to pay my bill and there he was, the same man. That's how I knew. When Frank came home that night, all excited, I asked him. Turns out he's given them some new information.'

'Gosh, I wonder what he knows.'

'Of course, Frank can't tell me anything else. It would be more than his job's worth.'

'Absolutely,' I said and changed the subject.
I had what I needed.

.

Chapter 11

'Well, I think it is very unfair to keep back facts from me.'
'I am not keeping back facts. Every fact that I know is in
your possession. You can draw your own deductions
from them. This time it is a question of ideas.'
The Mysterious Affair at Styles - Agatha Christie

The gods were on my side once more. Greg had agreed
to try out for the local pub darts team. They'd been on at
him for months to join them, but he kept coming up with
excuses. It wasn't until I pushed him on the subject he
admitted he was rubbish at darts.

'Just tell them then, they won't want a no-hoper on the
team.'

'You don't understand, I'm hardly likely to admit I'm
no good at something so simple. Everyone can play
darts, there's not much to it.'

'There must be something to it or you wouldn't have a
problem. And you're wrong, not everyone can play, I
can't.'

'I mean men. Ask any man and he'll tell you.'

'Well, you've got a choice. Either you come clean and
tell them you're rubbish, or you have a go and surprise
yourself. Practise makes perfect and all that.'

When I heard the knock at the door, I thought it was
him coming back early, but forgotten his key. I was all
ready to commiserate with him. Instead, I opened the
door and maintained an expressionless face when I found
Owen standing there.

'Hello,' I said.

'Janie, I hope you don't mind.'

'Good to see you, come on in. Greg's down the pub. They've been nagging him for ages to join their darts team. I shouldn't say, but I have a feeling they might be regretting it. Let's just say, he's unlikely to win them any trophies. He'll have fun though, which is the most important thing. Tea? Coffee? Squash?'

All the time I was rambling Owen remained standing in the hallway, looking decidedly awkward.

'Come through, have a seat. Will you have a drink?'

'Tea, two sugars, if that's okay.'

I guessed he had come to talk and wasn't sure how to get started. There was no safe ground I could think of to break the silence, but then he did it for me.

'I've come to apologise.'

'Apologise? What for?'

'I've haven't been completely honest with you.'

I handed him his tea and could see his hand shaking slightly as he took it from me.

'I told you it was two years since I've seen Zara, well that's not entirely true.'

'It's not?' For a moment I wished Greg was there to witness this, so I didn't have to say, *I told you so.* Although, depending on Owen's revelations there was a strong chance I wouldn't be saying a word to Greg, not about Owen's unexpected visit, or the confession I was now eagerly awaiting.

'You're her friend and I feel like I owe you the truth,' he said.

'You do?'

I settled down on the settee, while Owen fidgeted on the chair in front of me. As he spoke he looked down at his hands, which were clasped tightly together.

'Zara and I were more than friends. We dated for a while. More than a while, actually, five months and six days.'

'Oh, right, I see.' It was clear from Owen's demeanour this was no casual relationship, at least for him.

'I met her at an anti-nuclear protest meeting. The speaker was brilliant, he got a standing ovation and Zara and I pushed our way to the front to try to catch a moment with him at the end of the meeting. We both started talking at the same time and ended up laughing about it. By the time we'd apologised to each other the speaker had been ushered out of a side door and we lost our chance. We got chatting and well…'

'You went out for a while, but it didn't work out?'

'We were perfect for each other, it wasn't just our political opinions we had in common. We liked the same books, the same music. We used to talk for hours. She was passionate about justice and equality.' As he spoke about her his expression was intense, his jaw clenched and his eyes bright.

'It must have been wonderful to find you had so much in common. What happened? Did you just drift apart?'

He stopped talking and sipped his tea. Then he stood and walked to the window. It was clear he was struggling to choose his words and I was wondering what he was going to say next.

'I don't know what she ever saw in Joel.'

I thought back to a conversation I'd had with Zara, one summer's evening. We'd been walking along the seafront, then we wandered onto the beach, taking it in turns to throw pebbles into the gently lapping waves.

'Joel is so talented, Janie,' she said. 'He could easily get work in London, there are people there who would pay a fortune for what he does.'

'London, crikey. Would you go too then? If he moved to London, would you move with him?'

She just smiled and bent her head.

'His ambition is to open his own photographic gallery,' she said. 'He'll do it one day, I'm sure.'

'Portraits?'

'This is just a start for him, the weddings and all that. His real passion is telling a story with photos. He could make such a difference, you know. Making people see the world through his lens. It's exciting.'

I turned my attention back to Owen.

'You knew Joel?' I asked him.

'Yes, well, I knew of him. I never spoke to him, but I could see how Zara changed once he was on the scene.'

'She finished with you to go out with Joel?'

He hadn't sat down again, but was now pacing around the room, looking increasingly agitated. I sensed he was reliving his moments with Zara, wondering how much to tell me. He looked past me, with no real focus and then he said, 'I made a big mistake. I asked her to choose, I thought she'd come to her senses and tell him to back off, instead...'

'It must have been a difficult time for you.'

'I loved her, you see, I still do. When Zara broke it off with me my life fell apart. I'd rented a bigger house in Brighton, I wanted her to move in with me. She'd have none of it. She told me to forget about her, said she was moving in with Joel. It was all so sudden, so I came back to Tamarisk Bay. I needed to see her, to persuade her not to do it. He wasn't right for her, you must have seen that. You spent time with them both, didn't you? You and Greg?'

I was struggling to get my head around all that Owen was telling me. Zara had been living in Brighton until she moved in with Joel, but she hadn't mentioned Owen in all our conversations. I thought back to the day I packed Zara's tapestry bag, putting her diary in at the top. Perhaps there were clues inside that diary, but it was too late now, the diary disappeared the same day that Zara did.

'The end of a relationship is never easy,' I said. An image of Marjorie Proops' agony aunt column came into my head and I had to bite my lip to stop myself smiling. 'What happened?'

'I only saw her the once. I came for a weekend, stayed with my parents and hung around outside Joel's place, hoping to catch Zara on her own.'

'Did you?'

'Yes, but not for long. They came out of the flat together, it was lunchtime. They went their separate ways and I caught up with her outside Flay's.'

'The greengrocer's?'

'Yes.'

'What happened? She must have been surprised to see you?'

'We went for coffee, that was when she told me about you, that she'd met up with you after years and how pleased she was to have you as a friend.'

I wished I could take out a notebook and jot down everything he was telling me so that I could work out the timeline. I got the sense there was more to this than a straightforward break-up and the more he spoke the more anxious I felt.

'How did you recognise me? In the disco the other night…?'

'She told me you looked after the mobile library. I've been in once or twice. I had a crazy idea I could ask you to intervene for me, to talk to her about Joel, persuade her to leave him. She might have listened to you.'

'When you had coffee with her, did you ask her about Joel? If she was happy with him?'

'I was going to, but then…'

'What happened?'

'I lost my temper.'

'In what way?'

'I told her she was being stupid, that Joel wasn't the man for her, that he'd hurt her eventually. Men like Joel, well, you can just tell, they're only interested in one thing.'

I raised an eyebrow. 'I'm sure he really cared for her. I can see you might have been angry that he'd taken her from you, but Joel was a good man. He was always buying her presents, taking her out. They were happy together.'

'Ownership. He wanted to possess her, she was a trophy for him, that's all.'

'And you told her that?'

'Yes, she wasn't pleased with me.'

'I can imagine.'

'Anyway, we argued, she told me to mind my own business and to leave her alone. And that's when I did it.'

'What?'

'I hit her.'

He won't have missed my sharp intake of breath. I fought an impulse to distance myself from him, but instead I sat on my hands and studied his face. 'You hit her?'

'I'm not proud of myself. I don't know what happened, it was just hearing her talk to me like that, knowing she'd chosen him over me.'

'What did she do?'

'She got up and walked out of the café. I never saw her again.'

'Oh, Owen.' I didn't know what else to say. My mind was struggling to absorb what he'd told me and to work out if it had any bearing on Zara's disappearance. I couldn't think straight with him standing there in front of me, still appearing to be mortified by what he'd done. He bent his head and covered his face with his hands.

'And the people in the café? Did anyone tackle you about what you'd done?'

He shook his head and didn't respond. I sat still for a few moments, replaying the scene in my mind. My thoughts went to Greg, not just his gentle nature, but his imminent employment with the family of a bully, a woman beater.

'Don't tell anyone,' Owen said, his voice almost a whisper. 'I can't bear the idea of people knowing. I keep imagining what they'll think of me.'

I wondered if his parents knew anything about his relationship with Zara and about the difficulties their son had controlling his temper.

'Do you think Zara will come back?' he said.

'Right now, I don't even know where she's gone, but I'm going to do my best to try to find her.'

He sat down and picked up the cup of cold tea, twisting it around in his hands, but with no apparent intention of drinking it.

'Did you see the newspaper article about Zara's disappearance?' I said. 'Are you sure you don't know anything else that might help me track her down?' I said.

'No, like I say, I haven't seen her since that day. I read

about Joel's accident in the *Brighton Argus* and I was tempted to come back to see if I could help, to comfort her.'

'Might not have been your best idea?'

'I still love her.'

'Yes, I can see that, but she's had a hard time accepting Joel's gone. Whatever you thought of Joel, Zara cared for him.'

There was little more to say and I was keen for him to leave before Greg got home.

'If you remember anything else that might help me to find her, come and talk again,' I said. 'Although it's better if you drop into the mobile library, you're certain to find me there. I wouldn't want you to have a wasted journey.'

He stopped at the front door.

'Thank you,' he said.

'What for?'

'I've never done it before, you know. Hitting a woman like that. I hope you find her.'

'So do I.'

It was much later that evening before I had time to reflect on all that Owen had told me. I was grateful he'd felt able to be honest with me, but I got the sense he was still holding something back. His revelations had helped to plant a thought in my mind I wished I could shake off. Maybe Owen had done more than just hitting out at Zara. I fervently hoped I was wrong.

Chapter 12

Poirot gave me one look, which conveyed a wondering pity, and his full sense of the utter absurdity of such an idea.

The Mysterious Affair at Styles - Agatha Christie

Greg's sister, Becca, is the jewel in the crown of the Juke family. She'd been at college ever since leaving school and had accumulated more qualifications than I could dream of. Now she had just heard she'd got a place at Sussex University and it was all her parents could talk about. Becca, on the other hand, was surprisingly mute on the subject.

Greg's parents had planned a celebratory party, which sounded to me more like an opportunity to show off their clever daughter to various acquaintances and neighbours. As in-laws Jimmy and Nell Juke were okay, but I was frequently uncomfortable when they made their judgemental approach to life a little too obvious. I'd never said a word to Greg, knowing he would rush to their defence, which was completely understandable. It's easy for any of us to criticise our own family members, but we become like a vicious beast protecting their young if anyone else dares to.

Jimmy Juke was okay, in fact Greg was a lot like him, practical, hard-working and fair. But I got the feeling Nell believed the world owed her more than she had ever been given. She had a fairly ordinary family background, as far as I knew, but there was something aspirational about her. I'm certain when she first met Jimmy, who was a bank clerk back in the day, she had visions of his rapid promotion to bank manager and with it a comfortable middle-class life. Sadly, the war got in the way. After his spell in the army Jimmy returned to his job in the bank, but never rose beyond counter clerk. When Greg and then Becca came along, Nell had all the excuses she needed not to find herself a paid job. But with just one wage coming in, her hopes for an imposing, detached house in suburbia was out of the question.

Their modest semi in Roselands Avenue was homely, but Nell made it clear that it was a temporary measure and eventually they would move to a larger place. The temporary measure had lasted more than twenty years, but no-one dared to point that out.

With just three years between them, Greg and Becca were good friends, as well as brother and sister. Greg had always been the practical one, enjoyed being outdoors and active, but not one for sitting still for too long. Becca, however, thrived at school and was only happy when she had her head in a book. There was never any doubt she would eventually go to university. The only query was which one she would choose. We were both surprised she chose one so close to home, or maybe it was me who was more surprised. It was probably my vague antipathy towards Nell Juke that made me think if I was her daughter, I'd be on my way to Aberdeen or Dundee, given half the chance.

But the new university in Brighton sounded wonderful and offered Becca exactly the course she wanted, which meant taking book reading to a whole new level. I loved books, I spent most of my working week surrounded by them, but spending months deconstructing and dissecting a novel or play was not my idea of fun. I suppose it takes all sorts.

We'd visited Greg's parents a few days earlier to let them know their first grandchild was on the way. 'Well done, lad,' his father said, shaking Greg's hand so firmly I thought he would never let go. For a moment it was as though I wasn't involved at all. Then Nell came over and patted me on the shoulder.

'Oh, Jimmy, our first grandchild. You need to take care of her now, Greg. Spoil her a bit,' she said.

'What do you mean? I spoil her all the time,' Greg said. 'I even offered to bring her a cup of tea in bed the other morning and she turned me down flat.'

This wasn't the moment to go into details about my problems with tea, so I took Greg's hand and said, 'He's the perfect husband, don't you worry.'

'And you'll have to let us spoil that baby, you can't love a baby too much, that's what I say,' she flushed a little as she spoke, her emotions getting the better of her.

I dispelled any thoughts of Nell fussing around Bean, advising me to *feed on demand,* or scrutinising newly laundered nappies, ensuring they were *whiter than white.* Instead I just smiled and told her, 'It's a lucky baby to have such doting grandparents.'

'It's just as it should be,' she said.

We didn't reply, I had no idea what she meant and I don't think Greg was much the wiser.

'We'll always be available for babysitting, you know that,' she said. 'After all, your dad won't be able to…'

I held my breath, wondering how she would finish the sentence without dropping herself into a deep hole. Then Jimmy came to her rescue.

'We must have a get-together to celebrate, your dad must come as well, of course. Let's make a date on the calendar,' he said.

I smiled my sweetest smile and was pleased when Greg said we had to be going.

'Thanks, dad, we'll have a chat to Philip and sort some dates out,' Greg said, seemingly unaware that there was any tension to defuse.

'If dad comes, then so does Charlie and your mum isn't keen on dogs, is she?' I told Greg later that day, once we were home.

'Oh, she'll be fine. Don't take any notice of her moaning, it's all bluster with her.'

'Right, well, don't blame me if she complains about the dog hairs.'

Fortunately, neither Jimmy or Nell mentioned the get-together again and Becca's party provided Nell with another focus. The party was planned for a Sunday afternoon and was to be held at the Jukes' house. The forecast was for a glorious summer's day, which meant the chance for guests to overspill into Nell's well-tended garden. The menu centered around a delicate display of fish paste and cucumber sandwiches and little home-made scones.

I promised Greg I would lend a hand, so early on Sunday morning I turned up at Roselands Avenue, prepared to do whatever was needed.

'Here I am, your chief bottle washer and bread butterer, at the ready,' I said, as Nell answered the door. I wasn't surprised when she didn't smile, my jokes rarely raised a chuckle from my mother-in-law, but this time her expression indicated more than a lack of humour.

'Is everything okay?' I asked her, following her through into the kitchen where every surface was covered in part-prepared savouries and scones.

'It's Becca.'

'Is she poorly? What's the problem?'

'She won't come out of her room,' she said, wiping her hands on her apron. 'She's been in a mood all week and now she says she's not coming out and we can have the party without her.'

'Ah, so that's tricky then. Do you know why she's upset?'

'Upset? I'll give her upset. I've done all this for her and this is the way she repays me. Selfish, that's what it is.'

'Shall I get Greg? Perhaps he can talk her round? He was going to come over in a couple of hours, but I can go and fetch him now if you like?'

'Her father has already tried talking to her. I told him to give her an ultimatum, but he's far too soft with her. Stern words, that's what the girl needs. When I was her age I wasn't even allowed an opinion.'

'Maybe she'll listen to me? Would you like me to try?'

'Help yourself,' she said and waved me through to the hallway and then turned around and walked back into the kitchen without another word.

'Right,' I mumbled to myself, 'so I'll just go up then, shall I?'

I hadn't been in Becca's room before, but I knew it was opposite Greg's old room. The door was firmly shut, so I knocked gently at first and then a little harder when there was no response. After a few moments I pushed the door open a crack and popped my head around to see Becca curled on her bed with her back towards me and her arms up hiding her face.

'Go away,' she said, without turning to look at me.

91

'Are you okay? Can I come in?'

Without waiting for her response I walked into the room and closed the door behind me. I moved a chair that was beside the window and positioned it next to her bed to face her.

'Having a rough day?' I said.

'I told her, I don't even want a stupid party. What's the point of it? She hasn't invited any of my friends, just all her old cronies and nosey neighbours. She only wants to brag. Anyone would think she's the one going to university.'

'She's proud of you, that's all. She wants to show you off.'

'Show herself off, more like.'

'Greg and I will be there and it's only for a couple of hours. The three of us can sneak away into a corner of the garden. You don't want to disappoint your big brother, do you? He's looking forward to it.'

'No he isn't. He told me he was dreading it.'

'Well, the food looks delicious. She's gone to a lot of trouble.'

Becca sat up and swung her legs over the side of the bed. She brushed her hair away from her face, which was still wet with tears.

'Hey, it's not that bad. Just one silly afternoon and then she'll have got it out of her system. You must be so excited about your course, you've done so well, worked so hard.'

'I wish I was leaving today. There's still weeks to go before I start.'

'There must be loads to sort out. What about your books? Do you have to buy many? I would offer to check some of them out in the library, but I'm guessing our selection won't be quite what you're looking for.'

'The uni library is pretty comprehensive. We were given a tour when we went to their open day. You'd love it, although there's not many crime novels.'

The Juke family were well aware of my penchant for Agatha Christie and Jimmy often teased me about it. Greg told me once that his dad's pet name for me was Miss Marple. Thankfully, he'd never said it to my face.

'What about your digs, are they all sorted? Are you staying on campus?'

'I was going to, but then I had an offer of a house share.'

'With one of your friends?'

'Kind of. He's a friend of a friend. His name's Owen Mowbray. He rents a big house in Brighton and needs someone to share. My friend Melanie is moving in too. Should be fun.'

Becca was too busy studying her face in the mirror and re-applying her makeup to notice me flinch at her revelation. She was young and vulnerable. Perhaps my imagination was too fertile, but I couldn't sit back and say nothing and let Becca move in with someone who might be dangerous. The problem was that I couldn't think of a way to stop it happening, without showing my hand.

I rejoined the party and was just planning to move in on the sausage rolls, when Jimmy sidled over to me, extricating himself from one of his neighbours who had a high-pitched voice and a laugh that was more like a cackle.

'How are you keeping? Baby all alright?' he said.

'Yes, all good.'

'No more news about your friend? Terrible business. Still, it can't have been easy having her living with you all that time.'

'Has Greg said something?' I could feel the anxiety hiccups bubbling up.

'Greg? No, I just thought...all that moping about, she never stepped out of the door for a whole year by all accounts?'

'I'll just clear a few of these plates away, give Nell a hand in the kitchen.'

I couldn't decide which made me more angry; Greg moaning to his dad, or the fact that both of them were missing the point. We had tried to offer support to a good friend at a time of her life when she was at her lowest. In my book that shouldn't have come with criticism about how many times she went to the shops.

'Parties exhaust me,' Greg said, flopping down on the settee, once we were home.

'You are funny. Why? It's not like you had to do the food, or the clearing up. I noticed you suggested we left before your mum grabbed you for washing-up duties.'

There was no point saying anything to Greg about my conversation with his dad. It would have just started an argument and I didn't have the energy for it.

'All that mingling and small talk, it's boring. I'd rather be down the pub,' he said.

'Or here with your lovely wife?'

'Yeah, that too. You did well with Becca, talking her round. I'm sure mum was really grateful.'

'No more mention of the get-together with dad? To celebrate Bean's arrival?'

'There's no rush, though, is there?'

I laid in bed that night and tried to divide my worries into little filing cabinets. Greg, Bean, Becca, Owen, Zara. Sleep would have to go on the back-burner for a while.

Chapter 13

'I have a little idea, a very strange, and probably utterly impossible idea.   And yet – it fits in.'
The Mysterious Affair at Styles - Agatha Christie

Not wanting to push my luck, I had carefully avoided the subject of Mr Peters when I next met Nikki at the antenatal clinic. Fortunately, her mind was elsewhere, as the midwife had just told her she was expecting twins.

'Oh my,' was all I could think of to say, not knowing if she was delighted or terrified. Although the expression on her face soon told me it was the former.

'I've always wanted twins. Instant family,' she said, then launched into a ten-minute report of their plans for the babies' bedroom.

'Frank is thrilled. He says there's no way I can even think of working now. I'll have to be a stay at home mum. Do things properly.'

Her tone suggested she was revelling in the idea, clearly a change of heart from our recent conversations.

'Congratulations, I'm so pleased for you. Very exciting,' I said, thinking of my own dread of managing one little person, let alone two.

I had visited the paper shop and placed an order for a daily delivery. Neither Greg nor I were avidly interested in current affairs, but we loved crosswords, so I chose the newspaper with plenty of puzzles to keep us amused.

Mr Peters appeared to run the shop single-handedly. I hoped I could engage him in a conversation at an appropriate moment, without being disturbed by other staff, although there was no guarantee about other customers.

I left it a week and then arrived late on Tuesday afternoon to pay the paper bill. My hope was that by arriving just as Mr Peters was closing up there was more chance of catching him on his own. I had no idea how I would bring the conversation around to Zara, in fact, having any conversation at all would present a challenge.

As I reached the shop Mr Peters was sweeping, just outside his front door. He swept with gusto, his robust frame pushing the broom along in brisk strokes. His focus was entirely on the pile of dust, litter and leaves that had accumulated in front of the broom, so when I approached from behind and greeted him, he turned around and looked startled.

'Sorry, I've just come to pay my paper bill. I'm not too late, am I?'

He glanced at my increasing baby bump and smiled.

'Of course not, my dear, come on in. Take a seat if you like. I haven't started cashing up yet.'

It struck me that little Bean could prove as useful to me in gathering information as a dog can be for someone looking for love.

'I will take a seat, if that's okay. I'm finding I get tired more quickly these days.' I followed him into the shop and he disappeared out the back, returning with a folding chair for me.

'There you are, take the weight off for a few minutes. What's the name? I'll look out the bill for you.'

'Mrs Juke. I owe one week I think.'

He flicked through his accounts book and I seized the moment.

'I must say it's lovely to have the place open again. Before you took over we were buying our paper at the shop down Church Street, but this is much more convenient for us and it's ideal having it delivered. You've got the place looking pristine.'

Pristine, I thought, *what are you talking about? Who describes a newsagent's as pristine?'*

'Thank you, my dear, that's kind.'

'There must be so much to consider, ordering and so on. I expect you've been in the newspaper business for a while?'

Get a grip, Janie, you're waffling.

'I haven't, no. Well, I did help out now and again in the shop at the holiday camp.'

'Holiday camp?'

'Yes, I was working on the big holiday campsite over near Bognor. Been there for a season, but I thought it was time to come home.'

'Oh, sounds like fun. You're from around here then? What made you come back?'

'I heard about this place from an old friend. Thought it was too good a chance to miss.'

The conversation was taking the right direction, I just needed to push it one step further. 'I can understand you wanting to come back,' I said. 'I've lived here all my life and I love it. You feel so safe, nothing ever happens around here, which is a positive thing in my book.'

'Things are changing. You only have to read the local paper. Youngsters racing about on motorbikes, taking drugs, getting drunk. They talk about peace not war, but it's all talk. And there's no respect. I'm forever clearing up rubbish outside the shop, they just throw cans and bottles all over the place. I blame the parents. Don't get me wrong, dear, I don't mean nice young people like you, it's the teenagers, they come in here and the language. If my dad ever heard me using words like that he'd have given me a clout, that's for sure. I need to be so eagle-eyed, turn your back for a minute and they'll be stuffing their pockets with all sorts.'

I was happy to let him continue to rant while I thought of the best way of turning the conversation in the direction I was hoping for.

'You're absolutely right, of course,' I said, when he stopped speaking. 'My dad used to be in the police years ago and the worst thing he ever had to deal with was the odd case of scrumping. I can only imagine what the poor police have to cope with nowadays. Like you say, youngsters running riot.' I tried not to think about Greg's reaction if he could hear me talking like a fifty-year-old, otherwise I'd never be able to keep a straight face.

'I can tell you a thing or two about the police. If you ask me they have no idea how to treat decent people.'

'How do you mean?'

'I was in the police station just the other day. And do you know, instead of thanking me for coming forward, they treated me like I was the guilty party. I ask you.'

'Gosh, that must have been awful. What happened?'

'That missing girl, you know the case? She'd be about your age.'

'Er, yes, I know the one you mean. I heard the police had a new lead, so that was you, was it?'

'That's right, my dear, I saw her on the day she went missing. I'm the person who is helping the police with their enquiries.'

Mr Peters told me all I wanted to know without me asking him another question. He explained that on the day Zara disappeared he was visiting St Martha's cemetery. His parents are both buried there in a family grave he anticipates adding to, but not for many years, he tells me with a wink. His light-hearted approach to death made me uncomfortable.

He arrived late afternoon, which he explained was his favourite time, as the cemetery is usually empty.

'I like time to chat and it's better when there's no-one around. Some people think it's strange when you talk to the departed,' he said. 'I've always chatted to them, I use them as my sounding board. I was there that day to explain my plans to them, about taking on the newsagents. I was certain they were behind me all the way.'

At this point he looked at me as though he was challenging me to smirk in disbelief. I remained impassive and nodded.

'It was then that I saw her. I heard a rustling and looked up to see a young woman. She walked over to one of the headstones, knelt down and did something to the grave, but I couldn't see what. Then she got up, brushed herself down and left. I didn't see any flowers or anything. I like to think she was doing the same as me. The spirit world are always ready to listen, you know, and if you recognise the signs, then they'll often point you in the right direction.'

I could see Mr Peters getting side-tracked again, wondering off into his own world, when I needed him to focus more clearly on this one.

'And that's what you told the police, that you'd seen a young woman? What made you think it was the missing girl? I mean did you recognise her?'

'Pretty thing, no mistaking her. Olive-skin, beautiful eyes. Hang on a minute and I'll show you something.'

He disappeared out the back, returning with something rolled up under one arm. I knew exactly what I was going to see when he unrolled it. The bottom of the poster had been torn off, it was just Zara's face, staring out at me.

'I found this when I took over the shop. I expect they were everywhere when she went missing. You must have seen them yourself?'

'Er, yes, I do remember them, now you come to mention it.'

'Well, as soon as I saw her face, it triggered a memory, of that day in the cemetery. I went straight down to the police station and told them. And were they grateful? Oh no, not a bit of it.'

'I'm sure they were, I expect they're not allowed to say much, it being an ongoing case?'

'Ongoing case, my foot. No, they barely showed any interest. All they wanted to know is why I'd taken so long in coming forward, like I had something to hide. So I didn't tell them the rest.'

'The rest?' My heart started to thump in my chest and I hoped he wouldn't notice.

'I didn't tell them what she was carrying. It was a bag of some kind, large, like a holdall. She was too far away for me to see the bag in much detail, but it was multi-coloured, I'm certain of that.'

At this point my mouth fell open. It confirmed the seed of hope that I had clung to since the day Zara left. Now I had reassurance that she still had the bag when she visited Joel's grave. If she had planned suicide she would have dumped it somewhere, or maybe not even taken it. I realised how much worse it would be if I had walked into her bedroom that evening to see the tapestry bag still sitting on the chair.

'Well,' I said. 'That's quite a thing.'

'Is it?' he said. 'It doesn't seem like much, but it would appear that I'm the last person to see her, which is quite a responsibility. And I suppose if she had a holdall with her, well then she must have been going somewhere.'

'Yes, I can see that. You didn't mention the bag to the police?'

The question was out before I could stop myself.

'No, I remembered it afterwards, but they'd been so offhand with me. Well, I didn't want to go through that again. They just took my statement, read it back to me, got me to sign it and that was that.'

He paused and looked contemplative. 'It's a strange case though, isn't it?'

'Yes,' I nodded, 'it is.'

Having paid the paper bill, I left Mr Peters shortly after our chat. I'd got a little closer to finding out what happened to Zara the day she left our house. I already knew she'd packed all her things, so that wasn't news to me. The only surprising thing was that she'd left via the cemetery. I imagined the police felt the same way about Mr Peters' information. It was hardly a revelation. It got me wondering why the police had bothered to announce it as a 'fresh lead'. Perhaps Mr Peters knew more than he was saying.

Chapter 14

A "man of method" was, in Poirot's estimation, the
highest praise that could be bestowed on any individual.
The Mysterious Affair at Styles - *Agatha Christie*

Bitter irony is one way of describing what happened to
my dad. He was just a boy when the Second World War
ended, but old enough to be sent to fight. He survived
the worst of the death and destruction war brings with it
and then he steps out in front of a bus and ends up blind.
Dad never spoke about any of it. Not about the fighting
and not about the accident. I was five years old when he
crossed the road that snowy morning. It was the first
heavy snow I'd seen and dad promised to walk to the
park with me so we could make the biggest snowman.
We never got to the park and I've hated snow ever since.

My memory of that day is still crystal clear.

The bus was late and dad said it would be ages 'til we
had our tea.

'You wait here, Janie. I'll go and get some pink
doughnuts for my pretty pink princess,' he said.

'Don't be silly, dad, I'm not a princess and I'm not
even pink,' I said. Everything in my world was pink,
from my bedroom to my favourite pair of mittens.

Afterwards, the doughnuts were lying in the dirty
snow at the side of the road, beside the bus. It was funny
how the bus hadn't squashed the doughnuts, but it had
squashed my dad, well, his head anyway.

When it happened, I remember feeling vague, like
when you're having a dream and the dream ends and you
know you're awake, but you can't hear or feel anything.

There were people all around my dad and I could see

their mouths moving, but I couldn't hear what they were saying. Just before the bus came my tummy had been hurting, because I was so hungry and my hands and feet were freezing. Afterwards, it was like I didn't have a tummy or hands or feet, like I was sort of floating. But it wasn't a nice floaty feeling, because as soon as I felt my tummy again I knew I was going to be sick.

That was when I heard the noise from the ambulance and the police car and the people shouting. I heard all the noises at the same time and it made my head hurt.

A lady in a tea-cosy kind of hat smiled at me. She took my hand and led me to a bench to sit down.

'That wasn't a nice thing to see, was it? It's given you a shock.'

'Thank you,' was all I could think of to say. I let her hold my hand; well, she held my pink mitten, because my hands were in my mittens and they were still icy cold.

'Who are you here with love? Are you out with your mummy or daddy? Let's turn away, let's look over there at the park, see how the snow on the trees sparkles in the sunshine.'

'I don't like snow anymore,' I said. The snow had made the bus slide. It didn't stop. It just kept going. I didn't want doughnuts any more, I just wanted my dad. I pulled my hand away from the lady and ran to the ambulance. Two men with yellow coats were lifting my dad onto a stretcher.

'I need to come in the ambulance. I need to hold my dad's hand.'

I don't even remember the sirens and yet whenever I see an emergency vehicle racing along the road with lights flashing, I think of that day.

The first time mum took me to visit dad in hospital she got me ready as though I was going to a party. She put me in my best frock, tied ribbons in my hair and gave my face an extra scrub. She spent just as long getting herself ready. She wore her Sunday best dress, a cardigan that might have been newly purchased, or borrowed. Around her neck hung a string of pearls. I'd never seen those pearls before and I never saw them again after that day.

She took hold of my hand and we walked into the hospital ward together to see my dad lying there, with his eyes all bandaged up.

'Your dad can't see you anymore, Janie,' she said. It was a mystery to me as to why she had taken so much trouble over our appearance. I remember the expression on her face when she saw my dad. It was as though he had let her down, like she was the one who was suffering.

I ran over to his bedside and grabbed his hand. 'Hello dad, it's me, Janie,' I said.

'Hello princess.' His smile covered the whole of his face, an unshaven face, pale and drawn. 'Hearing your voice is the very best medicine your dad can have. Come and sit right here beside me and tell me all you've been up to.'

The back of his head took the brunt of the trauma and that's why he ended up blind. Later, when I was old enough to ask questions and comprehend the answers, dad told me it was his occipital lobe that had been damaged. If it had been another part of his brain, then he may not have walked out of that hospital. He could have died that day. His viewpoint was that blindness was a relatively small price to pay, when you consider the alternatives.

He never complained or railed against his fate and the day my mum moved out he never said a word against her. She'd given up pretending we were important to her and I have no idea what she's doing now. We have an address for her, somewhere up north, but she's not interested in our lives and the feeling is mutual.

When they were first married mum and dad couldn't afford their own place, so they moved in with dad's mother. I never met my grandmother, but dad has fond memories of her. Grandma died and dad took over the mortgage. It was the house where I grew up and dad still lives there. It's old, rambling, and badly in need of repair, but dad and I love it. The uneven floors and steep staircase aren't exactly ideal for a blind man, but dad knows every creak and groan of that place. On the days when I go back there to do dad's typing and housework it's like falling back into my childhood, but only the best bits.

My old bedroom looks out over the tiny back garden and the wallpaper is unchanged from my teenage years. When I was about thirteen I fell in love with everything orange and Aunt Jessica and I played around with wallpaper paste and paint brushes, getting more glue and paint on us than on the walls. Now and then, when I'm back in dad's house, I sit in my old bedroom, gaze out of the window and remember.

I stopped missing mum a long time ago, but now I'm pregnant I find myself thinking about her more than I used to. I wonder what it was like when she discovered I was on the way. I like to believe she and dad were happy then and still in love. It makes me sad to imagine dad being in a relationship with someone who didn't treasure how wonderful he is, he deserves much more than that.

When I was older and the yearnings of young love grabbed me, and I felt the excitement and desperation of fancying someone, I wanted those same emotions for my dad. Just because he couldn't see, didn't mean he couldn't feel.

'Do think you'll fall in love again?' I asked him once.

'Little Janie, all grown up. Listen to you talking about love.'

'That's not an answer.'

'I've got you.'

'Yes, you'll always have me. I'm not going to marry, I'll remain independent, forge a distinctive career, make lots of money and keep my dad in the manner he deserves.'

Instead, I met Greg, fell in love and failed to carve out any career, well paid or otherwise.

Greg's mum tries to overcompensate. She looks at me sometimes and I imagine she's thinking, *oh you poor thing, no mother there for you as you grew up and a blind dad as well, how have you coped?* although these sentiments are never voiced. There is a distinct possibility that Greg's desire to see me encumbered with a large brood is related to the whole *poor motherless Janie* scenario. As though becoming a bountiful mother myself will eradicate all that has gone before.

On my days with dad I make sure his paperwork and patient records are all up to date, as well as anything else I can do to make his life easier.

'Greg doesn't think I should get involved,' I said, as we sat in the kitchen, sipping our drinks. I had discovered hot water with lemon was a reasonable alternative to the usual cuppa.

'Looking for Zara, you mean?'

'Yes.'

'And what do you think?'

It's fair to say I am my father's daughter, present me with a challenge and I will be the proverbial terrier, not letting go until it's sorted. On more than one occasion as I grew up he'd discovered that to tell me not to do something was a sure-fire way to make sure I did it.

'She was my friend, dad. I owe it to her to help her out.'

'You helped her a lot, she lived with you both for a year, that would be above and beyond in some people's eyes.'

I told dad about Owen and Mr Peters. When I explained about Owen's violence, dad shook his head.

'That's not good, not good at all,' he said.

'It's a month now since the police announced their new lead and as far as I can see they are doing absolutely nothing. What if Zara is scared? Owen has been living in Brighton. That's where she was living before she met Joel. Maybe Owen was stalking her. It could be he frightened her so much she's hiding from him.'

'Do you think he's the kind of man who could really hurt her?'

'Well he hit her, didn't he?'

'But really hurt her?'

'I don't know.'

'What do you know?'

'Well, Zara and I were at school together, weren't we?'

'Do you know what I think?' he said. 'Take it back to basics. Blank out anything you know about her and start again. Be thorough, make lists.'

'Are you teasing me now?' Dad and Greg were forever teasing me about my inability to follow a system. Like I say, I am the least likely person to be a librarian, or an amateur detective, come to that.

'There's something else you can do.'

I waited.

'Make use of all those Agatha Christie novels you've read and re-read since you were a little'un.'

'What do you mean 'make use'?'

'Search for patterns, clues, that's what Poirot does.'

'Nice idea, but that's fiction. This is real.'

'It won't hurt to try.'

Dad's advice for me to start from scratch inspired me to get organised. His suggestion about Agatha's Poirot made me smile, but when I thought about it a bit more I realised it might just help. A few weeks earlier I'd started re-reading *The Mysterious Affair at Styles,* so I decided to scour the book to see if I could glean any tips from the wonderful Poirot and his sidekick, Hastings.

I wanted to approach this investigation in a professional manner, to forget that this was a search for a close friend. I bought a large notebook and started making lists. Much of what I wrote down were the avenues we explored straight after Zara's disappearance. We'd already spoken to everyone we thought might know her, but our enquiries got us nowhere.

We also visited her sister.

Until I met Zara and Gabrielle I didn't realise it was possible for identical twins to be so dissimilar. For every inward-looking aspect of Zara's character, Gabrielle was the polar opposite. It was as though together they made up the classic Jekyll and Hyde split personality. Perhaps if they'd been born as one child instead of two, this is how it would have been.

Zara and I first became friends when she joined Grosvenor Grammar in the fourth year. The twins arrived at the beginning of the summer term. Zara was put into my class and Gabrielle went into Miss Bone's class. It seemed a little odd to me that they were separated, but I just assumed they liked it that way. Zara and I hung around together during lunchbreaks, seeking out quiet parts of the school grounds. Gabrielle never joined us. She had her own circle of friends who had just one topic of conversation - boys. They would hang around outside Pam's Coffee Bar in the town centre on a Saturday morning. A few times Zara and I would walk into town together to listen to the latest hit singles. We'd stroll up Queens Road and there Gabrielle would be, with her two closest friends, Milly and Rose. Zara would link her arm through mine and walk briskly past them, calling out a brief hello. I thought it odd, but when I asked Zara once why it was they weren't close, she didn't reply.

After Zara and I met up again and throughout the year she spent living with us, we had nothing to do with Gabrielle. Zara mentioned that her sister had moved back to the area at the same time and I sensed that she wished she hadn't. I asked her whether they'd shared a flat when she lived in Brighton, but she just shook her head. It seemed they were as distant as they always had been.

So, when Zara disappeared we were certain Gabrielle's flat was the last place she would go, but it was still worth checking. Greg came with me and when I rang the bell for Flat 3C I heard a shout from above. Looking up, there was Gabrielle's face leaning out of the front window.

'Yes,' she said, 'what is it?' with her haughty manner she would have made an excellent hospital matron, although I couldn't imagine her wanting to get her hands dirty.

'It's Zara,' I shouted up to her. 'She's gone missing. We wondered if she'd come here, if she'd been in touch?'

'Here? Why should she come here?'

'We're worried about her,' Greg said.

'Well, she's not here,' she said and pulled the sash window down and that was that.

But now it looked as though another visit to Gabrielle was needed. As much as I didn't like the thought of being given short shrift again, I couldn't ignore the fact that Gabrielle was the only person who could tell me about Zara. I had no choice but to brave it, but this time I planned to go alone.

Chapter 15

'Tell me – you're drawn to something? Everyone is –
usually something absurd.'
'You'll laugh at me.' She smiled.
'Perhaps.'
'Well, I've always had a secret hankering to be a
detective!'
The Mysterious Affair at Styles - Agatha Christie

My home town of Tamarisk Bay lies to the west of
Tidehaven and could be described as its smaller
neighbour. It's strange to imagine it was originally set out
as a new town, back in the nineteenth century, with
elegant properties designed for the well-to-do. The
geography of the place sees it rising from the sea front,
sharply at first and then more steadily, as it winds up into
gentle slopes, with a scattering of parks and gardens and
wide roads.

Gabrielle's flat was in Sutherland Road, a trendy part
of town, favoured by arty types and musicians. The
architect who set out the original plan for the area also
worked on some of the properties in Bloomsbury, around
the end of the eighteen hundreds.

The road was lined with large Edwardian houses that
were now divided into three or four spacious flats. The
frontage of each was dramatic, with cornices and
decorative stonework around the large sash window
frames. I'd never been inside any of the flats, but I
guessed the interiors would be just as glamorous. I liked
to imagine the families who would have lived in one of
these grand houses in their heyday. Perhaps they had
servants, a drawing room with a grand piano, velvet-

covered sofas and a dining room that could provide a feast for twenty.

I walked up the stone steps and rang the bell for Flat 3C. The last time I attempted to speak to Gabrielle she'd shouted at me from a window and hadn't had the courtesy to let me in. This time I was more determined.

There was a padding of feet and a crunch as she drew back the lock and opened the door.

'Hello, Gabrielle. Can I come in?'

'I'm just off out,' she said.

'I'm sure you are, but before you dash can I have a quick chat?' I looked directly at her, challenging her to turn me away. 'Doesn't your sister deserve just five minutes? I won't keep you long, I promise.' Maybe it was a mistake mentioning Zara before being allowed inside, but the words were out and I couldn't retract them.

'You'd better come in,' she said, looking at my expanding midriff. She may have been taking pity on a poor pregnant woman, but whatever the reason I didn't need to be asked twice. I followed her up three flights of stairs and in through a heavy wooden door to the hallway of her flat.

Her home was as beautiful as I had imagined, perhaps even more so. We walked down the long hallway into a large sitting room where Chinese rugs covered the polished wooden floor. The high ceilings with deep architraves gave a sense of light and space. The walls on all sides displayed an eclectic range of photographs and paintings, as well as colourful wall hangings. She gestured to me to take a seat on one of the three armchairs. I sat gingerly on the edge of the chair, not wanting to lean back for fear of creasing the silk cushions.

'Drink?' she asked and, without waiting for a reply, she turned and went back out into the hallway. Her departure gave me a chance to examine her art and photographic display in a little more detail. I know little about art - modern or classical - but from what I could see Gabrielle had more than a passing interest. In the main it was French impressionism that featured, which was not surprising, given her family background, with a scattering of modern pieces as well. I didn't recognise the modern paintings, but then when it came to art I wasn't even a beginner, more of a non-starter. Some of the prints were framed, others were large posters. In-between them sat black and white photographs, providing a perfect contrast to their more colourful neighbours. Zara had inherited her mother's flair for style and fashion, whereas the pictures on display suggested that Gabrielle explored art in its more traditional sense.

As I studied the photographs in more detail I noticed that none of them showed faces. Most depicted people, rather than landscapes or still life, but each person or group was shown at a distance or from behind. A few expensive-looking ornaments were set out on the mantelpiece, but there was no evidence of any family photos, certainly not of Zara, but not even her parents. It was as though she had carefully created a world inside her flat where she had no need to relate to people.

I was looking at one of the Monet posters when Gabrielle came back into the room with a tray.

'Stunning, isn't it?' she said, putting the tray down onto the glass-topped coffee table. 'His attitude to light and shade is masterful.'

I couldn't think of a reply, so forced a weak smile and sat back down on the edge of the armchair.

'Milk or lemon?' she said, with the teapot poised over a delicate china cup.

'Um, lemon, thanks.' I was reluctant to explain my difficulties with tea and hoped Bean would behave and let me drink just one cup in peace, without forcing me to run to the bathroom. I was also anxious that my hiccups would start, now that I was face-to-face with Gabrielle. She had a way about her that belied her age and yet she was the same age as me.

'When did you develop your interest in art?' I asked. 'We didn't get to know each other at school, is it something you took up back then?'

'No, you were Zara's friend. Very pally the two of you. I'm surprised you didn't keep in touch when we moved.'

'I'm hopeless at writing letters, I can never think of anything exciting to say.'

'What is it you want?' she said, handing me the cup and saucer.

'Nothing, I don't want anything, except perhaps a chance to talk about Zara. I'm sure it would help me to find out more about her.'

'Why would it help you?'

I could see this was going to be an arduous conversation and likely one that would bear no fruit. I thought about walking out, which would at least get me out of drinking the tea.

'Gabrielle, I'll be straight with you. I care about Zara. I may not have been involved in her life for long, but that year she lived with us, with Greg and me, I formed a bond with her. And now I want to do everything I can to find her, to make sure she's okay. You're her twin sister, so you're her closest link. I just thought maybe you could

115

tell me a bit about the kind of person she was, I mean is. Those years between us leaving school and me bumping into her again. What was she doing? Where was she living? Did she have a job? Who was she hanging out with?' I paused, hoping my rambling would be persuasive enough to get her to open up.

'I have no idea,' she said.

'She's your sister, for goodness sake. Surely you must have known something about her life?'

'You need to understand something fundamental about my sister and me. We have no relationship. Yes, we are related by blood, but that's it. She's always made it clear she wants to live her own life. I respect that and I live my own life too. So, there you have it. You probably know her better than I do.'

'I doubt that,' I said, with irritation building up inside me. 'What about when you were children, weren't you even friends then?'

'That was a lifetime ago,' she said and looked away from me. 'I don't know what I can tell you that might help. I'll share with you what I told the police when they interviewed me if you like, if you think it will be useful.'

'Yes, anything at all. No matter how vague.'

'Well, Zara liked a cause.'

'How do you mean?'

'She liked to champion the underdog, protest against the evils in the world. She went on marches, waved banners. I've never seen the point myself. The world is messed up and no amount of marching will save us from ourselves. The human being will ultimately be responsible for its own demise. I concentrate on things of beauty, as you can see,' she gestured towards the paintings and photos.

116

'Was she a member of a protest group, a political party?'

'I have no idea. That's all I know and now I must ask you to leave or I'll be late for an appointment.' She stood up, indicating that was the end of our conversation.

As she stood, the shawl she'd wrapped around her shoulders fell away and for a moment there was Zara standing in front of me. At school, the teachers had struggled to tell the sisters apart, but for the fact that Zara maintained a short haircut and Gabrielle's long locks were usually plaited and wound tightly around her head. But as Zara's friend I was aware there was another distinguishing feature that marked her apart from her twin. She had a small, cherry-sized birthmark at the nape of her neck. I was reminded of this now when Gabrielle's shawl fell away, exposing her olive skin, with no sign of a birth mark.

'Will you let me know if you hear anything from her?' I said, as she ushered me towards the front door.

'I won't.'

'You won't let me know?'

'I won't hear from her. Trust me, I know my sister. She's probably gone to join a commune somewhere. I wouldn't worry about her. You've got other things to focus on anyway, haven't you?' she said, pointing at my midriff.

'Like I said, she's my friend and I want to know she's alright.'

'Well, you've come to the wrong person. Goodbye, Janie. See yourself out.'

Despite her antipathy towards me and her sister, Gabrielle had helped to confirm what Owen had suggested. Zara was passionate about inequality of any kind. She worried about the way the strong overpower the weak and felt sad to see peace and harmony destroyed by acrimony and bitterness. During the conversations we'd had as adults she often dropped hints that I should have picked up on. There was so much I could have learned from my friend if only I had been more aware, not least that it pays to be a good listener.

As I walked back down the stairs I was fuming and more grateful than ever to be an only child.

Chapter 16

'I say, what was the end of that message? Say it over again, will you?'
The Mysterious Affair at Styles - Agatha Christie

Waking early would appear to be a part of impending motherhood. Nature's way of getting you used to the sleepless nights and dawn feeds. As I swung my legs out of bed and into my slippers I had a fleeting thought that my next lie-in would be eighteen years away when Bean leaves home.

Greg muttered something under his breath about wanting to sleep, as I padded out to the bathroom. It was still dark. When I bought my bedside clock the advert promised 'luminous numbers'. It didn't take long to realise the promise was empty, but I couldn't be bothered to take it back to Woolworths and decided that time would soon be irrelevant. If my baby cries I'll need to get up.

Greg is a brilliant window cleaner but less than confident with all things plumbing. As a result, the noise from the toilet cistern when we pulled the chain was enough to wake the dead. I decided to wait until I'd checked the time on the kitchen clock before disturbing my husband further. Tiptoeing downstairs, carefully avoiding the squeaky floorboard, I turned on the kitchen light and discovered it was just 5.30. An hour at least before Greg needed to get up. A quiet hour for me to arrange my thoughts and make a few more plans.

I removed the whistle from the kettle before putting it on the gas and got my notebook from my bag. As I opened the notebook a photo of Zara fell out onto the table and I stared at it long and hard, willing it to give me some answers.

'Oh Zara, where are you?' I whispered, aware that even my dad would think me crazy if he heard me talking to a photograph. The kettle spewed a stream of steam, I made my hot lemon drink and sat down, holding the photo in my hand, remembering my conversation with Gabrielle. It wasn't just Gabrielle who seemed disinterested in her sister's wellbeing. Zara's parents appeared to be just as nonchalant.

I'd only ever met Zara's parents once. It was in our final year at school and she'd been chosen for the lead in *A Midsummer Night's Dream*. I was on the door checking tickets and taking coats. The parents of the main characters were to be shown into the front row, so I had to ask everyone for their name and tick them off a list. I guessed the couple who approached me were Zara's folks before they spoke, because her mother had the same almond-shaped eyes and olive skin. She could have been a model, perhaps she was.

'Mr and Mrs...?' I asked, as I took their tickets.

'Carpenter,' they said simultaneously. He smiled as he handed his ticket over, but she remained expressionless, as though a smile would be tiring for her.

'Oh, hello, you must be Zara's parents. I'm Janie, her...' I paused. Was I her best friend? I couldn't be certain. '...her friend,' I finished, anticipating a handshake at least. Instead she nodded and he smiled again and that was it.

'Cold fish?' my dad said, when I told him the next day.

'More like frozen,' I said, feeling deflated.

Zara was brilliant in the role of Helena. Her willowy figure, long legs and graceful movement suited the part

120

perfectly. She had me believing in her obsessive love for Demetrius and I was certain the audience felt the same way.

Once the play was over I went backstage. Zara was deep in conversation with her parents and I held back, not wanting to interrupt. Her mother went to put a hand on Zara's shoulder, but her daughter pulled away. As their conversation drew to a close, I wandered over to them.

'You were completely amazing, definitely the star performer,' I said.

'You see darling, this is what I was telling you. You have a real talent,' her mother said, with the most beautiful French accent.

'It's not real, none of it is real,' Zara said.

'Fantasy can often be better than real life,' her father said.

Zara was a regular visitor at our house, but I never got to set foot in hers. I didn't mind though, as I was always happy to be around dad, given half the chance. He didn't need me to watch over him, or anything like that. By then he had Charlie the 2nd, and the two of them were indomitable.

Charlie's predecessor had slowed up and deserved a relaxing retirement. A family just three streets away took him in, which meant dad and I could still visit now and then. When he first left us I popped round quite often. He'd been my mate for most of my childhood years and we had formed a bond, but I could see my visits caused some conflict. I suppose he had divided loyalties. In his new home he was trying to get used to a different way of life with a new family, no work to do, just gentle strolls and plenty of relaxing. Then I would turn up and he would be reminded of his work life and his duties with dad. After a while, I stopped visiting and contented myself with spotting him in the park, or around and about, when I would make a brief fuss of him and then wander off in another direction.

My relationship with Charlie the 2nd was coloured by the fact that I was a teenager when he came along and was more interested in fashion and music than rolling around the garden. His character was more serious than his predecessor. He took his duties to dad seriously and rarely strayed from his side. He was loyal to the core.

When Zara and I first became friends, she would come over two or three evenings a week and we'd fly through our homework and then put the transistor radio on and jig around the bedroom. But on some of her visits it was all I could do to get her to talk, let alone dance. She would flick through my singles, choose the most sombre record and put it on repeat. Then she'd sit on the bed, close her eyes and drift off into a dreamlike state. On those days it was difficult to know what was going on with her.

'Talk to me, Zara,' I said, on one of these occasions. 'You're off in your own world. Where do you wish you were? Is there something that's upset you? Or someone?'

She never replied and in the end I had to accept that there was a side to Zara that she wanted to keep private. Charlie was a good ice-breaker though, she'd chat to him as though he was a person.

'We have so much to learn from dogs,' she told me one day. 'They are far more intelligent than people.'

I raised an eyebrow.

'Don't laugh, it's true. Dogs instinctively know how to care for their young and for each other. Just because they can't speak doesn't mean they don't know what's going on.'

'Yeah, but they learn by copying, don't they? Isn't that what dog training is all about? Punishment and reward?'

'You don't hear about a dog starting a war, do you?'

'No, but you hear about dog fights and it's often the little ones who are the worst.'

It made sense that Zara wanted to champion a cause. It was clear she thought the world needed a good sort out.

In those early days my focus was fun. It was Zara who persuaded me to experiment with make-up and one day she grabbed one of my scarves, rolled it up, wrapped it around my head, tucking my unruly fringe inside it, leaving the long ends of the scarf trailing down behind.

'There you are, little one. All tidy,' she said.

She often called me 'little one', although I was only three inches shorter than her. After that night I was seldom without a hair band, although I had to remove it when in school uniform. It was considered inappropriate for a young lady. Not that I've ever really been that.

Wrapping my dressing gown tightly around me I got up to edge the draught excluder closer to the back door. Our house is full of draughts, more jobs required that Greg isn't confident about. On quiet days I'd flick through magazines with pictures of new houses with central heating, and dream. Our chances of affording such luxury were as likely as our chances of winning the football pools. But if he got the job with Owen's dad, well, who knows what it might lead to.

I sat and listened to the grumblings of the house. In truth I loved our home and wouldn't give it up to go and live in a soulless place, central heating notwithstanding. The creaks of loose floorboards were comfortably familiar, as was the buzzing of our little refrigerator and the distant rumble of trains. The railway line ran along behind our street, about half a mile away. I liked to imagine the travellers sitting in cosy carriages on their way to work.

As I got up to put the kettle back on the gas I heard the flush of the cistern upstairs, with the resultant banging of water as it travelled through the pipes. I grabbed another cup and saucer and got the teapot out ready for Greg's first cuppa of the day.

That's when I heard it. A rattle, rather than a knock. I stood quite still to see if I'd imagined the noise, or whether it was Greg making more fuss than usual closing the bathroom door. Then I heard it again and determined it was coming from the direction of the hall. It was still dark outside and I had no intention of wandering out to the front path. I went into the hall and, just as Greg appeared at the foot of the stairs, I spotted an envelope on the doormat.

'Morning,' he said and turned to go into the kitchen.

'Kettle's on,' I said, as he walked away. Greg is at best semi-comatose before he's had his first cup of tea. Strong, black, with two sugars and then he's ready to greet the day.

I bent down and picked up the plain brown envelope. I turned it over, not expecting much of a clue as to its contents from the handwritten scrawl across the front, which simply said, '*Want to make some money?*'.

It had been hand delivered, no stamp in evidence and

124

no address and I guessed the rattling I'd heard was the sound of its arrival. Unlocking the front door I peered out, looking up and down the empty street. Then, closing the door as quietly as I could, I stuffed the envelope into my dressing gown pocket and went into the kitchen to join Greg.

Later that morning, once Greg had left for work and I'd cleared away the breakfast things, I sat down in the kitchen with the mysterious envelope in front of me. I used my precious paper knife to slice it open. I'd always wanted my own paper knife, ever since I watched my dad using one, when I couldn't have been much more than four years old. It was such a grown-up way of opening a letter. I'd told Greg about it when we were reminiscing about our childhoods one day and the following Christmas he presented me with a shiny paper knife, with my initials engraved on the handle.

'There you go,' he said. Greg might not be one for romantic words, but he knows how to make me happy.

There were two pieces of paper in the envelope. The first was a folded press cutting. I opened it and saw it was the article that had been written straight after Zara had disappeared. The local newspaper had run the story for a week or two, with an editorial about the increasing dangers of our roads. They'd referred to Joel's accident and suggested a local campaign might help to get lower speed limits around the town.

It had annoyed me at the time they weren't more interested in helping to track Zara down. If they had put her photo on the front page of their weekly rag it would have helped, but no, the story got a couple of paragraphs on page 8. It seemed as though the press thought the same as the police, that Zara was an unhappy soul who had crawled away to end it all. It was as though I was the only person who missed her, the only one who cared. It made me unremittingly sad.

I unfolded the second piece of paper. It was a short handwritten note, which simply said:

'We are prepared to pay for any information that leads to the discovery of Zara Carpenter. We will contact you again soon.'

I read it through again, trying to discover more meaning. Who would be prepared to pay money to find out Zara's whereabouts? I folded up both pieces of paper and put them back in the envelope. I was certain I would hear from the mysterious letter writer again and until then I would wait and say nothing.

Chapter 17

'But, Poirot –' I protested.
'Oh, my friend, have I not said to you all along that I have no proofs. It is one thing to know that a man is guilty, it is quite another matter to prove him so.'
The Mysterious Affair at Styles - Agatha Christie

My days with dad weren't just about paperwork. He manages his life with organisation and precision and I don't need to look after him, but I do like to look out for him. Whenever I call in I check the fridge for out of date food and make sure the house and his treatment room are as clean as he would want them to be if his eyes were working.

My dad has never accepted pity. From the day of the accident, and all through the months and years when he had to learn to live a different life, he approached each challenge with determination.

When I was around ten or eleven, I reached the age when I was making comparisons. Until then dad had been my hero, regardless of his blindness. He was the one who taught me to love books, to be inquisitive, to cherish nature and to respect old and young alike. But towards the end of my days at primary school it was as though I'd been fitted with new spectacles; I started to see faults with my hero. I noticed for the first time when his hair was a bit straggly, or his stubble too long. I would lie awake late into the evening and listen to him coming up to bed and be irritated by the funny throat-clearing noises he made when he brushed his teeth. My hero had become a man and I started to compare him with other dads. It wasn't just dad I compared either. I'd compare our simply furnished little house with the more luxurious or eclectic furnishings of friends' houses.

Then one day I asked him, 'Do you wish you weren't blind?' Looking back, I can't believe I asked it and that he didn't even flinch before replying.

'There are worse things than being blind,' he said.

'Only being dead.' I remember being annoyed he was so calm about it. I wanted him to scream and shout and I guess I tried to provoke a reaction.

'There are lots of ways of dying,' he said. 'You can be alive and have your sight and all your limbs in working order, but you can be dead in your heart. Afraid to love life, afraid to treat each day like an adventure. The accident took away my sight, but it didn't take away all the other wonderful things that make my life precious.'

'What things?' I was probably fishing at this point, expecting I would feature prominently in his reply.

'Yes, you're number one on the list.'

'What else?'

'I had five senses, now I have four. That's all. I can feel the warmth of the sunshine, hear the birds, touch the flowers and taste the delicious apple crumble your Aunt Jessica makes. I can think and learn and dream.'

'But you can't see me anymore.'

'I have my imagination and my memories. I know just how you looked when you were five and I'm sure the image I have of you now, at the ripe old age of ten, is near to perfect.'

We had similar conversations a few times as I grew up and each time dad proved to me that, when it came to comparisons, I was the lucky one. His talents as a physiotherapist became well renowned locally. He always had more patients waiting to see him than he could fit in in a week and they would all rather visit him than anyone else, with their twisted knees, frozen shoulders and sciatica. He would have been wasted in the police force. Perhaps some things are just meant to be.

'Owen has offered Becca a room in a house share in Brighton. Greg's sister, Becca. For when she starts uni,' I told dad, as I moved around the treatment room, folding towels and wiping surfaces. Charlie was curled up in his bed under the window, keeping his focus on dad.

'Oh.'

'Exactly. I'm not sure what to do.'

'What are your options?'

'Tell Greg and risk an argument. Speak to Becca and risk frightening her unnecessarily, or say nothing, which isn't a viable option.'

'You could speak to Owen.'

'And say what?'

'Just be truthful, tell him you're worried about Becca, she's young and vulnerable and she might be better living on campus.'

'He'll think I'm being strange, won't he? What if I'm imagining all this and instead he's just a regular bloke who lost his temper on one occasion?'

'Speak to him. We'd all feel a lot better if you did. Detective work isn't all plain sailing you know. You have to deal with the swells and tempests as well.'

'Hm,' was all I could say, knowing dad was right, as usual.

The next day I watched Greg prepare for his visit to the builder's yard, donning his one and only suit and tie.

'You do know you're going for a job as a builder, not a

129

bank clerk, don't you? It's not a formal interview, he'll just want to chat to you, explain what's involved and make sure you're keen enough.'

'I want to make a good impression.'

'Well, if I was interviewing you there would be no doubt. In fact, I hadn't realised I'd married such a handsome beast. You should ditch those scruffy tee-shirts more often.'

'What do you think he'll ask me?'

'Can you bend and lift, get up early, make tea, that kind of thing.'

'Don't joke, this is my future we're talking about. Our future.'

'Ah, yes, my new house with the two bathrooms. Just go and be your delicious self and you'll walk it.'

'So says the girl who has never had to attend an interview in her life.'

'Some of us are just born lucky.'

I didn't tell him *I told you so* when he returned, beaming, as though he'd won the football pools.

'Brilliant, I'll start choosing my bathroom tiles, shall I? Seriously though, I'm so proud of you, as is Bean. Give me your hand and see if you can feel the fluttering. It's just like little butterflies trying to escape a cage, but soon I expect it'll be more like a footballer taking a goal kick.'

I took his hand and pressed it to my stomach, but as I did all went still and quiet inside.

'Typical. I'm sure Bean is getting used to an afternoon snooze, which sounds perfect to me. When do you start the new job then?'

'I told Jim and Nick I'll stay with them another month. It's only fair, I don't want to drop them in it, but Jim's already mentioned an apprentice he's keen to take on, so they'll not miss me for long.'

'How long before you'll know how to build a wall? I've got my eye on a little garden project to start you off.'

'Give us a chance.' He put his face down towards my midriff. 'Bean, your mother is a slave driver. My advice to you is stay where you are. It's the only way you'll get any peace.'

I didn't want to leave it long before confronting Owen again. As far as I knew, Becca hadn't told Greg or her parents about the house share, so the sooner I could intervene the better. I decided to call round to the Mowbray's house before Greg started to work for them. The house and builder's yard weren't that close to each other, but I didn't want to take any chances.

I chose a late Thursday afternoon, leaving dad's a bit earlier than usual. There was a strong possibility Owen wouldn't be in, in fact he may even have returned to Brighton. What I needed was a talisman, some kind of good luck charm.

As I approached the house, Mrs Mowbray was in the front garden.

'Hello there,' I said, 'weeding is a never-ending job, isn't it?'

She looked up from her kneeling position behind the front fence and then slowly got to her feet.

'Janie,' she said, in a tone that was not remotely welcoming and a distinct change from the kindly woman who was forcing jam tarts on me when I last visited.

'What is it you want?' she said.

'Er, I was just wondering if Owen was in? I popped round for a quick chat, but if this isn't a good time?'

'It depends.'

'Sorry, I'm not sure what you mean.'

'Are you going to upset him again?'

'Upset him?'

'He was that upset when he got back from yours the other day. Came in and went straight to his bed, didn't even want a hot drink.'

'Did he say what had happened to upset him?'

'He wouldn't talk to me. And there's no point his father trying to get anything out of him, because the two of them have been at loggerheads for years. His father has never forgiven him for not joining the family firm. I've told Owen I don't blame him, not for a minute.'

'You don't?'

'Well, he's got a brain, hasn't he? Might as well use it, rather than being outside in all weathers. It's back-breaking work, you know. Oh, it's fine when you're young, but after a few years, well, Mr Mowbray can barely bend to tie his laces some days.'

An image crossed my mind of Greg, a few years from now, laying on my dad's physiotherapy couch. It was not a pleasant thought.

'I'm so sorry, Mrs Mowbray, but I'm certain I didn't say anything to upset your son. In fact, as I recall, I said very little. He came round to tell me how much he'd cared for my friend Zara. Perhaps talking about it all stirred up the memories?'

'That girl has been nothing but trouble since the start.'

'Really? In what way?'

'He's easily upset is Owen. First she gets him all riled up with protests and what not and then she says she doesn't want to be his girlfriend. He was in pieces, you know. I didn't think he'd ever get over it. I won't have her name mentioned in my house and I don't mind telling you I'm pleased she's disappeared. Good riddance, I say.'

I was taken aback by her vehemence. It looked as though Owen took after his mother when it came to temperament.

'I'll go and ask him if he wants to see you,' she said, not hiding the begrudging tone in her voice. 'Wait here. Don't you mention that girl's name, or you'll have me to answer for.'

I felt suitably admonished and was desperately trying to work out how to approach the conversation so as not to alienate the entire Mowbray family. If there was the slightest risk I might jeopardise Greg's new job prospects it would be safer to walk away right now.

I hovered in the front garden, admiring the climbing roses running riot across the fence, as well as around the front porch. I imagined what it would be like to be a green-fingered, home-cooking mum, with several little children tugging at my apron. But the image was fleeting, as soon as I factored in the sleepless nights and busy days, with no time to immerse myself in a good book, or lie uninterrupted in a hot bath.

I heard footsteps over the gravel pathway and there was Owen, standing in front of me.

'You were deep in thought,' he said.

'Just admiring your mum's handiwork. She's a wonderful gardener.'

'Mum said you wanted to talk to me? I don't have anything else to say about Zara, I've told you all I know.' He avoided eye contact with me as he spoke and put both his hands in his pockets. Was this a guilty man? If he was guilty, then what had he done and why?

'You've met Greg's sister, Becca?'

133

'No, I don't think so.'

'It's just that she said you'd kindly offered her a room in your house in Brighton?'

'Oh right, no, I haven't met Becca, but she must be Mel's friend. Mel is mum's god-daughter. It was mum who organised it really. She told Mel there was room for another girl and I suppose Mel told Becca. Mum doesn't like the idea of me living on my own, she worries.'

'The thing is, Becca's parents would prefer her to live on campus. She's quite a shy girl, you see, so her parents would be happier if she was closer to the university. On-site, so to speak. No travelling involved.'

I realised I was waffling and that I sounded unconvincing. 'Parents, eh?' I added.

'My place isn't far from the university and she'd be with Mel. I would have thought that would be better?'

'They're just being over-protective, but what can you do. It's the first time she will have lived away from home.'

'Right. So, why didn't she tell Melanie, or my mum come to that?'

'She's embarrassed, doesn't want to let anyone down.'

'Well, it's not a problem. I'm sure Mel has other friends.'

'Thanks for being so understanding,' I said. He shrugged his shoulders and turned to go into the house.

'I'll be off then,' I said.

'Are you any closer to finding Zara?' he said, without turning around. 'I thought that's what you'd come to tell me. I think about her every day. The only positive thing to come from all this is that she's free of Joel.'

'I'm not sure she'd see it like that.'

'Trust me, he was no good for her,' he said, picking off one of the large rose blooms beside the front door and crushing it in his hand. 'Some things are not what they appear to be at first. Take this rose, its petals are delicate, but the thorns will stab you and make you bleed.'

Chapter 18

'Who? That is the question. Why? Ah, if I only knew.'
The Mysterious Affair at Styles - Agatha Christie

After my chat with Gabrielle I had a new reason to take an interest in the news. She had given me a little more insight into Zara's life, particularly the in-between years when we'd lost touch. There was just a chance that exploring Zara's interests during those years might lead me to a previously undiscovered group of her friends, people who might know more about where she had gone and where she was living.

My attitude to world affairs had always been one of disinterest. Dad took a keen interest in politics and current affairs and often told me off when I continued to chatter on during the radio news bulletins.

'If you don't know what's going on around you, princess, you can't have an opinion,' he frequently told me. I still doubted the value of having an opinion, as I could see it could get you into trouble. My problem is I am usually persuaded by both sides of an argument, so I find it less hassle to sit on the fence. What's the point of getting angry about things you can't change? There would always be inequality, people who loved war more than peace, people who had more wealth than they could spend in their lifetime and others who could barely afford to eat. Occasionally I would drop a few shillings into a charity collection box and walk on, without giving the beneficiaries of that charity a second thought.

Now my purpose was different. My focus was Zara and I believed it would help me to put myself in her shoes, to try to understand her passions. Each evening I would sit quietly as we watched the television reports of various atrocities taking place around the world. At first Greg commented he'd never seen me so quiet, but once I persuaded him I was preparing myself for the responsibilities of motherhood, he seemed happy.

'When Bean starts asking questions I want to have the answers, just like dad always did. It's no good if I don't know what's going on in the world. I need to think about our child's future,' I said. I was even believing my own argument.

But the news was all so depressing. There had been more race riots in America, and now British troops were trying to keep the peace in Northern Ireland. It had been a summer of love, with young people gathering in Woodstock, chanting peace and love and yet all around was death and destruction.

As well as finding out about Zara's interests and concerns, I hoped to learn more about her parents. It struck me the lack of any closeness between Zara and her mother and father must have been triggered by something. I couldn't believe they would have just drifted apart because of disinterest. Both Zara and Gabrielle were passionate characters and those traits must have come from one or other, or both of their parents. Passion and disinterest are unlikely to go hand in hand.

Zara had told me her mother and father had moved back to live in France some years ago. Perhaps Gabrielle was still in touch with them, although she hadn't mentioned them when we spoke. I'd missed an opportunity to ask her during my visit and I certainly didn't relish the idea of returning, to be met with her nonchalant air and icy stare.

There was one other person who knew Joel and Zara, albeit more as an acquaintance, rather than a friend. It struck me it would be worth having a conversation with Petula, the girl who worked in Joel's studio on Saturday mornings. She had worked for Joel when Zara moved into the flat above the studio.

Since the day of Joel's funeral I had only seen Petula once. She'd called round to our house to see Zara, but Zara had stayed in her bedroom. In those first few months after the accident Zara would speak to no-one, barely even passing the time of day with Greg and me. When Petula came to visit, I made her a cup of tea and we chatted for a while and when she left I promised to pass on her good wishes. Now I was desperately trying to recall that conversation and whether she had mentioned anything about looking for another job. I chided myself for being so inattentive.

Without any concrete clues as to where she might be working now I needed to try some of the more obvious places around the town. Spending a Saturday morning mooching around shops and cafés might be some people's idea of heaven. I was unequivocal about it, but either way it wasn't much of a sacrifice.

After an hour or so, I struck lucky. I walked up to the pick and mix counter in Woolworth's and there she was.

'Hello there. Petula, isn't it? I'm Janie, Zara's friend.'

At first, she looked blankly at me and then, as recognition dawned, a smile spread across her face. Her mass of copper-coloured hair and unblemished pale skin gave her a look of purity. I got the sense she would be surprised to be told she was pretty and embarrassed if a boy asked her out. I could have been wrong, after all I'd only met her a handful of times. For all I knew she could have a long line of admirers who she gaily strung along.

Luckily, there were no other customers needing her attention, so I felt safe to start chatting.

'You must miss your old job?' I said.

'I was lucky to get this one.'

'Had you worked for Joel for long?'

'Just coming up to a year, I was learning a lot. He was kind, let me handle his cameras, some of them were really expensive.'

'Have you kept it up, your interest in photography?'

'No, dad says it's an expensive hobby we can't afford. Not 'til I'm older, with a proper job.'

'Joel was a good boss then?'

'Like I say, he was kind to me, although…' she paused and blushed, turning away from me as a customer approached. I hovered for a while, amusing myself by filling a paper bag with liquorice shoelaces and sherbet flying saucers - joyous reminders of schooldays and pocket money.

'You were saying?' Once the customer had paid and moved away I handed my bag to Petula.

'I did feel uncomfortable sometimes, when he got a bit too friendly,' she said.

'How do you mean?'

'Well, at first I was quite flattered, him being older, but then he kept grabbing me. He teased me, saying he'd only give me my wages if I gave him a kiss.'

'He tried to kiss you?'

'And then when Zara moved in, well I thought he'd stop, but he kept saying it was just a game. Good fun, as long as we didn't get caught, he said. He showed me the developing room, I thought it would be a chance to learn, but then, well…'

139

'Crikey, Petula, did you ever tell anyone? Did you tell your dad? You know that what Joel was doing was wrong, you're only fifteen, he should never have taken advantage of you like that.'

'Please don't say anything, I shouldn't have told you. It was my fault really, he could probably tell I thought he was good-looking. I was flattered someone like him should take an interest in me.'

'You are a beautiful young girl and Joel should have known better. He took advantage of you in the most terrible way. You should be able to choose who you kiss and who kisses you, even with boys of your own age. Do you think Zara knew?'

'No, I'm sure she didn't. Although he seemed to like the danger, because sometimes he'd wait for her to come into the shop, then he'd call me out the back with an excuse.'

I didn't want to hear anymore. The pictures that Petula's words had conjured up in my mind were ugly. What she'd told me cast Joel in a new light, that was decidedly murky and unpleasant. I needed to talk to dad.

Dad's usual Sunday morning routine involved an early brisk walk with Charlie and then back home for breakfast, followed by a couple of hours listening to the radio. There were a few regular BBC programmes he enjoyed. Some, like *The Navy Lark*, made him chuckle and others, like the weekend news round-up, would have him listening intently.

I arrived at the house mid-morning. Greg had promised to spend the morning considering ways of draught-proofing the kitchen windows, as the rattles and leaks were now getting to be a real problem. I had my

140

doubts as to whether consideration would lead to any immediate action, but at least it was a start.

'Hello, it's only me,' I called out, as I let myself in the front door. Charlie came padding out to greet me and having made sufficient fuss of him I followed him into the kitchen, where I found dad sitting, holding a mug of tea and listening to the radio.

'Hello love, good to hear your voice. Tea? Or your strange concoction? The kettle's just boiled. Have a seat a minute. I just want to hear the last bit of this programme, it's about the protest marches in America. It's so sad, all those young men dying and there seems to be no end to it.'

I made my drink and sat quietly while we listened to the rest of the programme. For once I tried hard to pay attention to all the facts and the arguments for and against the war in Vietnam. This was a war that was happening so far away it had always been meaningless to me. I didn't even know where Vietnam was.

'This is exactly what I want to talk to you about,' I said, once I had his full attention.

'The war? You've never been interested before. What's changed your mind?'

I told him about my conversation with Gabrielle.

'Zara was passionate about causes, maybe she turned her grief into something positive. Perhaps she's out there somewhere trying to make a difference, to make her voice heard.'

Dad was quiet and looked thoughtful. 'You don't think she would have joined a cult, do you? I've heard about young people who have been persuaded to join a group and then they're brainwashed, encouraged to do dangerous things, to break the law.'

'You mean like a commune? Isn't that more of an American thing? I can't see Zara breaking the law, she's such a gentle soul.'

'You say she went on protest marches, that's what her sister told you? That chap Owen mentioned something about it too, didn't he?'

'Yes, but peaceful marches, as far as I can make out. If she was protesting about war she must have believed in peace, mustn't she? You might be right though, she could have joined up with a religious group of some kind. Perhaps her mental state left her open to influences?'

'Would you describe her as a weak character, from what you know of her? Do you think she could be easily led?'

'No, the opposite. She was gentle, but strong, if that makes sense. I'm certain she wouldn't let anyone force her to do something she didn't think was right, that she didn't believe in. But I can see now that she was so attracted to Joel that she didn't recognise the truth about him.'

'You know what they say about love.'

'Perhaps she hoped he would use his photographic skills to support her with her causes, a sort of candid reportage. In reality though, I reckon Joel just liked to ogle pretty faces, either through a lens or otherwise.'

'Well, I don't know love, but I do worry about you. In a few months you're going to be a mother for the first time. Shouldn't you be focusing on that, rather than chasing down a wayward friend? Perhaps there are things in Zara's life we will never know or understand and you may just have to accept that.'

'Dad, I'm fine and the baby is fine. It's bad enough having Greg trying to wrap me in cotton wool, without you doing the same. You've always taught me to follow my instincts and my instincts right now are that Zara is out there somewhere and she needs my help. I will be careful, but don't ask me to give up, not yet.'

'Poirot's take on the problem?' dad said.

'*Arrange the facts, neatly, each in his proper place. Examine - and reject. Those of no importance, pouf! - blow them away!* If only it were that easy.'

'One step at a time.'

Chapter 19

'I must confess that the conclusions I drew from those
few scribbled words were quite erroneous.' He smiled.
'You gave too much rein to your imagination.
Imagination is a good servant, and a bad master. The
simplest explanation is always the most likely.'
The Mysterious Affair at Styles - Agatha Christie

It was a typically quiet Monday morning in the library
van. I replayed what Petula had told me and thought
again about Joel. Dad's advice was to get back to basics,
so the next thing to do would be to revisit the site where
Joel died. My plan was to clear my mind of all
preconceptions and consider it with fresh eyes.

Fortune Park runs for two miles, with roads either side
of it. To the west is Upper Park Road, with Lower Park
Road to the east. Three smaller roads intersect the park,
dividing it into three distinct parts. The first part, nearest
the town centre is full of amusements for young and old,
a boating lake and a play area with a roundabout and
swings. Beautifully planted flower borders line the
pathways for families to stroll beside and admire. There
are plenty of benches and large grassy areas where dad
and I used to play ball before he had his accident. Mum
never came.

'You two go,' she'd say, 'it'll give me a chance to give
the house a good clean.' It was as though she couldn't
wait to sweep all trace of us away for a few hours and
have the place to herself.

The second part of the park is devoted to tennis courts
and the third is all woodland, with tracks that weave in
between the trees. This third part was my favourite. It

was here you'd see squirrels scurrying up tree trunks and rabbits racing into their burrows. When dad was first out of hospital and still recovering, I persuaded Aunt Jessica to take us there. She pushed dad in a wheelchair we had on loan from the hospital. I ran alongside them, shouting out with glee each time a white bobtail disappeared under a bush, or a swallow swooped through the branches. Dad would ask me questions, getting me to describe the trees, the shape of the leaves. It was on those walks I learned to be observant.

'Don't miss a thing, Janie,' he'd say. 'Study it carefully and you'll start to see everything afresh. Don't take anything for granted. Notice all the shades of green and brown. Remember them, because next time we come they'll be different again.'

It was a long walk and a long push for Aunt Jessica, so we only did it once with dad. A couple of times after that she took me on the bus and we left dad at home. On my return he'd quiz me for ages.

'Describe exactly what you saw. Draw a picture for me with your words.'

I may be impetuous, muddle-headed as well, on occasion, but if my one-word descriptor was 'observant', it would be well justified.

I got off the No 76 bus and walked along Lower Park Road, turning left into Cromwell Avenue, which was the site of the accident. There were three cars parked along Cromwell Avenue, all bunched up together at the end of the road. There were no houses on this road, it purely acted as an intersection between the second and third areas of the park. I guessed the car owners were visiting friends nearby and decided this was as good a place as any

145

to leave their cars. Most of Upper and Lower Park Roads had just been painted with double yellow lines, so if there wasn't an empty driveway then you were pretty much stuck.

Joel's accident had happened one evening in April. It would have been almost dark. The police had surmised that the hit and run driver hadn't seen Joel as he ran across from one part of the park to the other. We couldn't understand why he was out running at that time of night. He'd taken up running a few months earlier, but tended to run early morning, or at weekends. According to Zara he was constantly asking her to join him, but she was the least likely person to go running. She preferred to saunter through life; at least until the 10th April 1968.

I pulled my collar up and turned my back to the wind that had just picked up with a vengeance. Greg would be laughing at me all wrapped in the middle of August, but I was used to his teasing. The trickiest part of us being at either end of the temperature scale was finding a happy medium. The benefits were that I always had his hot back to warm my cold feet on.

I planned to retrace Joel's steps, as far as I knew them. I walked in through the entranceway to the park, neatly created with carefully clipped box hedging. I wasn't keen to venture too far in, but I stood for a moment to absorb my surroundings. Just beside the park entrance was a lamp-post that would have thrown a reasonable light onto the pavement and the immediate part of the road Joel stepped out onto. His body was found slumped partly on the pavement and partly on the road. Looking now at the scene of the accident, I realised that as he stepped out onto Cromwell Avenue he would have the benefit of the light cast from the lamp-post. Assuming the street light was working he would have been visible, despite the fact he was wearing dark clothes. I remember the police coming to our house to speak to Zara, going through it all again with her. One of the officers said how unfortunate it was that Joel wasn't wearing more visible clothing, as though it was his fault. I remember getting angry on Zara's behalf.

'The driver had headlights, didn't they? They must have seen him.'

Greg was there telling me to calm down, as I raised my voice. Given half the chance I would have screamed. This crazy person had run poor Joel down and hadn't even stopped.

'They would have felt his body hit the car,' I shouted at the police officer. By this time I was verging on the hysterical and he wasn't even my boyfriend. Zara sat silent throughout. It was as though she had lost all sense of time and place. I'm not sure she heard any of the details the police officer gave her. Even when I tried to hold her, to comfort her, she stood rigid, with her arms by her side.

'She's in shock,' the police officer said. 'It's to be expected.'

Being here again at the scene of such a terrible trauma I was reliving some of those emotions. I reminded myself of dad's words, *stay focused*. As I stepped into the park entrance I exposed all my senses. I smelt the odour from one of the nearby rubbish bins that had been left to overflow. I let my hand touch the sharp spikes of the berberis abutting the box hedging. I imagined what it would have looked like that night, any colour disappearing, leaving just grey and black.

147

I imagined myself into the shoes of Joel. He would have been running along the path, focusing perhaps on his timing and his breathing. Perhaps he had cramp and had stopped for a moment to relieve it and then, wanting to build up his pace again, he might have burst out through the park entrance. It was at that moment, as he stepped from the pavement to the road, the car had come from the direction of Lower Park Road and driven into him.

I stood still and looked again at the likely route of the car. My heart started to beat uncomfortably fast and I needed to take deep breaths to regain my composure. Right on cue the hiccups kicked in.

Why hadn't anyone looked at this before and realised the absurdity of it? A car turning left from Lower Park Road into Cromwell Avenue would have been on the left-hand side of the road. But when the young police officer found Joel in the early hours of the morning, Joel's body was laying across the road and pavement on the far side of the road. It didn't add up.

It wasn't possible for the car to have hit him unless he was running up from the lower part of the park. But that would mean his body would have been across the other kerb. The only other possibility was for the car to have been driving in the opposite direction, along Cromwell Avenue into Lower Park Road. If that was the case then the driver would have had longer to see him in the headlights and the streetlights, and Joel would have been alerted to the car coming towards him and stopped running or got out of the way.

I took out my notebook, drew a rough plan of the accident site and scribbled a few notes. I had no doubt I would remember all of it, but I wanted to be thorough

148

and prove to myself, and dad, that I wasn't just a scatty Gemini.

On the bus home I looked through my notes again. Perhaps the police had been mistaken when they explained the events to Zara, although this seemed unlikely. Policemen had to be thorough, that was their job. They would have made a detailed record of every aspect of the incident. There hadn't been any witnesses to the accident, which is why Joel wasn't found until the early hours of the next morning. Did Joel die instantly, or could he have been saved if someone had been there to call an ambulance?

When I got back home I said nothing to Greg about where I'd been. I let him assume I'd gone over to dad's to help with his paperwork. I knew what Greg would say if he knew the truth.

'You have to think of little Bean,' he was always telling me. Sometimes it felt that Bean was more important to him than I was and it hadn't even been born yet.

I had a sleepless night, replaying the accident scene over and over in my mind. I was so grateful when morning came. I was up, showered and breakfasted before Greg appeared, looking bleary-eyed.

'Blimey, Janie, you're early. Getting ready for those morning feeds? They say the body prepares you for sleepless nights, at least so Fred tells me. His wife's had four kids, with their fifth on the way.'

The subtext of his morning greeting did not pass me by. One little Bean was enough of a family for me and I certainly didn't intend to be a stay-at-home wife. I had other plans, but this was not the time to raise them.

'I promised dad I'd call in early, he needs help with a

149

patient.' I grabbed my bag before he could ask any more and called out goodbye as I scooted out of the front door.

I arrived at dad's to find him still out, giving Charlie his morning walk. I had my own key so let myself in and was just getting out mugs for our hot drinks when I heard them arrive at the back door.

'Kettle's on,' I called out.

'Morning,' was dad's reply, as Charlie pushed his wet nose up against my leg. Fortunately, my knee length boots took the worst of it, until Charlie decided to shake his whole body, giving dad and I a brief shower.

'Thanks mate,' I said and rubbed his head.

'Bed,' my dad said and Charlie padded off obediently, while we sat down to our hot drinks. I got my notebook out and reported all my findings to dad, who listened without interruption.

At the end he said, 'What's your next step?'

'I don't have a clue, I was hoping you'd tell me. You're the one who used to be a copper remember.'

'Yes, but this time the ball's in your court. You fancy yourself as an investigator, so investigate. Start by determining all the reasons that the scenario might not be what we thought.'

'The police made a mistake?'

'Well, that's one possibility.'

'Unlikely one?'

'I'd like to hope so.'

'If the car was coming towards Joel on the other side of the road the driver would have seen him, he would have had time to slow down and Joel would have time to get out of the way.'

'Okay, so why would the car not have slowed down?'

'The driver was distracted? The car's brakes were

faulty?'

'Yes, two realistic scenarios. What else?'

I put my cup down and looked at my dad's face, trying to read his expression. I knew what he was thinking, but I couldn't bear to say the words aloud.

'It wasn't an accident. The driver meant to run him down,' I said.

He nodded and held his hand out to me.

'I think we have to count that as a distinct possibility.'

Chapter 20

'Pardon me, madame, for recalling unpleasant memories, but I have a little idea' – Poirot's 'little ideas' were becoming a perfect byword…
The Mysterious Affair at Styles - Agatha Christie

I'd achieved part one of my attempt to protect Greg's little sister from a threat that may have existed only in my imagination. Now I just needed to work out the best way of telling Becca the change of plan, without alerting her to the problem.

There was a chance I had dug myself into a hole for no reason. Although the image of Owen cruelly crushing the flower in his hand made me determined to see my plan through. There was a dark side to Owen and I wasn't going to risk Becca finding out what was at the heart of it.

'Let's invite your parents round for supper at the weekend, to celebrate your new job,' I said to Greg that evening. 'It'll save them worrying about organising another get-together.'

'I thought we'd go out, make the most of being free before Bean arrives.'

'Sounds good, but it's ages since we invited your family round. We could ask Becca as well, talk about her plans for uni?'

'Becca won't want to spend a Saturday night with us, she'll be out dancing with her mates.'

'Well, let's just ask. She can always say no.'

I called round to the Juke household and luckily enough caught them all in. I still felt uncomfortable calling Greg's parents by their first names, although calling them Mr and Mrs Juke felt weird. I couldn't get used to the idea that I was Mrs Juke too. Giving up my maiden name felt like giving up on my dad and secretly I still thought of myself as Janie Chandler.

'Greg would love it if we had a get-together, to celebrate his new job.'

'We can toast our new grandchild. Excellent idea. When were you thinking of?' Greg's mum asked. 'I could bring a pudding, if you like.'

'This Saturday evening?'

'Count me out,' Becca said, 'I'm seeing Mel. We're going to *The Saturn Club*, she's got free tickets.'

'Oh, that's a shame. Greg will be disappointed. He was just saying this morning how much he enjoyed your party.' I hoped I wouldn't be struck down for telling such lies. 'It's quite a big change for him, this new job. It would give him a real boost if you could be there.'

Becca tutted and looked away from me, making a point of studying her brightly painted nails.

'Melanie can manage without you for once.' Nell said. 'Janie's right, your brother needs your support. You'll be off soon enough and then we won't see you for months on end.'

'Tell you what,' I said, trying desperately to salvage the situation, 'how about you pop in for an hour or so? Bring Melanie as well, if you like. You can have some nibbles, give your brother a hug and then go off to your nightclub and leave us oldies to it.'

Having succeeded in getting them all to come, I now needed to work out the next part of my plan. I'd never met Melanie, so I wasn't sure how easy it would be to convince her about what I had in mind.

Saturday morning was spent shopping and cleaning, leaving the whole afternoon free to prepare the food. I have no idea how anyone can enjoy entertaining on a regular basis. Greg just laughed at my constant sighing and sat and watched as I scooted around with the vacuum.

'At least go in the kitchen, out of the way,' I said, 'or go out completely?'

Instead, he just grinned and lifted his feet as I vacuumed underneath them.

'If you don't go out, then you can help. Peel potatoes and carrots and polish the glasses.'

'I'm just popping out, won't be long,' he said, with a cheeky grin on his face.

I poked my tongue out at him as he grabbed his jacket and left. In truth it was easier to have the place to myself.

Our guests were due at 6pm. I was ready, with an hour to spare, so there was time for a soak in the bath before getting changed. Greg returned with some beers and cider and a bunch of flowers.

'Blimey, are they for me?'

'Well, they're not for me. I'm allowed to treat my wife, aren't I? Besides, you deserve a thank you. You've worked hard all day and I haven't. But, I don't feel guilty, 'cos I work hard all week, while you read books for a living.'

'Be extremely careful, or your dinner may end up in the bin, together with those beautiful flowers.'

I wrapped my arms around his waist, pulled him to me and planted a kiss on his lips. 'You're right though, about the books. And soon I'll be having cups of tea all day,

154

while singing nursery rhymes. And you'll be carrying hods.'

'Er, possibly, although I have yet to find out what a hod is. I expect it will be one of my first lessons. The kiss was nice, can I have another?'

'No, Mr Juke, you may not, as I have to prepare myself to greet my guests.'

The Jukes arrived on time and Melanie and Becca went straight into the kitchen, while Greg organised drinks for his parents.

'You two can help, if you like?' I said to the girls. 'I'm not used to feeding so many all at once. Becca, can you check the roasties, they might need basting? Use the oven gloves, our oven is pretty fierce.'

Melanie stood to one side and I handed her a tea towel. 'It's probably rude to ask my guests to help, but I'm hopeless at all that protocol stuff. How did you manage to get free tickets for *The Saturn Club*? That was a bit of luck.'

'Yeah, friend of a friend, he knows one of the bouncers. Have you been?'

'*Aquarius* is more our scene, it's where Greg and I met.'

'I don't suppose you get out dancing much now?' she said, nodding her head towards my midriff.

'It won't be long before I can't, but we managed to get out recently. Just to remind ourselves we aren't quite over the hill yet. In fact, we bumped into someone you know.'

'Oh right, who was that then?'

'Owen Mowbray, I think his mum is your god-mother, is that right?'

155

At this point Greg came into the kitchen to see what was keeping us. 'Mum and dad are wondering if there is anything they can do to help?'

'No, tell them thanks, but the girls are being a big help. We'll be through in a minute. Don't leave them on their own though, take these peanuts.' I handed him a bowl of nuts and tried not to make it obvious that I was ushering him out of the kitchen. 'Stay here too long and you'll be enlisted.'

'Don't you like cooking then?' Melanie asked me, as I took the joint out of the oven and contemplated the best way to carve it.

'Let's just say I'm not exactly a natural.' I rifled through the drawer looking for a half-decent carving knife. 'You two must be looking forward to uni. It's ideal you're going to be together, are you taking the same course?'

'Mel's taken different options to me, she's doing French as well,' Becca said.

'Owen was telling us how disappointed he was he couldn't help you out with accommodation. Seems he might not be staying in his house for much longer,' I said, surprising myself at how accomplished I was becoming at telling lies.

'How do you mean?' Becca said, anxiety making her voice quiver slightly. 'Did you know that, Mel?'

'No, he hasn't said anything to me. Oh, God, now what are we going to do. We've only got a month or so before we start. That's typical of him, I've always thought he was a bit weird. I didn't even want to share his stupid house, but mum and Mrs Mowbray go back years and once mum has decided something then we all have to follow her plan. This is a complete nightmare, now what

156

are we going to do?'

'He just mentioned it to me in passing,' I said, trying to sound reasoned and calm. 'I get the sense he's a bit embarrassed about it, didn't want to let you down, but couldn't think of a way of telling you. I suppose when he bumped into Greg and me he saw the perfect opportunity.'

'Now what?' Becca said, frustration evident in her expression.

'If I were you I'd sort out digs on campus and then just let him know, without making a fuss. If you make a big thing about it it'll only upset everyone.'

The girls stayed for the first course, made their excuses and went off to prepare for their night out. As I tucked into the roast dinner, which I had to admit had come out well by anyone's standards, I gave myself an imaginary pat on the back. I had averted a potential disaster and hopefully everyone would come out of it unscathed. I doubted Mel or Becca would want to have a detailed conversation with Owen about the whys or wherefores and once the new accommodation was in place I was certain both families would be content. Owen certainly wouldn't be happy, but I had to hope that the Mowbray family wouldn't be too annoyed by my interference. It was clear that the more I got involved in this amateur sleuthing lark, the more tact and diplomacy was needed. The community of Tamarisk Bay was close-knit. Many of the families were connected, either by blood or friendship and now that Greg was planning to work for the Mowbray's I needed to tread carefully, or I would have one very unhappy husband to deal with.

Once the Jukes left, Greg helped me clear away the dishes and then we wandered through to the sitting room.

I was so deep in thought I didn't notice I'd left several dirty glasses on the sideboard, until Greg started to collect them up.

'Were you ever jealous of Becca?' I asked him.

'What kind of a question is that?'

'It's just that your mum makes such a fuss of her, with her university place and all that. I just wondered.'

'Why would I be jealous? University is my idea of a nightmare. You know what I'm like. The thought of being cooped up in a classroom for hours on end. It was bad enough at school.'

'Your mum is proud of you, you know. Even though she doesn't show it often.'

'I'm not sure what point you're trying to make. Trust me, mum and me are fine as we are. Dad and me too, come to that. Becca gets to do what she's always dreamed of. Good luck to her.'

He picked up the local paper, suggesting that that particular topic of conversation was over.

'If I had a sister, I'd want to be close to her, to be mates,' I said, pushing his feet out of the way so I could sit beside him.

'For goodness sake, we are friends, we don't need to see each other every five minutes. Becca's got her own friends and I've got you.'

'I know, I was just thinking about Zara and Gabrielle. It's so sad they're not friends. I understand you and Becca like different things, but they're twins. I keep going over it in my mind and it doesn't make any sense.'

'You think too much.'

'Probably. When's your next darts match? Do you want me to come, for moral support?'

'Thanks, but no thanks. If I'm going to make a fool of

myself I'd rather not have an audience.'

I curled my legs up onto the settee and nestled up against him. He put his arm around me and dropped the paper to the floor. 'Is that what this is all about then?' he said, turning to look at me.

'All what?'

'You and Zara, your fixation with tracking her down. Is it because you wish you had a sister?'

I didn't answer him, because I couldn't. I didn't know the answer.

Chapter 21

'Not now, not now, *mon ami*. I have need of reflection. My mind is in some disorder – which is not well.' For about ten minutes he sat in dead silence, perfectly still, except for several expressive motions of his eyebrows, and all the time his eyes grew steadily greener. At last he heaved a deep sigh. 'It is well. The bad moment has passed. One must never permit confusion. The case is not clear yet – no. For it is of the most complicated!'
The Mysterious Affair at Styles - Agatha Christie

I'll admit I was feeling a little overstretched with everything that had been going on. Dad had had a busy few days with patients, so I hadn't had much time to think about my detective work, or to talk to him about my progress, or lack of it. I kept my notebook to hand and in the rare quiet moments I glanced through it to see if anything jumped out at me that might be worth exploring.

It was the beginning of a new working week, but I was already shattered and as soon as I got home from dropping off the library van I ditched my bag on the kitchen table and went upstairs to run a bath. All day I'd been looking forward to a long soak and a read of some light-hearted nonsense. With the bubbles floating around me I flicked idly through a magazine, glancing at the pictures. I heard the front door go and Greg's voice calling out hello, followed by him clattering about in the kitchen.

'You okay?' I shouted down to him, but then the radio went on and I knew I'd never compete, so I laid back in the warm water and hummed along. Midway through the

160

track, the music stopped and I heard Greg's footsteps on the stairs. The bathroom door opened and he stood glaring at me, holding my notebook in my hand.

'What the hell is this?' he said, looking angrier than I'd seen him in a long time.

'My notebook,' I said, tempted to dip down under the water to avoid what I thought would soon follow.

'This is crazy. You're expecting our first baby, you're driving around in that library van and you're still working for your dad and now you've set off on a one-woman campaign to hunt down someone we barely know.'

'We do know her, she lived with us for a whole year.'

'Yes and probably spoke twenty words in twelve months.'

'Don't exaggerate.'

'I'm really cross with you. Don't you care about Bean?'

'Don't be ridiculous, of course I do.'

'You are the one being ridiculous. Does your dad know about this madcap scheme of yours?'

I didn't want to involve dad, so I chose not to answer, although I did wonder whether Greg would be less angry if he knew dad was monitoring my exploits. He had a lot of respect for my dad and the feeling was mutual.

'I'm not doing anything dangerous,' I said, 'I'm just trying to think laterally and to explore areas the police might not have thought of.'

'Oh, please, don't tell me you haven't shared any of this with the police.'

'Well, I…'

'You do know that if you keep anything from them you could be charged for withholding valuable evidence. Do you want our baby to be born in prison?'

'Oh, now you're just being silly. Let me get out of the bath and you put the kettle on and we can continue this discussion downstairs. The water's getting a bit chilly.'

He left me to get dry and dressed, making a point of slamming the bathroom door as he left. By the time I arrived in the kitchen he was sitting at the table holding tight to a mug of tea, with a drink for me being distinctly inconspicuous by its absence.

'Greg, come on, let's not argue. This is important, the police have just about given up, you must admit that.'

'They've got new leads, they're on the case.'

'No, they have one new lead and that's the sighting Mr Peters told me about. As I far as I know they've done nothing about it.'

'I need you to promise me you'll stop this nonsense. Zara will either be found by the police or she won't, it's not your responsibility to search for her.'

'But she's my friend, our friend.'

'And you're my wife.'

'Oh, for goodness sake, this is the 1960s, not the 1860s.'

The argument was getting out of hand and soon one or both of us would say something we regretted.

'Greg, I love you and I would never do anything to jeopardise the health of our baby, I promise.'

'Do you promise to stop looking for Zara?'

'No love, I can't do that. I promise I'll be careful though and not take any risks.'

I slid my hand across the table towards his, but he quickly moved away from me and stood up.

'I'm going to the pub, I'll eat there.'

'Well, that will help a lot, won't it. Just go and get drunk and then sulk for days on end.'

Before I finished speaking, he'd grabbed his jacket and left.

I was in bed before Greg returned home later that evening. I'd been dozing on and off, so when he got into bed I turned over to give him a hug. Instead he turned his back to me and edged further towards his side of the bed. Within seconds he was snoring loudly and I was left alone with my thoughts.

By the time Greg came downstairs the next morning I'd laid the table for a proper cooked breakfast, hoping a full English would help persuade him to see my side of the argument.

'Smells divine,' he said, lifting up the lid I'd put over the frying pan to stop the bacon spitting everywhere.

'Morning, husband,' I said and slid my arms around his waist. 'You do realise Bean is quite literally coming between us and it's not even born yet. Sit yourself down and let me spoil you for once. What would sir like, coffee, tea?'

Over breakfast we chatted about insignificant trivia, both of us carefully avoiding anything contentious.

'I'll wash up,' Greg said, once we'd shared the last slice of toast. 'I know you don't want to talk about it anymore and nor do I, but I just want to say I love you and I worry about you, that's all.'

'I know you do.'

'It's all very sad, of course it is. Anyone could see how happy Joel and Zara were together. No wonder she went off the rails when he died.'

'Yes, they were happy, weren't they?' I was starting to doubt everything, even my memory of the last few

163

months of Joel's life.

'Take that morning when I saw them out running together, they just looked so much in love.'

'Running? When was that then?'

'You remember, I'd gone off early to the Mansion House job. They had a big function coming up and they wanted the windows sparkling before the weekend. Anyway, I drove up Upper Park Road and there they were, running together, alongside the park.'

'Joel and Zara running together, early in the morning?'

'He was always on at her to run with him, don't you remember? He kept teasing her about it.'

'Yes, I know, but she hated the idea. I'm sure you've never told me this story, I would have remembered it. So, you saw them running together?'

'Well, not actually running, but they were both in running gear, at least he had his usual shorts and singlet and she was wearing jeans and a T-shirt, but when I saw them it looked as though they'd just stop for a breather. Mind you, there was more kissing and cuddling going on than breathing, if you get my drift. The point is they looked so happy, so in love.'

I thought a lot about Greg's remarks. He might have been inferring Zara and Joel showed their love for each other in a way we didn't, but that wasn't what bothered me. Greg and I were fine and once he'd stopped worrying about my detective antics he would agree. We didn't need to shout our love from the hilltops, ours was a quiet love and for my mind all the more solid as a result.

The real focus of my thoughts was that I had never given Zara's relationship with Joel much critical consideration. She'd met him, fallen in love and moved

164

into his flat. On the few occasions we had been out as a foursome they seemed happy. She would always hold tightly to his arm as they walked. I thought it was rather sweet to see her doting on him. So when he died, I wasn't at all surprised she fell apart. But now I had to factor in Owen's relationship with Zara, as well as everything Petula had told me about Joel's behaviour. Plus, there was something of a contrast between Zara, the doting girlfriend, and Zara, the girl prepared to go on protest marches, with strong opinions of her own.

I couldn't help thinking I was missing something. There was a niggling thought at the back of my mind that wouldn't go away. For now, I jotted a few notes down in my notebook. Fortunately, I'd retrieved it unscathed from Greg and made a mental reminder to stash it away in a safer place from now on.

The information I had gained so far provided me with background, but I was no further forward in tracking down my friend. Mr Peters had confirmed that the day she went missing she went to the cemetery. It made sense then to revisit the cemetery to see if it held any clues.

Joel is buried in St Martha's cemetery, which is walking distance from our house. It was a surprise to me when his parents chose not to take their only son back to Scotland with them, but then the more I discover about people, the more I realise I understand nothing.

The proximity of the cemetery to our house was one of the reasons we thought it strange Zara never visited during her whole time with us. Not a single visit in a whole year, and yet on the first anniversary of Joel's death it was the last place she had been seen. Perhaps she visited him to say goodbye. Perhaps it was to tell him she'd be with him again soon. I tried to dispel such thoughts from my mind. Zara had to be alive, I wasn't prepared to countenance the alternative.

St Martha's is a peaceful place, as I suppose most graveyards are. It's a place where the dead can rest in peace and the living can visit for quiet moments of reflection. Wandering around the cemetery I read a few of the inscriptions. *'Gone but not forgotten'*, *'Heaven has another angel'*, *'Always in our thoughts'*. All words designed to help the living.

I've never thought much about death. On the odd occasion the subject came up during conversations with Zara, I sensed she'd spent time searching for a solid belief system. Although her mother was a strict French Catholic, Zara told me quite early on in our friendship that she'd rejected Catholicism as soon as she was old enough to be allowed her own opinion. When we were at school together she'd made a few remarks about the hypocrisy of Sunday churchgoers. It struck me that she was battling some kind of inner demon that made her withdraw into herself. Whether it was to do with religion or politics, or her struggle to find her place in the world, I could never work out.

Then, when I met up with Zara again as an adult, I could tell her interests in George Harrison and John Lennon went much further than the music. Once I caught the title on the cover of a little book she was reading, before she slipped it away into her bag; Buddhism was mentioned. I wish now I'd spoken to her about her thoughts on the afterlife. Perhaps it would give me some pointers as to why she might have needed to run away.

Cemeteries are not my favourite place, nevertheless I'd made a point of regularly visiting Joel's grave. Despite him being well thought of locally, it was doubtful that grateful customers would think to commemorate him and with his parents back in Scotland there was no-one else. On all the visits I'd made since his death I'd never seen any other flowers in the brass vase, except for the ones I brought.

I walked up to it now and for a moment thought I'd made a mistake. I always approached this part of the cemetery from the top path, but today I'd walked the long way around and came upon it from another angle. But, no, I wasn't mistaken. For the first time since Joel's death someone else had visited his grave. The little brass vase contained a bunch of chrysanthemums.

I stood beside the headstone and thought about Zara. Perhaps she had visited again, which meant she must be somewhere nearby. I went through a mental list, trying to guess who else might have brought the flowers. Joel's parents were back in Scotland and I was certain they would have contacted me had they decided to make a trip south. Petula had been at the funeral, but after what she'd told me I couldn't imagine her visiting his grave.

In the end, I wrote an entry in my notebook with today's date and then put it out of my mind. The chances were a kindly stranger had a few flowers left over and felt sorry at the sight of a young man's grave looking bare and unloved. I looked around and spotted a man in a grey raincoat a little distance away from me. He didn't appear to be walking with any purpose in mind, it was as though he had chosen the cemetery for his afternoon stroll, which was odd.

I unwrapped the flowers from their newspaper wrapping and took the vase over to the water fountain to refresh it. I spent a few minutes rearranging the chrysanthemums and mixing them with the carnations I'd brought and then I bent down to return the vase to its holder at the side of the marble headstone. I'd left a little cloth stuffed in a crack between the vase holder and the headstone. I used it to wipe the marble down every now and then. As I pulled the cloth out something fell to the ground. It was a small piece of card, torn from a cereal packet or similar. One side was coloured, but on the other side were just three handwritten words, '*Please forgive me*'.

Once the man in the raincoat was facing away from me I put the card in my pocket, feeling guilty, but this was evidence and would be more useful to me than poor Joel. When I looked up again the man had gone.

Chapter 22

I hesitated. To tell the truth, an idea, wild and extravagant in itself, had once or twice that morning flashed through my brain. I had rejected it as absurd, nevertheless it persisted. 'You couldn't call it a suspicion,' I murmured. 'It's so utterly foolish.'

The Mysterious Affair at Styles - Agatha Christie

The next time I called in to pay the paper bill I wasn't expecting Mr Peters to remember our brief conversation. I couldn't have been more wrong.

'Did it help at all?' he asked, as I handed over a note and some change.

'I'm sorry?'

'What I told you about your friend?'

Either I had been less discreet about my investigations than I thought, or Mr Peters knew more than he had led me to believe.

'You mean Zara Carpenter?'

'You're her friend, aren't you? You must be keen to find her. The police don't seem to have done much since I gave them my statement.'

'They have their own methods, I guess. But, yes, I'm keen to find her. How did you know we were friends?'

'Oh, you hear all sorts working in a paper shop. I might be able to help, if you'd like me to?'

There was something vaguely distasteful about Mr Peters and ordinarily I would have kept him at arm's length, but if he could help then I wasn't going to turn down his offer.

'Yes, any other information you might have…'

'Tell you what, meet me here at the shop tomorrow at

5pm. Once I've locked up we can go over to the cemetery together and I'll tell you exactly what I saw. It might trigger something, give you some clues.'

By the time I got home I was regretting having agreed to the meeting, but decided half an hour spent in the company of an oddball wouldn't be much of a penance if it got me closer to finding Zara.

The next afternoon, when I arrived at the shop, he was standing outside, looking keen. He was dressed in what could have passed as his Sunday best, with his hair slicked down with Brylcreem and an overdose of aftershave I could smell as I approached. I was still tempted to abandon the whole idea.

'You came. Good. Well, it's just a walk to the cemetery from here. Are you happy to walk?' he said.

We set off at a steady pace and entered the cemetery at the top end, which meant a longish walk downhill to the area containing Joel's grave. St Martha's cemetery had expanded over recent years, synonymous with the expansion of the town. The top part, nearest to the little chapel, was flat, with rose bushes and small trees lining the pathways. Then there was a reasonably steep descent to the newer areas, which were more sparse. This lower part looked out over the valley, offering no protection from the prevailing easterly winds, which made it bleak, even on a summer's day.

'Cemeteries are fascinating places, don't you think?' he said, as we walked past a young family visiting one of the graves.

'Well, I...'

'I come here all the time, whenever I have time to spare. There's so much you can learn from a gravestone.'

'Yes, I suppose so,' I replied, increasingly doubtful about the purpose of our visit.

'Take a look here, for example, this lady died in childbirth. Do you see, that's the date she died and right next to her is the grave of her daughter, showing she was born on that very day. Fascinating, don't you think?'

'So sad,' I said, hoping Bean couldn't hear this strange man's words.

'It's social history, that's what it is. See this family grave. Stand just here and you'll be able to read the words.' He went to take my arm, but I moved away from him just at the right moment, leaving his hand to wave without purpose.

'Three sons, all died in the same year, probably consumption, or even influenza. There was a time when even the common cold could kill you.'

'Yes, of course. Mr Peters, I don't mean to hurry you, but you mentioned you had more information about Zara. It's just I need to get back to make my husband's tea.'

'Ah, yes, your husband. Well, he's a lucky man, I only wish I had a lovely wife to make my tea.'

I was distinctly uncomfortable now and wished I hadn't agreed to come to the graveyard with him at a time of day when there were few people about.

'Shall we walk down to Joel's grave? Where you saw Zara?' I said.

We walked down past many headstones adorned with fresh flowers, and many more covered in algae, looking sad and unloved. I let him go slightly ahead of me and I could hear him muttering, but couldn't catch his words.

'Here we are, this is where I saw her,' he stopped at Joel's grave and turned to face me. 'You come and stand

171

here,' he said and once again reached out to manhandle me into position. I stood back out of his reach.

'It's okay, I can see what you mean. This is where she stood, when you saw her?'

'Yes, just here.'

'And you were?'

'Over there, by my family,' he pointed to some headstones about fifty yards away, shaded by a group of newly planted elm trees.

'And it was in the afternoon?'

'Yes, late afternoon, I like coming then, it's quieter, easier to talk. I tell them everything. I know they can hear me. There's so much we don't know about death, it's not the end, you know. I'm certain of it.'

'And you just saw Zara come to the grave and then leave again?'

'Yes, I looked up and saw her arrive. I watched her for a while, I reckon she was chatting to him. Then she left.'

'That's all you know? You didn't see where she went from here?'

'No, she was carrying a big bag, like a holdall. I told you about the bag, didn't I?'

'Yes.'

'Well, she put it down on the ground.'

'Nothing else then?'

'There is something, actually.' As he bent down I realised what he was hoping to find. He put his hand down behind the gravestone and ferreted around for a few moments.

'I don't understand, it's not there,' he said, his forehead creasing with a frown.

'What's not there?'

'There was a note. A piece of card, I saw her stuff it down behind the gravestone and when she left I came over to see what it was.'

'You took it out? You read it?'

'You think I shouldn't have, that it was none of my business? Well, you're right, but like I say, there's so much to learn from a cemetery. I just looked at it and then I put it back. What I don't understand is why it's not here now. It's been moved, maybe she's been back, taken it away?'

'Did you tell the police about the note?'

'No, she seemed like a nice girl, I didn't want to get her into trouble.'

'Why would it get her in trouble?'

'Because of what it said.'

'What did it say?'

'*Please forgive me.* Just those three words. You do see, don't you. If I told the police you can imagine what they might think.'

'What?'

'Well, it sounds like a confession to me.'

I was tempted to cancel our newspaper delivery after the cemetery visit. Inevitably, going into the shop to pay the bill was going to invite more questions and conversations with the strange Mr Peters. An alternative was to send Greg every now and then, but the last thing I wanted was for him to get embroiled in it all.

The more I thought about Zara's note, the more I worried about her state of mind. I couldn't imagine why she felt she needed forgiveness. The only way to know more would be to find her.

I didn't want my distrust of Mr Peters to cloud my

judgement, and was keen to remain objective. Perhaps there was a link between Mr Peters and Zara's disappearance. Maybe he saw an opportunity to make some money when he saw her that day in the cemetery. Blackmail is an evil thing, the blackmailer using his power over the vulnerable. Although if that was his intention wouldn't he have taken the note to prevent anyone else finding it?

Quiet days in the library van gave me a chance to mull over all that I'd discovered to date. The more information I was gathering about Zara, the more I was getting sidetracked and confused. So far I'd learned about an ex-boyfriend who was handy with his fists and a strange cemetery dweller who had a fascination with death. Either of them could have given Zara a reason to run away. The only way I would know for sure was to encourage a confession, which was highly unlikely, or to find Zara. So, in reality, I'd travelled several miles in various directions and returned to the beginning.

Just before packing up for the day on Friday the door of the van opened and in walked Phyllis Frobisher.

'Not too busy?' she said, glancing down at the books spread out on the counter in front of me.

'It's lovely to see you. It's been weeks. What news do you have for me?'

'My garden is free of all weeds and looking perfect, and I'm getting bored. The doctor says boredom is a positive sign, as it means my energy levels are finally returning. Between you and me I don't think they ever went away, it's just that my body hadn't realised it needed to keep up. What's been happening here? How's your dad?'

174

I hesitated before telling her about Zara, wondering what she might think about it all.

'Still enthralled with Agatha?' she nodded her head towards the books.

'There's a reason for it. I'm learning the tricks of the trade.'

'Which trade would that be? Decided to be an author now then? Well, that would make sense, you were always one of my best pupils. Not that I would have told you that at the time, wouldn't have wanted you to struggle to fit in your beret,' she said, with a wink.

'Not writing, detecting,' I smiled, thinking she might assume I was joking.

'You're looking for your friend, aren't you?' She had always been one step ahead of me.

'Yes, but not getting far. Every approach I take uncovers more questions than answers.'

'I hear the police have a new lead. Did it come from you?'

'No, but I know who has spoken to them. It might be relevant, I can't decide.'

'Why not leave it to the police, now they're on the lookout again. I'm assuming they are on the lookout again? And I'm guessing you might need to be taking things a little easier now?' she gestured towards my expanding waistline. 'Congratulations in order, I think?'

'Yes. Greg would like to see me put my feet up, but if anything I'm livelier than ever, well at least I'm waking up earlier than I ever have done, so there are more hours in the day than there used to be.'

'Be careful, Janie. Sometimes it's best not to meddle. I'm sure your friend will find her own way through her problems, whatever they are.'

Now I had two people advising me to drop the search and only dad encouraging me to carry on. But I'd gone so far now that even without dad's support I couldn't let it lie.

Chapter 23

Poirot did not answer me for a moment, but at last he said: 'I did not deceive you, *mon ami*. At most, I permitted you to deceive yourself.'

'Yes, but why?'

'Well, it is difficult to explain. You see, my friend, you have a nature so honest, and a countenance so transparent, that – *enfin,* to conceal your feelings is impossible!'

The Mysterious Affair at Styles - Agatha Christie

I've given a lot of thought to the day Zara left. I've thought about the day before and even the week before, to determine if there was anything unusual in her behaviour, anything that could have triggered her decision to leave, apart from the obvious trauma of having to accept a whole year had passed since the death of the man she loved.

For three or four months before her disappearance she started to show the beginnings of recovery, but before that, since the day Joel died, it was as though she had a critical illness. I felt helpless as I watched her body close down. She didn't want to eat, she barely drank and even when she was awake she appeared to be asleep, her eyes glazed and her face without expression. I frequently attempted to get her talking about everyday trivia, but the most I would get in response was a nod or shake of her head. Greg suggested I leave her be.

'Everyone reacts to grief differently. We don't know what it's like. Let's hope we never do,' he said.

All our grandparents had died before we were old enough to get to know them, so the most Greg had had to deal with was the loss of a hamster when he was about six years old.

The day my mum left was traumatic, but at least she was still alive. She had recently sent a brief note confirming she'd received my letter about her forthcoming grandchild. It was short and emotionless, much like my relationship with her. I doubted I'd experience much grief if she died, I'd dealt with the loss years ago.

But in the last few months Zara was with us she gravitated from the closed, quiet period of her grieving to a state of almost permanent agitation. She hardly slept and would pace around the house at all hours. She drank copious cups of coffee, but still barely ate. She had always had a slim figure, but now she was pencil thin and I could imagine her walking out in a strong wind and being blown right over.

Joel's parents had overseen the disposal of his studio and flat. They made all the arrangements before returning to their home in Scotland. Once all the legalities had been resolved they arranged for a removal firm to go into the flat and pack everything up.

They kept in touch with us and suggested Zara might want to check through everything, in case any of her possessions were still in the flat.

'The last thing we want is for her belongings to be swept up, and never seen again,' Mr Stewart told me. 'See if you can persuade her, she'll listen to you.'

His confidence in me was welcome, but unfortunately misplaced.

'We need to go round to the flat, Zara,' I told her, 'you'll have to come, because I won't know what's yours and what's his.'

She was resolute, she wasn't going to enter the flat and nothing I could say would persuade her.

'Just my clothes,' was all she said. 'Nothing else.'

'Books, records, photos? Don't you want some reminders of your time together?'

'Just my clothes,' she repeated.

Greg and I went over and filled one of our old suitcases with anything that looked as though it belonged to Zara and the next day the removal men came in and emptied the place.

Another photographer took over the studio and I suppose a deal was done over Joel's equipment. I wondered if his dad might have liked to keep some of it, but perhaps the memories were too painful. Such a sad way for a life to end.

Try as I might, I couldn't remember anything unusual about the day Zara went missing. I was up quite early and wasn't surprised to find her in the kitchen already. Most mornings we would exchange a few words, about whether she had managed to sleep, or about the weather. I had been on at her to go out, I was worried she had become almost agoraphobic. On brighter days she would go into the back garden and sit under one of the cherry trees, shading herself from the sun. Her skin was so pale and even her hair had lost its shine. Perhaps I was being too gentle with her, maybe I needed to be firmer, to take her arm and drag her out with me for a walk, or to the shops. Each time I thought about it, I reminded myself I had no idea how grief might affect someone and if it was me, having to deal with losing Greg, then I would probably take to my bed for a year.

That Thursday was always going to be more difficult than other days. I could imagine her reliving every moment, from the arrival of the police who told her the man she loved was dead, to leaving Joel's flat and curling up in our spare room. I was never going to stop her replaying those dreadful memories. I found it hard enough to cope with and selfishly I wanted nothing but distraction. It was easier for me to go out with Greg and think about brighter things, blanking out all thoughts of my poor friend left behind with her grief. Perhaps my feelings of guilt were the real reason for my passionate search, maybe it was all about making amends.

When Zara first went missing we let the police take charge of her search. We weren't ever kept in the loop about any of the specifics of their investigations. After all, we were only friends. We'd assumed they kept Gabrielle informed, as she was Zara's immediate next of kin. But as Gabrielle didn't exactly offer up a hand of friendship we could hardly delve too deep. Any questions we asked her were likely to remain unanswered.

As the days passed and there was still no news, we decided to take matters into our own hands. We assumed the police had questioned everyone in our immediate neighbourhood, as well as checking with all the local hospitals. The next obvious move would have been to widen the search to the nearby towns.

I found a recent photo of Zara, a studio portrait she'd taken to give to Joel as a present. She'd told me about the portrait, but swore me to secrecy.

'Do you think he'll like it?' she asked me. 'I mean, do you think it's strange I'm giving him a photo of me as a present?'

Zara was never wholly aware of her beauty, which enhanced her attractiveness even more. I told her I thought it was a wonderful idea and Joel would be thrilled.

Zara gave me one of the smaller versions of her portrait and it was this one I took to a local photographic studio. I asked them if they could enlarge it and use it to make fifty posters. I wrote out the wording for them to add, which was as simple and clear as I could make it:

Zara Carpenter is missing
Anyone with information about her whereabouts, please contact
Janie Juke, at
7 Flint Close, Tamarisk Bay

We didn't have the advantage of a telephone at home, we couldn't justify the expense. Dad had one installed to help his patients make appointments, but I didn't want dad to be bothered with what would inevitably be crank calls in the main. If anyone had genuine information, then I prayed they would take the trouble to write a letter, or visit in person.

Greg helped me circulate the posters. We asked pub landlords and newsagents to put them up in their windows. We visited the central library and pinned one on their noticeboard. We tried to focus on places where Zara may have been in the past, where she might have made friends or got chatting to people. Realistically anyone who knew Zara would have already known about her disappearance from the coverage in the local paper, so we knew this was a long shot. But the way I saw it we had nothing to lose.

When Zara left I went through the house and removed

any photos or reminders of her, as looking at them on a daily basis was just too distressing. I was certain something bad had happened to her and I couldn't bear the not knowing. But I kept a few of the posters, rolled up and stored out of the way. If only I'd discovered my new thorough approach to investigating when we did the original poster campaign, I would have had a detailed list of all the places we'd displayed the poster. As it was I had to rely on my memory. Greg would probably remember, but asking him would only set alarm bells ringing and we'd end up arguing.

We'd blitzed the immediate area, but we hadn't gone as far as Brightport. The sleepy seaside town had never featured in our lives until that point, which was strange, as it was less than five miles away. Maybe it was because if we went out for days we'd go inland, or east. Brightport didn't have much to offer, apart from the seafront, and Tidehaven seafront was always going to win hands down, with its amusement arcades and chip shops. On the rare occasion we travelled west we caught the train and visited the larger seaside towns further along the coast, bypassing Brightport completely. Looking back I realised how stupid we'd been to ignore somewhere on our own doorstep.

By the time I got home on Friday, Greg was soaking in the bath.

'Good day?' I said, as I poked my head around the bathroom door.

'Tiring,' he said.

'Difficult job or annoying customers?'

'Both,' he said and submerged his head under the water, blowing bubbles before re-emerging.

'Never mind, tomorrow is another day and all that.'

'Yes, that's what I'm worried about.'

'Soak all those cares away and I'll make a start on supper. Don't fall asleep and drown, or I'll have to eat it all myself.'

'You're all heart,' he said, as I closed the bathroom door.

Before preparing supper I decided to get one of the posters out. I was studying it and developing a plan when I heard Greg pull the plug on the bath. As the water gurgled down through the pipes I rolled up the poster again and put it back in the drawer. I served up supper, but didn't have much of an appetite; so much for the idea of eating for two.

'You're quiet,' Greg said, as he polished off the last of the sausage and mash. 'Your dad alright?'

'Um, oh yes, he's fine. Busy, which is always good.'

'Bean alright?'

'Yes, perfect,' I said and took his hand, laying it on my stomach, so he could feel the early flutterings of our precious creation. 'It tends to be quite fidgety after I've eaten. I think it's going to be a chef. Intrigued by my masterpieces.'

'What, bangers and mash?'

'Yes, well,' I said and dug him in the ribs.

My first opportunity to visit Brightport was Tuesday. I popped Zara's photo in my bag, together with a notebook and pen and walked down to the bus stop. I told dad my plan and said I'd be with him later in the afternoon to catch up with his typing work.

On Thursday I went to Brightport again. I showed Zara's photo to anyone who could be bothered to look.

Then, come late afternoon, I got the bus back and visited dad to fill him in on my day's successes and failures. In fact, just failures. Everyone I spoke to shook their head. Some said they might have seen her but youngsters all looked the same nowadays, didn't they. Others said they kept themselves to themselves and didn't go poking around in other people's business and I should do the same. I wasn't sure how being observant equated with being nosy, but I kept a civil tongue, despite being frequently close to losing my temper.

Dad calmed me down each day and told me to persevere.

'It's legwork, Janie, the basis of thorough police work is legwork. You might well have a breakthrough and even if you don't, you can be sure you've been thorough. After Brightport, perhaps you should do the same around Tidehaven again. The story being back in the news might have jogged people's memories.'

Greg didn't seem to notice that anything was amiss, although it was a close call one day when I caught a glimpse of his van passing me, just as I was stepping off the bus on my way to dad's. He didn't mention it when we were home together that evening, so I guessed he hadn't seen me. There was no doubt he would disapprove of my amateur sleuthing, not least because I was returning home more and more exhausted. It was like having two full-time jobs.

My lunchtimes in Brightport were spent having a drink and a sandwich at a different café, chatting to people and hopefully spreading the net as wide as possible. I had my copy of *'Styles'* with me and flicked through it regularly to see if Poirot's talents might rub off on me.

After my second visit I reckoned I was wasting my time. I told dad that would be my last Brightport trip.

'What's the point?' I said, making no attempt to hide the irritability in my voice.

'Nothing you are doing is a waste. You just never know.'

'There's no way she would have stayed so close to home. She could be anywhere, even in France for all I know. And if she's moved back to Brighton, then I don't stand a chance. What made me believe I could ever track her down.'

'I know it's disheartening, love, but you're doing the right thing. What about the back streets, away from the town centre? Why don't you just give it one more day?'

It's not the first time my dad's advice has made the difference in my life between failure and success. It was on the next visit to Brightport I struck gold.

Chapter 24

Poirot, I noticed, was looking profoundly discouraged.
He had that little frown between the eyes that I knew so
well. 'What is it, Poirot?' I inquired.
'Ah, *mon ami,* things are going badly, badly.'
The Mysterious Affair at Styles - Agatha Christie

It was the back of her head I saw first. Her hair, once
rich and silken, was tangled and greasy. Her head was
bent forward. As I stood in the doorway and watched
her I wondered whether she could have been asleep,
resting her head on her hands. I had seen her sleeping in
that position day after day, in those first months after
Joel's death. But as I approached, I noticed her hands
were wrapped around a steaming mug of hot liquid. Her
gaze was down towards the drink.

The café was warm, steamy even, with an all-pervasive
smell of fried bacon. Zara was wearing a heavy coat and
a thick woollen scarf around her neck. Now we were
into September, the mornings could be chilly, but her
clothes looked overly wintry, even by my standards.

I watched her for a while and noticed how still she
was. It was as though she was in a trance. Instead of the
relief and exhilaration I thought I'd feel, having finally
tracked her down, I felt only sadness to see her brought
so low.

I walked towards her, searching with every step for the
right words that might cheer her, to lift her from the dark
place she had sunken into.

'Hello Zara,' I said, as gently as I could, while coming
around to the other side of the table to face her. 'Can I
join you?'

She lifted her head slowly and directed her gaze at me. She squinted, as though she was standing in a long tunnel looking out at a bright light. Her hair fell back from her face, exposing pale skin. I had always been envious of Zara's olive skin, she could sit in the shade and still get tanned. Now, seeing her so pale, made me think she must have been living in the shadows.

'Janie,' she said. There was no emotion in her voice, she just stated it as a fact, as though she had expected to look up and see me standing there.

'Yes, it's me,' I said and reached out to take one of her hands, but they remained motionless, holding her mug. I pulled out a chair and went to sit down and at the same moment a waitress appeared at the table.

'What'll it be, luv?' she asked, in a broad Liverpool accent.

'Another drink, Zara, or something to eat?'

Zara was still looking at me and for a moment I wondered if she had taken a drug of some kind. She seemed to be oblivious to the waitress, who was fidgeting beside the table, anxious to take our order.

'Just one coffee, please,' I said, hoping this would send her on her way.

The waitress had been holding a pencil and pad in her hand, anticipating a significant order. Now, with just a cup of coffee to remember, she sighed, dropped the pencil and pad into her pocket and walked off to a neighbouring table.

'It's so good to see you.' I moved my hand across the table so that it rested beside hers, not quite touching. 'We've been worried about you.'

I searched her face for any expression that might tell me what she was thinking, or how she was feeling, but all

I could see was the dullness of her eyes, once vivid and bright. Her lips were dry and cracked. It was as if she had just returned from a polar expedition and was numb from the feet up.

The waitress arrived with my coffee and plonked it down in front of me with such gusto that the dark brown liquid slopped over into the saucer, pooling around the base of the cup.

'Great, thanks,' I said, hoping she wouldn't miss the sarcasm in my voice. She mumbled something and shuffled off back to the counter.

'How are you? You look...' I hesitated. It was difficult to sum up all the things she looked; tired, lonely, sad, unwell, were just a few of the words at the tip of my tongue. 'Greg sends his love. He's been missing having you around the place, now he just has to put up with little old me.'

More customers came in, bringing with them a draught of fresh air. I noticed Zara shiver and wanted to wrap my arms around her, but it was as though she was surrounded by an invisible wall.

'Where are you staying?' I said. 'Shall we walk round to your digs? Hey, I could get some bits to eat on the way. Do we pass a shop? I reckon you could do with feeding up.' I wondered at what point she would start to talk to me and how soon I would run out of topics for my pathetic monologue.

'No, I don't think so,' she said, pushing the mug away.

She stood and walked up to the counter, took a few coins from her pocket and gave them to the waitress. By the time I had paid for my coffee and waited for the change, she was out of the door and halfway up the road.

'Hey, Zara, wait. My legs aren't as long as yours,

188

remember,' I called after her. She carried on walking ahead of me and didn't turn around. I increased my pace to brisk and within a few minutes I was up beside her. She turned into an alleyway and I wondered where she was heading, then suddenly she stopped and turned around.

'Janie, go away. I don't want you here.'

'I'm your friend, I miss you and I want to help you.'

'You can't help me. It's too late for that, much too late.'

'Come back with me. Come home, whatever needs sorting out we can do it together. That's what friends are for.'

'No, Janie, I mean it. You need to go now and not come back.'

She stood with her eyes fixed and defiant, but everything else about her posture shouted exhaustion. Her shoulders were slumped forward and her arms hung at her side.

'Okay, I'll go for now, but I will be back. I won't let you go through this on your own.' I turned and walked away. As I reached the end of the alley I looked back to see which way she'd gone, but there was no sight of her.

A walk around the town helped me to get the thoughts straight in my head. At least now I knew my friend was alive. My first instinct was to tell dad I'd found her and ask him what he thought my next step should be. But this was my search and it was up to me to plan from here. I stopped at one of the bus shelters and sat on the bench for a while. A couple of buses came and went while I looked through my notebook and thought long and hard about what to do next.

Chapter 25

'Poirot,' I cried, 'I congratulate you! This is a great discovery.'
The Mysterious Affair at Styles - Agatha Christie

On my next visit to Brightport I arrived at the alleyway early. Most of the properties looked like small warehouse units. A few had signs displayed outside, announcing their owners. I glanced along the doorways to see if there was any sign of a familiar name, or even evidence of a doorway leading to a flat or house. I felt sure Zara had gone into one of the entrances along the alley, but the more I looked, the more unlikely it became.

At one end of the alley there was a large covered entrance to one of the lock ups, where I could stand and be reasonably secluded. After standing there for ten minutes undisturbed, a delivery van pulled up and I realised I was in front of some loading doors.

'Mind yourself, love,' a burly chap called out, as he opened the van doors, loaded his sack-barrow with boxes of crisps and started to walk towards me.

'Sorry, yes, will do. Morning, by the way.'

By moving out of the way I would be in full view of anyone walking up and down the alley, so I walked around the van and stood to one side of it. From this position I could see all the doorways down the alley, but couldn't be seen by anyone approaching. Of course, this only worked as long as the driver wheeled his sack-barrow back and forth from the van to the loading doors. After a while he was all done. He folded up the barrow, shoved it into the back of the van and slammed the doors shut.

'You waiting for someone?' he said, walking past me to reach the driver's door.

'Um, kind of. Do you know the area well? Are there any flats down here?'

'Not down here, love. There's the club, the one I've just been delivering to and the rest are small warehouses, well, storerooms more than anything.'

'There's no-one living down here then? It's just I thought my friend gave me this as her address. I must have got in a muddle.'

'Living? No, unless you mean those scroungers who are squatting in the disused Walker's place,' he nodded towards the far end of the alley. 'Disgusting if you ask me. Shouldn't be allowed.'

As the van driver pulled away I walked towards the entrance of Walker's storeroom, wondering what I was going to find inside. I pushed the old wooden door and at first it seemed to be locked, but it was just the warped timber that was blocking my way. I gave the door another shove and I was in.

A narrow corridor led out into a large expanse. I peered through the gloom and tried not to gasp as I took in the degradation that met my eyes. The walls were covered with patches of damp and black mould. Paint was flaking off the ceiling. Although we were at ground level there was only one small window, which looked as though it was boarded up from the outside, with a little light coming through in-between the slats. It crossed my mind that Greg would have a fit, certain that Bean was being exposed to toxins just by my standing here, breathing in the musty air. I moved forwards gingerly, making sure I didn't touch the walls.

191

As my eyes became accustomed to the dim light I could make out four old mattresses, yellowed and stained, retrieved from a rubbish dump perhaps. Old, torn blankets and coats were scattered randomly across the mattresses, offering minimal warmth in this cold, damp place. There was a girl laying on one of the mattresses, turned away from me, her body covered in an old raincoat, her hair pulled back and roughly tied with some string. Another lad was sitting on his mattress, looking directly at me. He had blonde hair and could have passed for Norwegian, or Dutch. And there was Zara. There was a threatening intensity to the way the blonde lad looked at me. Was Zara being held against her will?

I walked over to her and spoke quietly, hoping the others wouldn't hear me. 'What are you doing here, Zara? Come home with me, please. I can't leave you here in this place, it's...'

She shook her head and motioned for me to sit down beside her. She was sitting on the edge of one of the mattresses with her legs tucked up underneath her. Bizarrely, she looked more at home here than she had ever looked during that long year at our house. I was trying to come up with an excuse not to sit down, certain I would find myself bitten with fleas, or worse. As if he could read my mind, the blonde-haired lad came over and held out a folding wooden chair, a deckchair of sorts. Perhaps he'd pinched it from the seafront.

'Oh, thanks,' I said, as he opened it for me and walked back to his mattress.

'No wonder you're so thin,' I said, continuing to keep my voice to a whisper. 'What have you been eating? What are you living on? You don't have any money do you? Oh Zara, I can't bear to see you like this.'

My voice was clearly not quiet enough because as though on cue the blonde-haired lad got up again and handed me an opened packet of biscuits. I shook my head and watched Zara as she smiled at him in gratitude.

'You won't understand, Janie, so I'm not even going to try to explain. Just go home, go back to your cosy life and leave me to mine.' The bitterness in her voice was not something I'd heard before. Grief, yes, but never anger.

'You've probably noticed I've had a development since I last saw you,' I said, trying to lighten the mood. I pointed to my midriff and smiled.

'I'm pleased for you, Janie, really I am.'

It felt as though we were worlds apart. There was nothing I could say to her to bridge the gap. I wished dad was here, or Greg, or anyone who might be able to get through to her. I was getting nowhere.

'Is there a danger of you being evicted from here?' I asked her, remembering what the van driver had said about scroungers. If he knew about the squat I guessed other people did too and it wouldn't be long before the authorities would have something to say about it.

'Are you planning to tell someone about us? We're not harming anyone you know.' The anger had gone from her voice now and she sounded more like the Zara I remembered from our schooldays, wistful and full of dreams. Just as I was recalling the fun times we used to have together, listening to music and dancing, the blonde-haired lad picked up a guitar that had been laying on the floor next to his mattress and started to strum it. The sound immediately softened the atmosphere and I noticed Zara's face relax. She closed her eyes and moved her head in time to the music.

'Do you remember when we danced together, Zara? We had some fun times when we were at school together, didn't we?' Perhaps by reminiscing about positive days I could encourage her to accept my help, just as she did when she was told about Joel's death.

'It was a long time ago, I'm not the same person now. You've never known the real me. Trust me, you won't want to.'

'You've got so much to offer the world, you know. All the chats we've had, you've taught me a lot. You've shown me a new way of looking at things. Make Joel proud, move forward with your life. Don't waste it hiding away here.'

'Go home, Janie, just go home.'

I stayed a little longer, but knew I was achieving nothing, except potentially putting myself and Bean at risk from the damp and acrid stench of the place. As I left I promised her I'd be back. She remained sitting on the mattress and as I turned at the door to wave goodbye she had her eyes closed and her head bowed.

On the way back on the bus I took deep breaths, trying desperately to bite back tears. Once I was home I had a bath and put all my clothes to wash before Greg got back. Even after bathing, the rancid, smoky smell lingered in my memory.

When I closed my eyes that night the pictures in my mind would be Zara, living in squalor. The sense of powerlessness was overwhelming.

I wasn't the only one to have been disturbed by all I saw and smelt. Bean was clearly disenchanted with my visit and decided to give us all a fright, which meant I didn't return to the squat for several days.

The morning after my visit to Zara I woke with sharp tummy pains. I didn't say anything to Greg and let him go off to work unperturbed. He'd started his new job at Mowbray's and was keen to make the right impression, so the last thing I wanted was to worry or distract him. But once he left I managed to dress and get myself round to dad's.

'Oh, princess, you should never had gone,' dad said, as soon as I explained. 'I did tell you. Goodness knows what bugs you might have picked up.'

After a sit down and a couple of glasses of water I felt a little better, but the tummy cramps were still fairly regular.

'I'm sure it's nothing. I probably shouldn't have had that curry last night,' I joked, hoping to allay dad's fears, although I hadn't gone anywhere near the curry and had settled for a ham salad. 'I'll just lay out on the sofa for a while, close my eyes. Is that okay? Have you got clients this morning?'

'I want you to phone the doctor, get him to call in on his afternoon round,' dad said.

After a particularly strong cramp that almost took my breath away, I decided to take dad's advice. Dr Filbert called in early afternoon, examined me and told me that bed rest for a few days should do the trick.

Phyllis Frobisher would cover for me, now she was fully recovered from her heart attack, so the library was in good hands. But the library was the least of my concerns.

'What am I going to tell Greg?' I asked my dad. I didn't want Greg to worry and start to treat me with kid gloves.

'He's your husband, so what goes on between you is nothing to do with me. But I would like to think you will tell him the truth?'

Dad was right, but there are different levels of truth. I would apply the 'need to know' approach and tell Greg I was a bit under the weather and needed to rest up for a few days.

It was frustrating not being able to go straight back to see Zara. I was worried she would believe I had given up on her. Dad tried to convince me to tell the police I'd found Zara, but I couldn't risk her being evicted and thrown out on the streets. There was little to be positive about when I thought about the bleak place that Zara had found to hide herself away in, but at least she wasn't sheltering in a doorway, or sleeping on a park bench. She had chosen to hide herself away and I needed to find out why. I used my days of rest and relaxation to plan my next steps.

Chapter 26

A vague suspicion of everyone and everything filled my mind. Just for a moment I had a premonition of approaching evil.
The Mysterious Affair at Styles - Agatha Christie

Following my few days of rest I was longing to return to the squat. I was determined to persuade Zara to come home with me, but knew I'd need some kind of lever.

A few days earlier I'd spotted a poster in the town advertising a clairvoyant, aptly called Crystal, who offered to unravel all the mysteries of the future. I've never believed in all that mystical nonsense, but these were desperate times, requiring desperate measures. I added 'Contact Crystal' to my jobs list.

Apart from enlisting the support of the spirit world, Gabrielle was the only person I could approach who might be able to help. It was a risk telling her anything about Zara. Their mutual antipathy meant she would be just as likely to tell the police about the squat to spite her sister.

I decided to visit Gabrielle and hope to get her talking, but would tell her nothing about the squat, or about seeing Zara. Although Gabrielle's nonchalant attitude irritated me, she was my best link to Zara's past. I was still convinced it was her past that would provide the trigger I needed to get her to leave the squat and return to a safer place.

There was a chance Gabrielle's reaction would be more favourable if I didn't arrive on her doorstep unannounced. The best way to advise her in advance was to write a letter, but it felt too formal. In the end, I sent a postcard. I chose a neutral scene of Tidehaven Pier, carefully avoiding the humorous cartoons of seaside antics. I kept the message simple, writing that I'd appreciate another quick chat with her and I'd call round on Saturday morning about 11am and hope to catch her in. I realised this pre-warning would give her the perfect excuse to be out, but it was worth the risk.

As I dressed that morning I found myself worrying about what I was going to wear. I was limited to one of two dresses, as none of my trousers or skirts would fit. I chose the most flowery of my Indian cotton smocks that I could wear over a warm tee-shirt, imagining the look of disdain on Gabrielle's face at my lack of style. The butterflies in my stomach had nothing to do with Bean. I'd told Greg I planned to do some clothes shopping, as everything in my wardrobe refused to fit around my ever-expanding bump. It wasn't a lie, as I intended to have a quick peek in a couple of shops on the way back from Gabrielle's. Greg was happy to have a few hours to himself and kissed me as I left, which made me feel even more guilty.

The walk to Gabrielle's flat was mostly uphill and by the time I arrived I was out of breath and sweaty, despite it being a cloudy day. I kept reminding myself this was not an interview, it was just meant to be a friendly chat, although 'friendly' may have been pushing the possibilities a little too far.

I rang the bell and wondered how long I should wait before abandoning the whole idea. Instead, two seconds later, the door opened and there she stood.

'Come in Janie, can I take your wrap?'

I'd grabbed an old cardigan before leaving home to

add another layer of warmth, which had proved unnecessary. Gabrielle was either being kind, or she was making a point. Either way it didn't help to put me at ease.

'Thanks,' I said, handing her my cardigan. I followed her along the hallway into the sitting room.

It was difficult to see Gabrielle looking poised and stylish, when just a few days ago I had seen her twin sister dishevelled and alone. The contrast was stark between Zara's dark, dirty living quarters and this glamorous sitting room, which oozed wealth and taste.

'I received your postcard,' she said, looking at me expectantly. It was then I realised I hadn't prepared my opening lines. My focus had been on getting through the door, now I was here I wasn't quite sure how to start.

'I appreciate you seeing me,' I started, pausing when I realised how formal I sounded. What I needed was to relax the atmosphere between us. She looked at me and waited and I found myself praying for a clue about how to break the ice, which was threatening to freeze me into silence.

'I love your choice of paintings,' I said. 'It's not just the prints themselves, but the way you've arranged them. You certainly have an artistic flair. Have you done any painting yourself?'

She smiled and shook her head. This was not going to be easy.

'Have you lived in this flat for long? It's so homely, it must have taken you ages to get it looking the way it does.'

'Let's concentrate on why you're here, shall we?' she said, fixing her gaze on me.

'Of course. It's just you were so helpful when I came to see you last time and I was wondering if there was anything else about Zara you could share with me. About her past?'

'You don't need to butter me up. I wasn't helpful then and I probably won't be now.'

'Have the police been in touch with you?'

'No.'

'Nothing since the information from Mr Peters?'

'Mr Peters?'

My mouth had run away with me. There was no way I wanted her to know I'd spoken to Mr Peters. Perhaps it wasn't too late to backtrack.

'I have a feeling that was the name they mentioned on the news?' I said. 'There was a man who came forward with a new lead. I'm probably wrong about his name, it could have been Powell or Purcell. You say the police haven't updated you?'

'Why would they? I made it clear I'm not interested in whether Zara is alive or dead. It makes no difference to me.'

'How can you say that?' My heart started thumping and any minute now I expected my hiccups to start with a vengeance. I was grateful she hadn't offered me tea, although her lack of hospitality hadn't gone unnoticed.

'Easily,' she said, her voice steady and objective. 'Any connections that might have existed between us were destroyed a long time ago. She lives her life and I live mine. She has never forgiven me you see.'

'Forgiven you? For what? What did you do?'

'I saved her life.'

I couldn't find any words, so I remained silent.

'When Zara was fourteen she tried to kill herself,' she paused either for effect, or because she was remembering how distressing it was. I liked to think it was the latter.

'I should have seen it coming, I suppose,' she continued. 'But at that age I was more worried about hair and makeup.'

'What can have made her so unhappy at just fourteen? Did you really not notice? Isn't there supposed to be a special connection between identical twins?'

'It's a fallacy, at least for us, we were just like any other sisters, some things we shared and others we didn't.'

Knowing Zara had been brought so low before, made me even more anxious about her current state of mind. I had a terrible image of arriving at the squat to find Zara laying unconscious. For a moment I felt like leaving there and then and going straight over to Brightport to make sure she was alright.

'What happened?' I said, taking short breaths to steady a rising sense of panic.

'His name was Samuel. He was Jamaican. His parents came to England after the war. His dad had fought with the British and loved the idea of bringing his family to the Mother Country. What they didn't know was how much hatred there would be. He was Zara's first boyfriend. They met in a coffee bar or some place like that. I don't know much of the detail, to be honest.'

'Did he end it, was that what happened?'

'No, quite the opposite. Our parents found out and forbade her to see him. They said it would only bring misery to them both.'

'They were fourteen for goodness sake. Surely it was just a friendship, it wasn't as though they were about to run off and get married. Anyway, your mum's French, she should know all about the importance of acceptance.'

'All I know is my parents' minds were fixed and for a while there were endless screaming arguments. I spent most evenings up in my bedroom with my transistor radio turned up as loud as possible.'

'Did you talk to Zara about Samuel? Did you ever meet him?'

'I met him a couple of times when they were together in town. He seemed like a sweet boy.'

'What happened? Did she agree to stop seeing him?'

'The decision was taken out of her hands. Samuel was the victim of a vicious attack. Some local boys beat him up, he spent some time in hospital. They cut his face with a broken bottle. It was horrible.'

'Oh God, poor Zara, poor Samuel.'

'It was dreadful for his family of course and they were worried for Samuel's younger sister, so they moved back to Jamaica. Zara took it badly, she didn't speak for weeks after the attack. She stopped going to school. Then one day I came home from school and decided to persuade her to come out of her bedroom, to go for a walk. She hadn't been out of the house for ages. I suppose I felt sorry for her, she was miserable all the time. I knocked on her bedroom door and when she didn't reply I pushed it open and that's when I found her.'

As she recounted the story to me there was no emotion in her voice or her expression. It was as though she was describing a scene from a mildly entertaining film.

'She was laying on the bed,' she continued. 'She'd put one of her shawls over her face, she was so still that at first I thought she was dead. There was an empty bottle of pills on the bedside table. I panicked, I shook her hard and then I could see she was breathing, her chest was rising and falling. I started screaming at her, "Wake up, for God's sake, wake up," but she didn't respond. Mum and dad were out and we didn't have a phone in the house. I knew I'd have to leave her to go to the phone box. I was terrified she would die as soon as I left her, I knew I'd get the blame. I ran to the phone box, phoned for an ambulance. They arrived in minutes, whisked her off to hospital and pumped her stomach. Said she was lucky I found her when I did.'

'Why would she hate you for saving her life?'

'Because she wanted to die.'

I was struggling to take it all in, but I was grateful I was finding out about this terrible time in Zara's life after I had seen her at least alive, if not well.

'After that we moved, came to live here,' she continued. 'Mum and dad said we all needed a fresh start. It was because of Zara's stupidity that I had to leave my friends behind. Mum and dad were fixated with Zara, what she was doing, how she was feeling. I might as well have been invisible for all they cared.'

'So, the suicide was before she moved to Tamarisk Bay, just before I met her?'

She nodded. 'Then, no sooner had we finished school we had to move again. No-one asked for my opinion. At least now I get to choose where I live and who I see.'

She glared at me, which was my cue to leave.

The images of poor Zara lying comatose on her bed while Gabrielle tried to save her made my mind reel and my stomach churn. The days when I struggled to shake Zara from her sadness all made sense now. There were too many similarities between the loss when Samuel was

203

taken from her and the loss she must have felt after Joel's tragic death.   I had to get Zara out of the squat and into a brighter place where I could keep an eye on her.   I knew what I needed to do, but I had no idea how I was going to do it.

Chapter 27

I heard Poirot chuckle softly beside me. 'How did you
know?' I whispered.
The Mysterious Affair at Styles - Agatha Christie

Greg's first week at Mowbray's went well. Each evening
he came home full of enthusiasm for what he'd learned,
with plenty of amusing anecdotes. He'd hit it off with the
rest of Mowbray's team, and I could tell that they were
pleased to have him onboard. Listening to him chattering
away over supper was a perfect antidote to the anxious
thoughts that were running through my mind. When I
started my search for Zara I thought that tracking her
down was my sole challenge. Instead, now I had found
her, it was clear that I had a whole host of further puzzles
to solve. It was like being lost in a maze.

It appeared that reading had gone out of fashion, with
another quiet day in the mobile library. A quiet day was
just what I didn't want. After everything Gabrielle had
told me about Zara's attempted suicide, I was more
anxious than ever. I couldn't return to the squat until I
had a definite plan. Until then what I needed was
distraction and busyness, but each hour seemed to drag.
Then the door opened and in walked a woman and as
soon as I saw her I guessed who she was.

'Can I leave these leaflets in here, dearie,' she said.
'This spot on the desk will do just fine.'

I didn't need to read the front of the flier to realise this
was Crystal, the local clairvoyant, whose posters were
plastered all over the notice boards in town.

'Um, sorry, no, we aren't supposed to have advertising
in the library, unless it's about talks, lectures, that kind of

thing.'

'Well, that's what I do. Talk, not lecture though, dearie, oh no. I don't pass judgement, that's for the spirits, they'll let you know if they're not happy.' I wondered if the tattered shawl wrapped around her shoulders and her dangly earrings were all part of her act, or if this was her normal dress code.

'Right, yes, but I'm sorry, I still can't let you leave the leaflets. You could try the paper shop, the one on the corner of High Street and Waterstone Avenue. Mr Peters is the owner, I'm sure he'd be happy to help.' It struck me Crystal and Mr Peters would make a well-matched couple, both in love with the spirit world and fascinated with the afterlife.

'I'll keep one for myself though, if I may?' Desperate times required desperate measures. I'd been crazy enough to wander around a cemetery with the weird Mr Peters, so paying for a half-hour session of palm readings, or whatever else she did, might not be a bad idea.

'I won't forecast the sex,' she said, nodding her head towards my midriff. 'I'm careful with mothers-to-be, it's a precious thing, childbirth, not to be messed with.'

'Right, yes.'

'But I'll help you with your search.' Perhaps there was more to Crystal than I had first thought.

'What makes you think I'm searching?'

'Oh, we're all searching, dearie. That's what this life is all about, looking for answers, for love, for forgiveness. It's not 'til you reach the next life that it finally makes sense. I just help folk along the way. Well, not me, you understand, it's the spirits, they talk to me.'

'I see, yes,' although I really didn't, but I was fascinated to hear what Joel might have to say to her from the other side.

'Will I see you then, dearie? Will you make an appointment now? Afternoons are best, shall we say tomorrow?'

'Er, yes, okay, why not. 3pm?' I had nothing to lose, except for the silver needed to cross her palm.

As I left dad's the next day I told him about Crystal. He couldn't stop chuckling and made me promise to come straight back to tell him the outcome.

'It'll be better than a chapter from one of your murder mysteries,' he said.

Crystal's place of work turned out to be a little caravan, tucked round the back of one of the many junk shops in Tidehaven Old Town. Any ideas about the inside of a clairvoyant's caravan were quickly dispersed when she opened the door and bid me inside. This was no homely mix of brightly decorated floral china and shiny brassware, instead the walls were patchy with mildew and the strip light was so covered with grease it barely cast any light.

Crystal indicated for me to sit opposite her on a blue plastic chair, that wouldn't have looked out of place on a rubbish dump. She was ensconced in a threadbare armchair that fitted snugly around her rotund figure. Between us was a small wooden table covered with a piece of lace, yellowed with nicotine stains, or age, or both. The faint smell of cigarette smoke lurked, partly disguised by some joss sticks that had just finished burning.

'Are you ready, dearie?'
'Er, yes, I think so.'

'If you can pay me then. I like to get the money out of the way first.'

'Yes, sorry.' I handed over the required sum and she put it into a large pocket in the front of her flowery apron. She pulled her shawl around her shoulders, bent her head and started humming. I guessed this was all part of the act, but had to grit my teeth to stop myself giggling. After a few moments she picked up a pack of cards from the table and handed them to me.

'Shuffle please.'

I looked at the cards, which were larger than normal playing cards and wondered what to do. I'd never been adept at shuffling and had visions of the cards spraying out around the caravan.

'Sorry, I don't know how to.'

'Just cut then, like this.' She took the cards and divided the pack several times, then handed them back to me. I repeated the action and put them down on the table.

'Cut the pack and choose a card,' she said.

I lifted some of the cards up and uncovered one, handing it to her.

'The Tower, yes, that makes sense.'

'Does it?' I said, feeling increasingly foolish.

'Choose another.'

I repeated the action a couple more times until there were four cards laid out in front of me.

'The Tower, that represents change, so no surprise there. You need to look after your health, take things easy now you have a little one to think about. The Moon, now that tells me you're finding things a tad confusing. Had a few heated words with your husband? Don't say a word, I don't need to know. All I'd say is pick your battles and be prepared to lose some of them. Now here's an interesting one, the Hanged Man.'

'Oh great, so now you're forecasting capital punishment are you?'

She gave me a sharp look, intending to put me in my place.

'The Hanged Man signifies you are at a crossroads, you need to learn to let go, see where fate takes you. You can't always be in control of things, in fact, I find that none of us are ever in control.'

'Right, okay, and what about this last one, it looks like a devil? If it's anything bad, I'd rather not know.'

'It's in your hands.'

'What is?'

'The Devil is nothing to be scared of, it's showing you not to give up hope, don't take things at face value, dig deep to find the real truth of a situation.'

'So, to summarise, you've told me I might have the odd quarrel with my husband, I need to take it easy, remember I can't control everything and don't give up hope. It's hardly fortune telling, you must say the same thing to everyone.'

'No need to be rude, dearie, I'm only telling you what the cards say.'

'Nothing else? Nothing about a tall, dark stranger, or a big pot of money?'

'I don't take kindly to sarcasm, I'm no fraud. I've been telling fortunes since I was a wee girl, just like my mother before me. It's in my blood, been in my family for generations.'

'Well, that's fine, but I expected a bit more for my money. Seems like an easy way to earn a few shillings, it would save me going to work.'

'I'd like you to go now.' I'd upset her, clearly her sensibilities were more fragile than I thought. She stood and walked past me to the door. As she opened it I spotted a young girl coming down the alleyway towards the caravan.

'Looks like your next customer is here. Maybe she'll be better at shuffling than me.'

As I passed the girl I smiled. 'Good luck,' I said. I was tempted to say a lot more, but decided Crystal gave her customers exactly what they came for. A chat and a little bit of hope that tomorrow might be a better day.

Chapter 28

Amid breathless excitement, he held out three thin strips
of paper. 'A letter in the murderer's own hand-writing,
mes amis!'
The Mysterious Affair at Styles - Agatha Christie

Now I had more insight into Zara's past I believed I
could get her to talk to me and hopefully persuade her to
come back with me to enjoy a safe haven, at least for a
while.

At the next opportunity I took the bus to Brightport
and wound my way through the streets to the alleyway.
Revisiting this bleak place, littered with broken bottles
and rubbish bins spilling over with refuse, was depressing.
I knew the inside of the squat would be just as
demoralising, but I clenched my fists to remind myself
why I was there and, filled with new resolve, I pushed
open the door into the darkness.

Since my last visit there had been a change around, as
there were now only three old mattresses on the floor.
Once my eyes had become accustomed to the gloom I
saw Zara laying with her back to me. The blonde-haired
lad with the guitar was sitting plucking at the strings, with
his eyes closed as though in a trance. The third mattress
was unoccupied, with just a couple of ragged blankets
thrown across it.

I moved slowly towards Zara, wondering whether she
was sleeping, but as I knelt down to touch her shoulder
she turned over and sat up.

'Janie,' she said, sweeping her hair away from her face.
She looked as though she hadn't known a proper night's
sleep for a long while. 'I told you not to come back.' Her

voice was slurred, possibly from drugs or alcohol, or a mixture of both.

'I need to talk to you, but not here, the air doesn't suit my little one,' I said, patting my midriff. 'Will you come outside and walk with me a while? We could grab a coffee somewhere? My treat?'

She sighed, as though she didn't have the energy to argue. Standing up she grabbed a thin grey jacket and a woollen hat. I thought about the stylish Zara I remembered and wondered if she would ever be that person again.

We walked out into the alleyway in silence. I was desperate not to say the wrong thing and have her close the shutters down again, but I wasn't sure what the right thing might be. She stopped at the first café we came to and pushed open the door to release a waft of greasy fry-ups and cigarette smoke. I sent out a silent prayer that the odours wouldn't mean me spending the next half hour in the toilet throwing up.

This must have been her regular haunt, as the burly chap behind the counter poured her a mug of tea without her asking and pushed it towards her.

'What'll it be for you, love?' he said.

'Coffee, black, please.'

She took a seat at a corner table and I sat opposite her. She ladled two teaspoons of sugar into her mug and stirred it for several seconds, her gaze permanently down.

'How are things?' I asked.

She shrugged and took a sip of tea and finally she looked up at me.

'What is it you want from me?' she said.

'Nothing, I just want you to be okay.'

'You need to understand, the life I had is over. This is

212

the life I've chosen, the one I deserve.'

'Why would you deserve to be miserable? You're the victim of a terrible accident as much as poor Joel, but it's not your fault.'

'Yes, it is my fault, that's just it.'

She took a sip of her drink and looked directly at me, as if to challenge me to answer. I wondered if she thought she was meant to be punished in some way for trying to take her own life. I wished I had experience in counselling or anything that might guide me, give me a clue about what to say next.

'Charlie had to go to the vet,' I said.

She looked at me, but it was as though I was speaking another language, or talking about another world.

'Dad's dog, Charlie,' I continued. 'The crazy animal decided to tread on a sleepy wasp, poor thing. He made such a fuss, limping around. But he's okay now.'

There was still no reaction, so I tried again.

'Do you remember how you envied his hair? You told me girls would pay a week's wages for those chestnut locks with golden highlights. Any hairdresser would kill to be able to achieve that effect, you used to say. And then I told Charlie his Auntie Zara had gone a bit crazy.' Everything I said seemed to be making the situation worse. Perhaps it made more sense to focus on the truth.

'Zara, I've spoken to your sister.'

'Why?'

'I thought she might be able to give me some insight about how I can help you.'

'Janie, will you do something for me?'

'Anything.'

'Leave now and don't come back. Don't speak to my sister again. Just pretend you never met me.'

'I can't do that, I'm sorry.'

'You have a new life to look forward to. My life is tainted, it's black and it will only bring you sorrow.'

'It's too late, I'm already involved. I can't just walk away and forget I ever knew you. We've been good friends, we are good friends. You are like the sister I never had.'

'Be careful what you wish for,' she said. Still I was getting nowhere.

'You've been to Joel's grave, haven't you?' I said.

She looked at me and then looked down at the table. The café door opened and as a customer entered he brought in a blast of cold air that made me shiver.

'Joel's death was my fault.' As she spoke she picked at the cuff of the old jacket she was wearing, still avoiding my gaze.

'What are you talking about? You don't drive,' I said, trying to absorb her words.

'I was there.'

'He was knocked down by a car, no-one was there. Nothing you're saying makes sense.'

'I was there that night. I followed him, we had an argument.'

She stood up, dipped her hand into the cotton bag she'd looped over the back of the chair and took out some coins. 'Like I say, you don't want to get involved in my mess, it will take you to places you'd rather not know about,' she said.

I put my hand on hers and gently pushed it away and then went up to the counter and paid. Once outside in the chill north-easterly wind, it was evident that Zara was getting little warmth from the thin cotton jacket she was wearing.

'What happened to the warm coat you had last time we met?'

'I gave it to Dee, her need was greater than mine,' she said, as she started to walk ahead of me.

'Slow down, there was a reason you used to call me 'little one', remember?'

'I want you to go now, Janie,' she said, as she turned the corner into the alleyway. The thought of her returning to the darkness of the squalid squat and the misery of the life she'd chosen weighed me down with sadness.

'I'll be back, I'm not leaving you, not like this.'

It was time to enlist support. This was a bigger problem than I could deal with on my own and I believed what they said about a problem shared.

Dad was just saying goodbye to his last patient of the day when I arrived.

'Hello love, I didn't expect you today. Is everything okay?'

'I need your help,' I said, as I walked through to the kitchen. I poured a glass of water and sat down at the little Formica table that had always been the focal point for our chats.

'I've been to see Zara again and she's in a dark place.'

'The squat?'

'Yes, but in her head too. She's told me stuff that...I don't know what to believe to be honest. Dad, will you come with me to see her, help me talk her round?'

'You know I'll help, but I'm still not convinced you should be doing this without involving the police.'

'I can't tell the police, not yet. The thing is dad, Zara believes she's to blame for Joel's death.'

'Oh, Janie.'

'No, don't you see? She can't be, she doesn't even drive. For some reason she's blaming herself and I can't get her to listen to me. I thought perhaps with you there, it would be a calming influence. She might be more prepared to listen. We need to persuade her to leave that place, to come back and stay with Greg and me, at least for a while.'

'Have you spoken to Greg about any of this?'

'I can't, not yet. But I will, I promise.'

Dad had been standing, leaning against the kitchen counter and now he eased his way over to one of the chairs and sat opposite me. Charlie had been laying at my feet, watching dad's every move and now he adjusted his position to sit beside dad, pushing his head up against him.

'That's Charlie informing me it's time for his afternoon stroll. Will you join us?'

'I'd love to, but I should be getting back. I want to be home before Greg, otherwise he'll worry. Will you think about it? I can't bear to leave her there.'

'Yes, love, I'll think about it. I'll give you my answer when you call in Thursday.'

I stopped at the corner shop on the way home and bought a few bits for tea and as I turned down into our street I noticed someone walking away from our house. Although I only saw them from behind there was something familiar about them I couldn't quite place. I pushed open the front door and saw an envelope laying on the mat. There was no stamp, so it had been hand delivered and at first glance I was fairly certain the envelope was identical to the one I received a few weeks

216

earlier.

I took the shopping through to the kitchen and looked at the envelope more closely. I retrieved the other envelope from my bedside drawer and put them side by side. Sure enough they were a match, both written by the same person. Any detective, Poirot included, would investigate the handwriting, work out a way to match it to a potential suspect. But I didn't have any suspects, just a few suspicions. And I wasn't a detective, real or fictional.

Opening up the envelope I had just received I expected to see another press cutting, instead it was a handwritten letter.

'I know something about your friend that I'm sure the police would be interested in. Perhaps you'd like to make me an offer to keep my mouth shut. I'm not greedy, so I'm sure we can come to a sensible arrangement. I'll contact you again when you've had time to think about it.'

The letter wasn't signed or dated. It looked as though someone knew something about Zara that might get her into trouble. More than that, this person must have been following me, or at least they knew about my friendship with Zara. I read the letter through again, feeling increasingly uncomfortable about what it was intimating.

Just then I heard Greg's key in the front door, so I shoved both envelopes into my coat pocket and started busying myself with putting away the shopping.

'Hi love,' I called out. 'You're home early. All okay?'

'Yeah, fine. Tired is all. How's my girl?' Coming into the kitchen, he threw his lunchbox into the sink. 'Hug?'

'Yes please,' I said.

'You've got your coat on. I thought you weren't going

to your dad's today?'

'No, I needed to get a few bits from the corner shop, left it last minute. Saturday tea okay?'

'It's Tuesday.'

'I know, but I thought egg and chips would be just the thing for a growing lad.'

'Me or Bean?'

'Both of you.'

It wasn't until much later, after we'd eaten, cleared up and caught the news headlines, that I was able to think again about the envelopes. The more I thought about it the more it looked as though both letters had been sent from someone who knew something about Joel's accident, or thought they did. It sickened me to imagine that someone wanted to make money from someone's misfortune and as I lay in bed that night I rehearsed several conversations with this evil individual. If blackmail was at the heart of it and if I could prove it, then he would get his comeuppance with a spell in prison. But guesswork and solid evidence are two different things.

I would tell dad about the letters. His eyes might not work, but I'd learned over the years dad didn't need sight to work out what was going on.

Chapter 29

'Poirot,' I asked earnestly, 'have you made up your mind about this crime?'

'Yes – that is to say, I believe I know how it was committed.'

'Ah!'

'Unfortunately, I have no proof beyond my surmise, unless...'

The Mysterious Affair at Styles - Agatha Christie

Thursday morning the rain was lashing down and I was tempted to stay curled up under my warm blankets. Then I thought of Zara and any selfish thoughts vanished.

When I arrived at dad's he was already hovering by the front door with his jacket on and Charlie sitting alert beside him.

'Just out walking? It's a bit late for his stroll, isn't it?' I said.

'No, that was two hours ago. We got soaked. Now we're all dried off and ready and waiting for you. We're going to see Zara, aren't we?'

'Have I told you recently how much I love you?'

'Maybe, but it's always nice to hear.'

'Thanks dad, really. It means a lot. I know you're not comfortable with this, but I'm certain you'll make a difference.'

'Come on, let's get going. I've only got one patient today at 3pm, so we've plenty of time.'

Although dad was confident walking around the town, he rarely caught a bus. At least if he did then I made sure I was with him. Charlie did a great job, but negotiating a dog as well as bus fare could present a challenge.

The bus was on time and fairly empty, which was a surprise given the weather, but also a relief. We sat near the front and made sure Charlie's long legs weren't blocking the route to the back of the bus. Dad was quiet and I guessed he was feeling apprehensive.

'We'll try to get her talking, I'm sure with you there she'll be more relaxed,' I said. 'She's always liked you. For those last couple of years at school she spent more time round our house than her own.'

'Yes, I remember all that music drowning out my wireless,' he said, smiling. 'Let's just take it a step at a time, but don't expect too much. She's been through a lot and I'm sure her emotions are struggling to keep up with events.'

Dad was right, I always had high expectations and then had to cope with being let down when things didn't go the way I hoped. Whereas Greg and dad rarely had preconceptions - perhaps it was a man thing.

As we approached the squat we had to negotiate our way through the litter and general debris, making sure that Charlie didn't step on any of the broken glass laying in the gutters.

'Okay, this is it. We're here. Shall we all go in together or should I go in first and tell her you're here?' I said.

'Let's go in together, Charlie may ease the situation for us.'

I pushed the door and we walked into the gloom. The stench of stale smoke and body odour was as strong as ever and it took me a while for my eyes to adjust to the darkness. The three mattresses were still on the floor, with the tattered blankets thrown in a pile in one corner of the room.

'Hello again,' the voice came from the far side of the squat and looking over I realised it was the blonde-haired lad I'd met on my previous visits. 'If you're here for Zara, you've had a wasted journey,' he said. 'She's not around.'

Even in the dim light I could tell Charlie was longing to explore the musty smells and probably fancied his chances of snuffling up remnants of food. Instead, he was on his best behaviour, standing close to dad, looking up at him.

'Do you know where she's gone?' dad asked.

'This is my dad, he's known Zara since we were at school together,' I said.

'Sorry, I can't help you. I don't know where she is.'

I wanted to sit on the floor and cry, except there were two pressing reasons not to, the first being the dirt, and the second being the definite probability that I wouldn't be able to get up again. Bean was increasingly impeding my movement, or I was eating too many biscuits. Nevertheless, tears came; I'd found Zara only to lose her again and the whole thing was starting to overwhelm me.

'Has Zara spoken to you much since she's lived here?' my dad asked.

'We don't intrude on each other's lives, we just share a living space. I'm Luke by the way. I know she's been sad, when she's not asleep she spends a lot of time crying.'

'Who else lives here with you? There's a third mattress?' I said.

'It's spare now. It used to be Dee's, but she moved out.'

I remember Zara mentioning she'd given her overcoat to someone called Dee and I wondered if she'd gone to find her.

'I don't suppose you know where Dee went?'

'Dee's family had money, but they threw her out when they found out she was taking drugs. She's had a difficult time of it, worse than the rest of us.'

'The rest of us?'

'Yeah, we've all tried a bit of this and that, but Dee got caught up with a bloke, he introduced her to the hard stuff.'

'LSD?'

'I think so, yeah.'

'She's trying to turn her life around. Zara was a good friend to her. Perhaps Dee went back home. Anything's possible. Is it okay if I say hi to your dog?'

Dad made a small hand gesture, indicating to Charlie that he could move forward and Luke bent down to stroke him.

'What about you, son?' dad said.

'I'm okay. Just trying to work out the meaning of life.'

'That might take you a while then. How do you live, where do you get the money to buy food?'

'I play this,' he said, strumming his guitar. 'I do alright, enough to get by.'

'We wish you well,' dad said.

'How long have you been blind?' Luke said.

'Oh, a few years now.'

'Is it hard, not being able to see the sky?'

'I can still see it, I've got my memories.'

'There's things I've seen I wish I hadn't.'

'It's been a pleasure meeting you, son,' dad said, holding out his hand. Luke stood and held dad's hand in his.

'Likewise,' he said. 'If Zara comes back I'll tell her you came. I can see why she talks about you both, you're good people.'

We left the squat and walked in silence back to the bus-stop.

'What now?' I asked dad, once we were on the bus.

'I have no idea,' he said. 'Maybe we need her to make the next move?'

'But that means doing nothing.'

'Sometimes that's all you can do.'

'If I could find out more about Dee, that would give me a lead.'

'You heard what Luke said, he doesn't know where Dee has gone. If she's gone back to her family to try to sort herself out, then the last thing you want to do is interfere.'

'The only way I'm going to find Zara is by doing just that. Interfering.'

The bus took a corner a bit too fast and dad and I were both thrown forward in our seats. Charlie made a quiet bark, as if to reprimand the driver.

'You okay?' I said, once we were back on the straight again.

'I'm fine. You don't need to worry about me. What about you? You didn't bump that baby of yours, did you?'

'No, Bean is hardy. Takes after its granddad.'

'I like the sound of that.'

'Granddad, or Gramps? Any preference?'

'Let Bean decide, shall we? Crikey, what a thought. My little Janie, a mum.'

'Er, yes, strange thought, isn't it? Do you think I'll be any good at it?'

'You will be perfect. And don't forget that husband of yours, he's going to make a great dad.'

'You don't believe Zara would be silly enough to take hard drugs, do you?'

'I don't know, love, but whatever she has decided to do you need to accept it's her decision. We're each of us responsible for the choices we make.'

When we got back to dad's I remembered the envelopes. I took them out of my jacket and laid them on the kitchen table.

'You remember I told you about an envelope that turned up a while back, with a press cutting?'

'Yes, why?'

'Well, I've had another one.' I read the letter out to dad while he drank his tea.

'Some guttersnipe trying to make money out of someone's misery. It's a nasty thing and the product of a sick mind,' he said.

I sighed a little too loudly. I didn't want dad to worry about me, but as each day passed I felt like I was losing my grip on the situation. I wanted to take a trip in Dr Who's tardis back to those easy schooldays, when everything was possible and the most complicated thing to concern me was which shoes to wear.

'Don't lose your focus,' dad said, reading my mind. 'Talk me through what you've found out so far.'

'Joel is run down by an unknown person. Zara claims she is responsible. But you know what Poirot says? That the first instinct of the criminal is to divert suspicion from himself - or herself in this case. If Zara had done it she'd hardly be admitting it now, after all this time. There's no way that Zara is a criminal, I'm certain of that, if nothing else.'

'Okay, what's next in your synopsis?'

224

'Greg saw Joel and Zara out running together, happy and in love.'

'Anything else?'

'Zara runs away from our house and on the day she leaves Mr Peters sees her at the cemetery, putting a note behind the gravestone, which I've found. Mr Peters doesn't report the sighting until months later.'

'Why do you think that is?' dad says.

'Because he didn't know people were looking for her?'

'Maybe.'

'What? You think there's another reason? Do you reckon Mr Peters knows more than he's saying?'

'Maybe.'

'C'mon, tell me what you're thinking. You're the ex-detective remember. I'm just a probationer.'

'Well, it could be Mr Peters has seen more than he's letting on. Maybe, just maybe, he's worked out a way of making a bit of cash on the side. There's not much money in running a newsagents. The last couple went bust, didn't they?'

'Oh, crikey, dad. What about Owen? I need to factor him in somewhere.'

'I'm surprised you've had time to come to work. You're not letting your library work suffer, are you? You were lucky to get that job, you need to hang on to it.'

'Owen was in love with Zara. Still is, I'm sure. He hated Joel and we know he has a temper. Maybe he had something to do with the accident? His dad said the last time he came back to visit was about three months ago. That's the same time Zara went missing.'

Dad shook his head, his expression showing more than mild concern.

'Another idea I've had,' I said, reflecting that perhaps I had achieved more than I thought.

'Which is?'

'Petula. What if her dad found out about Joel, perhaps he wanted to teach Joel a lesson for treating his daughter so badly. It could be that it all got out of hand?'

'Okay, this is the point at which you really do have to involve the police. I mean it, Janie. It's getting too dangerous for my liking and Greg would have an absolute fit if he knew the half of what you've been up to. Promise me you'll take these envelopes and their contents to the police and let them pursue it.'

'I promise.' I didn't need to cross my fingers behind my back when I agreed. I said I'd take the letters, but I had no intention of telling the police about the squat. I had to protect Zara for as long as it took to find out the truth.

Chapter 30

Then, suddenly, he asked: 'Are you a judge of finger-marks, my friend?'

'No,' I said, rather surprised, 'I know that there are no two finger-marks alike, but that's as far as my science goes.'

'Exactly.'

The Mysterious Affair at Styles - Agatha Christie

The officious Detective Sergeant Bright made me wait fifteen minutes before showing me into the same airless room we'd sat in before. Once again he brought with him a dirty ashtray and a packet of cigarettes. I had to smile when I realised he also had a glass of water in his hand. He put it down in front of me and I nodded my thanks.

'I understand you've something to tell us about Zara Carpenter?'

'Well, yes, kind of,' I said and placed the two envelopes in front of him. 'I received this one a few weeks ago and this one the other day.'

'You do know that withholding evidence is a crime?'

'I'm not withholding them, they are here in front of you.'

'You've taken your time to show these to us. Why is that?'

'Well, I didn't think anything of it. At least not the first one, I thought it was just a childish prank. Then, when I got the second one I wondered if there might be more to it.'

'I see,' he said, taking off his glasses and peering more closely at the envelopes. I went to pick one of them up.

'Don't touch them,' he said, in a voice well suited to an army sergeant major.

'I was only going to point out how the handwriting is the same on both of them. Do you see? And it's the same writing on the letter that's inside this one.' I pointed, taking care not to touch anything.

'Fingerprints, you see. We can get a lot of information from fingerprints,' he said.

'I've already touched them, I've opened them and shown them to my dad.'

'Your father? How is he involved?'

'He's not involved, he's just my dad. He used to be a policeman, so he's switched on about evidence and all that stuff, in fact he was the one who told me to bring them here to show you.'

'Well, he did the right thing there. Used to be a policeman, you say? Local, is he?'

'Yes, but it was years ago, before your time.'

'Couldn't stick it, then?'

'He was a brilliant detective, actually,' I could hear my voice escalating in pitch as I rose to my dad's defence. 'He had an accident, he's blind. So that makes police work kind of difficult, as you can imagine.'

'I'm sorry to hear that. Now, let's concentrate on the matter in hand, shall we?'

He took a pair of thin plastic gloves from his jacket pocket and put them on. Then he carefully opened the first envelope and slid out the press cutting, smoothing it out flat on the desk.

'It's about Zara.'

He said nothing, but continued to open the second envelope and was quiet as he read the letter.

228

'How does this person know about my friendship with Zara? It's clear they're trying to scare me,' I said.

He didn't reply, but put the contents back in their respective envelopes and removed the gloves.

'I have a theory,' I said.

The detective shrugged his shoulders. 'So did Einstein,' he said, with sarcasm.

'Blackmail.'

'That's a serious accusation.'

'It's a serious crime.'

'We need proof.'

'You have it there, in front of you.'

'This is proof of nothing, except someone who has decided they'll have a laugh at your expense and give you a bit of a runaround. Take my advice, Miss...'

'Mrs.'

'My advice to you would be to leave this to the professionals. Don't go meddling in things you don't fully understand. Go home to your husband and let us make our own enquiries.'

'That's just it, you don't. What have you done since you had the new lead?'

'That's not any of your business, now is it? I think we're finished here. I'd just like to take your fingerprints if I may and your father's if he agrees, to eliminate them.'

'Do you think they will help you?'

'I beg your pardon?'

'Will the letters help you with your search for Zara?'

'I'm not at liberty to discuss the case with you, but I thank you for bringing this evidence to our attention. And now, Miss, I bid you good-day.' He stood up, pushed his chair back from the table and looked at me expectantly.

'Will you let me know what happens, if you work out who sent them?'

'The desk sergeant will take your fingerprints and if you could ask your father to come in to the station as soon as possible?'

'Right, yes,' I said, as he ushered me out of the room and handed me over to the desk sergeant. Having my fingerprints taken gave me a rush of excitement, before I reminded myself this wasn't a game or a scene from a drama, it was real and scary. Zara could be in danger and I wouldn't be able to rest easy until I knew she was safe.

My best chance now was for Zara to turn up again at the squat so I could try to understand why she thought she was to blame for Joel's death. Hercule Poirot would have solved the case long before now.

I wondered if I should tell her I knew about her attempted suicide. Owen's violent streak was also on my mind; Zara was the only person who could explain the truth about the day Owen hit her. But I didn't want to scare her. At this stage I was scaring myself with the thought of what might have happened.

My Friday session in the library van was so busy I barely had time to think, but just as I was tidying up ready to close for the day I had a last-minute customer.

'Hello, it's Janie, isn't it? Gran told me you'd taken over from her. Says you do an excellent job.'

'Thanks, you must be Libby. Phyllis has told me a lot about you, you're her favourite grandchild.'

'Yes, well, her only one.'

'And you're living down in Devon?'

'Cornwall, near Falmouth. At least I was, I've decided to move back here. I miss Gran too much and my job down there is boring. I need a new challenge.'

'You're a journalist, is that right?'

'Yes, I've been on a local rag down there and the most exciting thing to happen is when one of the locals catches a prize-winning fish. I thought there might be more going on here. I've managed to get a job with the *Tidehaven Observer*. You never know, I might get the chance to report on a juicy murder.'

I hoped she was joking, but let the remark go unanswered.

'Well, it's lovely to meet you, I'm sure your gran will be pleased to have you nearby. She's a special lady,' I said.

'I know, I'm lucky to have her. She's got a soft spot for you, you know. Always on about your undiscovered potential. Am I too late to choose a book?'

Meeting Libby meant I had the means of publicising all the discrepancies concerning Joel's death and Zara's disappearance, but I couldn't risk it. For one thing the police would probably charge me with interfering in a criminal case and then there was the problem of letting people know I'd tracked Zara down. I had to keep that discovery secret until I could determine for sure whether Zara was at risk. And right now the whole truth felt even more elusive.

Greg suggested a Saturday night out at the pub. A few of his darts mates would be there and I guessed they were hoping to talk tactics before the next match. With the thought of a night out, I'd spotted a closing down sale in one of the clothes shops the last time I was in Brightport. So, I planned to combine a shopping trip with a quick visit to the squat in the hope Zara might have returned, or at least that Luke might have more news.

It was a crisp, sunny morning and Brightport town centre was buzzing with people who were glad to see blue skies, despite the chilly start to the day. I got off the bus in Town Hall Square and planned to walk round to the squat before browsing for clothes. A crowd had gathered around a young musician and as I edged my way through to the front there was Luke, sitting on a small fold-up stool, playing his guitar. He'd put a cap on the floor beside him and people had already shown their appreciation by half filling it. He finished playing, to rapturous applause and more tossing of coins. I ferreted in my bag for my purse, moved forward to put the money into the cap and then someone caught my eye.

As soon as I turned to get a better look, she also turned and started to walk away.

'Zara, wait,' I called out.

A couple of people looked over at me, but she didn't turn around and despite my fastest pace I couldn't catch up with her.

'Zara, stop.'

Perhaps it was the urgency in my voice, or perhaps she felt sorry for her poor pregnant friend. She stopped walking and waited while Luke's admirers filtered past.

'How are you? Have you been staying with Dee? Luke said he thought you might have been there?' I gestured to a bench, encouraging her to sit beside me.

We sat side by side and I watched her as she looked into the distance, her focus on the skyline. 'Yes, Dee is a good friend, she's had a tough time of it, but I'm sure she's through the worst of it now.'

'I hope I'm a good friend too?'

'Yes, of course, I didn't mean…it's just that Dee has

been coming off drugs, she's made it up with her parents, they've been great. I stayed with her, helped her through it, at least I like to think I helped.'

'I'm sure you did, you know exactly what it's like to be in a dark place. You can understand better than most.'

She was wearing a brightly coloured Indian cotton dress, with a burgundy woollen shawl wrapped around her shoulders.

'I love that dress, it brings out all the very best in you.'

'It was a gift from Dee, the positive news is she is really back on track. She's off the drugs completely and even talking about going back to college.'

'That's down to you. Sounds like she's been through a lot, but then so have you. Will you let me help you, just like you helped Dee?'

'You've already done a lot for me. You and Greg. You put up with me for a year, it can't have been easy.'

'What made you go that day, Zara? Did something happen? Did someone threaten or scare you?'

She looked at me and shook her head. 'I'd been a burden on you for a whole year, it wasn't fair.'

'Was that the only reason? Are you sure you weren't scared of something, of someone?'

'A year had passed and I felt exactly the same. The pain didn't get any easier. I relive every minute and it never changes, it's always black. I knew I had to get out of your lives.'

'Zara, can you bear to tell me what happened that night, the night of Joel's accident. The thing is, well I've found out a few things, there are other people who might have wanted to harm Joel.'

'No-one else was there,' she said, but there was a hesitancy in her voice.

'Tell me what happened.'

She took a deep breath and then started to speak and as she did her whole body seemed to relax, as though she was relieved to be able to share the dreadful memories.

'You remember Joel had taken up running. Well, a few times he'd gone out late, when it was almost dark, and when he got back there was a smell about him that was nothing to do with sweat. It was a smell I knew too well, a perfume. So that evening I followed him. I kept back in the shadows, he didn't know I was there. I was right of course.'

'Right about what? What did you see?'

'Not what, who. My sister. Joel and Gabrielle hugging and kissing, that's what I saw.'

'Your sister? But surely she wouldn't…'

'Oh, my sister would and has, with every boy I've ever loved.'

'But Joel, he doted on you. He wouldn't have cheated on you, and with your own sister?'

'He would and did. I knew, at least I suspected. I waited until they'd finished their assignation. She walked off and when she was out of sight I caught up with him, confronted him. We had a blazing row. He shouted at me, told me I had no right to follow him, said I didn't own him, he could do what he wanted and there was nothing I could do about it.'

'It must have been terrible.'

'Then I started pleading with him, I told him I loved him, that he'd hurt me and that I'd forgive him, provided he promised never to see her again.'

'What did he say?'

'He laughed at me. Then he grabbed me and kissed me, long and hard on the lips. There was no love in that

234

kiss, it was the last kiss we had.'

'Oh, Zara, you poor thing. What happened next?'

'I don't know, that's just the thing. I left him there laughing, I could hear his laughter as I ran away. I still hear it now, at night, it's inside my head, sometimes I think I'm going mad.' She grabbed the edge of her shawl and twisted it into a tight ball. Her voice was shaky and her breathing heavy.

'It wasn't your fault, don't you see. He must have just run out in front of the car, you can't blame yourself.' I tried to take her hands in mine for reassurance, but she pulled away from me and stood up.

'If I'd stayed with him, then it wouldn't have happened. Or if I'd never gone there in the first place, if we hadn't argued. It's my fault, Janie, I killed him.'

Chapter 31

'Don't say it! Oh, don't say it! It isn't true! I don't know
what put such a wild – such a dreadful – idea into my
head!'
'I am right, am I not?' asked Poirot.
'Yes, yes; you must be a wizard to have guessed. But it
can't be so – it's too monstrous, too impossible.'
The Mysterious Affair at Styles - Agatha Christie

I had all I needed and there was just one person I had to
confront. I noticed a taxi parked outside Gabrielle's flat
when I arrived. I rang the bell and heard her call out, 'I'll
be right down.' I was about to ring again to announce
myself, when the door opened and there she stood,
wearing an emerald green coat and carrying a multi-
coloured bag.

'Oh, it's you,' she said.

'Yes, I want to ask you a few more questions, about
Zara.'

'I can't stop, that's my taxi and he won't want to be
kept waiting.'

'Are you going for long?' I nodded towards the bag,
which she handed to the taxi driver.

'A few days, maybe longer, it's not fixed.'

'I'd like to talk to you, when you're back?'

'There's nothing I can tell you that I haven't already.
To be honest with you, you're becoming rather tiresome.
Zara will appear if or when she wants to. I have my own
life to lead and she has hers. Now I must go.'

'Right, yes, well,' I said and with that she got into the
taxi.

There has been more than one occasion during this

search when I wished I had a camera with me. I didn't yet know the implications, but I did know that a photograph of Gabrielle's bag, now in the boot of the taxi would have piqued the interest of the police. The tapestry bag was identical to the one I packed for Zara on the day Joel had died, the same one that sat on the chair beside her bed all the time she lived with us. The same bag that Mr Peters had mentioned that Zara was carrying the day he saw her in the cemetery, the day she disappeared.

I opened the car door and slid onto the back seat, next to Gabrielle.

'What do you think you're doing?'

'I'm coming with you. I'm staying with you until you give me some answers, until you tell me the whole truth.'

'Where do you get off poking your nose into other people's business? You're not a policewoman, you're just a pathetic librarian. Go back to your books, Janie, and leave me in peace.'

The taxi driver was waiting for an instruction to pull away, either with or without his additional passenger.

'I'm going nowhere, at least I'm going wherever you're going,' I said. 'Where is that? The driver is waiting for you to tell him.'

'Tidehaven Railway Station, please driver.' Gabrielle's voice quivered with irritation.

'Where are we going from there?' I kept my voice firm and steady, but was beginning to wonder what would happen once Gabrielle stepped onto a train. I could hardly follow her once she'd left Tidehaven, or I'd be returning to divorce proceedings.

'I've nothing more to say to you. You can keep asking, but you'll get no more from me,' she said.

'How is it that you have Zara's bag?'

'What?'

'Zara's bag, the holdall you gave to the driver to put in the boot. I know it's Zara's because I packed it for her the night Joel died, the night she came to stay with us.'

'It's not Zara's, it's mine.'

'I don't understand.'

'We're twins, our mother delighted in buying us identical presents. So lacking in originality.'

'You both have tapestry bags?'

'You're not that sharp, are you? No wonder you can't find Zara.'

'That's where you're wrong.'

'Am I?'

'Yes, I've found her. I've known where she is for a while now.'

'Where is she? I'm her sister, I'm entitled to know.'

'You are not entitled to anything. I have no intention of disclosing her whereabouts.'

'Have you told the police?'

'No.'

'You can be charged for withholding evidence. Perhaps I'll tell the police. I'm sure they'd be pleased to hear from me.'

'Yes, why don't you do that. I'm sure they'll be very keen to hear what you've got to say. In fact, we could go to the police station together. I can tell them what I know about what really happened the night Joel died, and you can fill in the rest.'

'What do you know? You weren't there.'

'No, but your sister was, wasn't she? She followed Joel, she saw him and you kissing. She found out about the two of you and your seedy affair.'

'My poor sister. Her first boyfriend gets beaten up and

238

her last one gets run over. It's quite funny when you think about it.'

'Funny? You think it's funny what she's had to go through?'

I'd been trying to keep my voice level and calm, but now I was so incensed I wanted to shake her. I noticed the taxi driver looking anxiously in the rear-view mirror and guessed that he couldn't wait to reach the station so he could finally rid himself of the pair of us. We passed the rest of the journey in silence. I let Gabrielle pay once we arrived and kept close to her as she walked through the covered entrance into the railway station.

'You think she's whiter than white?' she said. 'Poor little Zara, always the victim. Well, the truth of it is that she's manipulative, controlling and selfish.'

'Selfish? What's she ever done that's been selfish?'

'She knew how I felt about Joel. He and I could have made a real go of it, we were both the same, driven, ruthless. He knew what he wanted and so did I. But Zara, oh no, she wasn't prepared to let him go. She wanted him for herself, even though they'd never have been really happy. She was too much of a pushover for a man like Joel.'

'You stole him from her though, didn't you?'

'She probably threatened him, told him she'd kill herself if he ended it. Whatever it was, he fell for it.'

'I don't understand, what is it you think happened?'

'I don't think, I know. I saw them.'

'What did you see?'

'I saw him kiss her. He'd promised me, he said he'd finish with her, but he lied to me.'

We stood to one side of the ticket office. People were milling around us, but thankfully no-one was within

239

earshot.

'What did you do, Gabrielle?'

'Why do you think I did anything?' She glared at me, her mouth set in a thin line, her forehead creased with tension.

'You can't run away from this. It will haunt you for the rest of your life.'

She started to walk away and I followed her to an empty bench near to the ticket barrier.

'I only meant to scare him, to let him know I'd caught them together, teach him a lesson. I was so angry.' Her voice was quieter now, uncertain, almost childlike.

'It was you? You drove into him?'

'I was raging. I must have pressed too hard on the accelerator.' She looked beyond me as she spoke, as though she was back in that moment, behind her steering wheel, heading towards the man she professed to love.

'You stupid woman, you're the one who's not that sharp,' I said, so angry I wanted to shake her. 'There was no love in that kiss, he was taunting your sister, he never loved her.'

She stared at me, unblinking, in shock. Then, she took a deep breath and all her haughtiness fell away, leaving a pathetic figure.

'You could have saved him,' I said, 'instead you were too worried about saving your own skin. You left him to die.'

People brushed past us on their way to the platforms, but neither of us moved.

'He must have seen you driving towards him.' The dreadful waste and injustice of what I was being told made me seethe.

'I see his face. When I close my eyes I can see the

240

disbelief in his eyes. He didn't move, he just stood there.'

As I looked at her face all the beauty of Zara reflected back at me.

'It was you who Mr Peters saw in the cemetery that day, you who put the note behind the gravestone, wasn't it? He thought you were Zara.'

'How do you know about the note?'

'I found it. I still have it. I'll be giving it to the police. You know you'll have to confess, don't you?'

'No-one knows, only you. You could let me go, I'm not a killer. I didn't mean to do it.'

She went to grab my hand, to plead with me, but I stood back from her.

'That day in the cemetery, why did you have your holdall with you? I thought it was Zara who Mr Peters saw, because of that bag.' I pointed at the tapestry holdall that now sat beside her.

'How do you expect me to remember what bag I had with me?'

I could see now that she was devious enough to make any scenario work in her favour.

'Just tell me one thing, why did you stay in Tamarisk Bay? You could have moved far away. You might have got away with it.'

'I needed to be near him. I did love him, you know.' Her head was bowed now and her voice quiet and wavering.

As I looked at her the remaining pieces of my unfinished jigsaw slotted into place.

'You wrote the letters, didn't you? You tried to point the finger at your sister. You steal her boyfriend, run him down, leave him for dead and then you try to frame her for it. You are evil. You don't deserve to have a sister.'

241

'You can't prove any of it,' the vitriol was back. Any contrition she might have felt was short-lived and now she was begging for her life once more. 'Anything you tell the police I'll just deny. It'll be your word against mine.'

'What about fingerprints?' I said. 'Your fingerprints will be all over those letters. That will be all the police need to prove you planned to frame your sister. You are the only person who knows the truth about what happened that night and that's because you did it, you murdered Joel.'

I wished I had handcuffs so that I could cuff her there and then, but she made no attempt to move. She said no more and in the end, I think she was relieved the truth was finally out.

I called the same taxi driver over and asked him to take us to the police station. He was reluctant at first, I'm sure he was loath to get mixed up with the strangest customers he must have had that day.

As I handed her over to the disparaging Detective Sergeant Bright, I allowed myself a moment to feel smug. It would have been nice if he'd given me a pat on the back for my efforts, but I wasn't holding my breath. For all I had learned from Poirot, one distinct difference between us was that I had no desire to jump for joy that the crime had been solved. Uncovering the truth was the right thing to do, but it gave me no pleasure to know such evil could hide away in someone's heart.

While Gabrielle was being processed, I asked to speak to DS Bright in private and we returned to the little airless room that I'd sat in on two previous occasions.

'There's something that's been puzzling me all along,' I

242

said, anticipating a stonewalling by way of reply.

'You know I can't talk about the case. We're grateful for what you've done, but that's as far as it goes.'

'It's just that I don't understand why you announced the new lead.'

'Which new lead?'

'Well, you only had one, didn't you? Mr Peters, the chap who said he'd seen Zara the day she left our house. At the cemetery. Although it turns out it wasn't even her, it was her sister.'

'I'm not at liberty to explain to you the machinations of the police force. However, one good turn deserves another, I suppose. The information Mr Peters gave us wasn't significant in any way. Miss Carpenter left your house that day and if she went via the cemetery, well, it didn't give us any pointers as to where she had gone from there.'

'Why was it on the news then? You must have thought it important to announce it to the press?'

'The decision was a tactical one. Our investigation into Miss Carpenter's whereabouts had drawn a blank. It's unusual for someone to disappear like that, with no indication she was planning to leave. That, together with the circumstances in which her boyfriend died, it left a question mark, it made us believe there was more to the case.'

'And every time I came in here you made out I was making a fuss, that it was perfectly normal for her to just disappear.'

He didn't respond to my accusation, but instead, he continued, 'When Mr Peters came to us with his report we released the news to the press because we hoped a television broadcast may flush Zara Carpenter out.'

'You talk as though you thought she was to blame. She's the victim here, Gabrielle didn't only run her boyfriend down, she tried to frame her sister for it.'

'Joel Stewart was the victim. We realised there was more to his death when we found the note.'

'Which note?'

'The one hidden behind Mr Stewart's gravestone.'

'You found that note? But how?'

'When Mr Peters told us he'd seen Miss Carpenter in the cemetery we did a fingertip search of the area. We found the note, which indicated Mr Stewart's death was not a straightforward road traffic accident.'

'Why did you leave the note there? Wasn't it evidence?'

'We thought the perpetrator may have had second thoughts and returned to the grave to retrieve it. And then you came along.'

'You knew I'd taken it?'

'We've been keeping a watch on the gravestone. Murder is a serious crime, Mrs Juke.'

'So you used me? You knew I'd have more luck in finding Zara than you.'

'I'll admit it, you've helped us a lot. We were hoping the news coverage would flush out something, someone. We just didn't quite know how, when or who.'

'Did you know about the antipathy between Zara and her sister?'

'We guessed. When a much-loved sister goes missing it doesn't normally result in the level of disinterest Miss Gabrielle Carpenter showed whenever we spoke to her.'

'You thought I'd have more luck in extracting a confession than the might of Tidehaven police force?'

'As I said earlier, we're very grateful for all you've

done. You have a flair for seeking out the truth.
Perhaps you've inherited it from your father? You said he
used to be a detective, isn't that right? Or maybe from
those books of yours? Of course, she'll need to repeat
her confession to us, there's no saying whether she'll
change her story. You've been extremely helpful, Mrs
Juke, but this is where we take over. Your role in this
case is now over.'

'You know Gabrielle wrote the two letters, the ones I
gave you. It was never about blackmail, she just wanted
to point the finger, to cast doubt. Her own sister, can you
believe it?'

'You'd be surprised at what people will do. We see the
worst of human beings in this job. I'll repeat my advice
to you, stick with the day job. Books won't let you down,
they won't get you into dangerous situations, or give you
sleepless nights.'

I didn't know whether to be irritated by all DS Bright had
told me, or proud I'd been able to bring a successful
conclusion to the case, a case that had stumped the police,
whatever he said. His words about the darker side of
human nature reminded me that real life could be as bleak
as some of the tales I'd spent years reading. Maybe more
so.

I'd done all I could and whatever punishment was to
be meted out to Gabrielle was out of my hands. My
intention had always been to look out for my friend and
that's what I'd done, so now I could rest easy. But first
there were a few people I needed to speak to and a few
apologies I needed to make.

Chapter 32

All the things that one had read a hundred times – things
that happen to other people, not to oneself.
The Mysterious Affair at Styles - Agatha Christie

I wanted to let dad know the outcome of the day's events
and I needed to come clean with Greg. But first I had to
tell Zara the truth about Joel's death so she could stop
blaming herself.

This time I found her and Luke sitting on a bench on
Brightport seafront. I'd walked towards the squat from
Town Hall Square, not expecting to find them en route.
They were deep in conversation as I approached.

'Hello again, mind if I join you?'

'We were just talking about you,' Zara said.

'Nothing too awful, I hope.'

'I was trying to persuade Zara to go a bit easier on you,
you're on her side and she's lucky to have a friend who
cares,' Luke said, taking Zara's hand in his. There was
something brighter about her, not just what she was
wearing. I noticed her face was less pale and there was a
light back in her eyes. Perhaps she felt easier since
unburdening herself just a few hours earlier.

'I'm sorry I've made it difficult for you, Janie, I'm
grateful for all you've done, really I am.'

It was as though she had worked through some of her
fears and sorrows and although she wasn't quite out of
the tunnel yet, at least she could see the light at the end of
it.

'I have some news for you. It will be difficult for you
to hear, but now I know what happened to Joel that
night.'

'You do?'

Part of me wanted to save her from any more sadness, but she would hear from the police soon enough and it was better for her to hear it from me, rather than an objective stranger.

'I'm really sorry, Zara, it's worse than any of us could have guessed. You told me earlier that Gabrielle was there that night.'

'Yes, I saw them together and then she left.'

'Well, that's just it. She didn't leave. She saw you together. It seems Joel had promised her he was going to break it off with you, to come clean and to make a life with her. It wasn't just a fling, at least not from her point of view. So, when she saw him kiss you it made her wild.'

'Don't tell me, I don't want to know.' She buried her face in Luke's shoulder.

He stroked her hair and then said quietly, 'you need to hear this Zara, you need to know the truth about that night so that you can move forward with your life. Otherwise the not knowing will haunt you forever.'

I told them both all that Gabrielle had told me, maintaining as gentle a tone as possible. All the time I spoke Zara didn't lift her head from Luke's shoulder.

'What will happen to her?' Luke asked.

I shook my head. 'It's up to the police now. She's confessed, so that will stand in her favour. It wasn't premeditated, I suppose the French would call it a crime of passion.'

'All this time I thought it was my fault, that if I hadn't followed him that night then the accident wouldn't have happened. I was jealous of Gabrielle, but I can see now that what she felt for him was more to do with possession than love. If she had really loved him she could never

247

have done such a dreadful thing. Maybe she's right, she and Joel are the same kind of people, if he hadn't cheated on me with my sister it would have been someone else.'

I wasn't going to mention Petula, Zara had enough bad news to absorb without learning that her boyfriend had taken advantage of an innocent young girl.

'What about my parents, will they have to be told?' Zara sat up, exposing her tear-stained face and bloodshot eyes.

'The police will need to inform them. Gabrielle might like their support? There'll be a court case, of course, we'll both have to explain what we know. But I'll be beside you all the way.'

'She told you, didn't she?' Zara said.

I waited for her to explain.

'Gabrielle told you about my attempt at suicide?'

I nodded and let her continue.

'My parents never forgave me. All religions believe in the sanctity of life, but for Catholics suicide scores highly in their list of sins. I thought true confession would lead to forgiveness, but I don't think my mother saw it that way. Do you think she will be any less angry with a murderer?'

'Do you forgive your sister then?' I asked.

'No, but I feel sorry for her. She's destroyed three lives, Joel's, her own and mine.'

'She's only destroyed your life if you let her,' Luke said, gripping her hand in his. 'You have a chance to start again.'

'If I were you I'd grab that offer with both hands,' I said. 'Just think of all that serenading you'll enjoy and you won't even have to throw a coin in his hat.'

I hugged them both before I left and as I turned back

248

to wave they didn't even see me. They were turned towards each other, both of them smiling. It was the perfect picture.

All that was left now was for me to relate what had happened to the two most important men in my life. I decided to cheat by telling them at the same time, in the hope dad would come to my rescue if Greg lost his rag.

By the time I got home all I wanted was to sink into a bath, but that would have to wait.

'Greg, do you mind if we don't go out tonight? Dad's got a problem with his kitchen tap. I said you'd take a look at it,' I told him, as soon as he walked in the door.

'I can pop round tomorrow, if you like.'

'No, it's urgent, he can't even make a cuppa. I said we'd call round this evening.'

'I was looking forward to taking you out.'

'Well, you will be taking me out, it's just that it'll be to dad's. I'll cook while you fix the tap.'

'Oh blimey, Janie, I'm hopeless at plumbing, you need someone who knows what they're doing. Alex at work, I'll ask him to call in.'

'No, dad doesn't like strangers calling in.'

'He's not a stranger, I know him. Anyway, he has patients calling in every day - he doesn't know them.'

'Don't be awkward, come on. We haven't all had supper together for ages. It'll be fun.'

When we arrived at dad's and Greg watched him fill the kettle from a fully working kitchen tap, I knew I'd have to come clean pretty quickly.

'What's going on? Philip, your daughter has got me round here under false pretences. Do you know what it's all about?'

'Sit down, both of you,' I said. 'I need to tell you a few things. Greg, I need you to stay calm and listen, don't interrupt.'

They sipped their drinks while I recounted all that had happened over recent days. I skipped over anything to do with Mr Peters, Owen or Crystal, as it turned out none of that mattered, now I knew the truth.

When I finished speaking Greg shook his head and was quiet.

'What are you thinking? Are you cross with me?'

'I'm thinking I hope Bean isn't twins.'

'It's grim, isn't it? Like DS Bright said, there are some gruesome folk out there.'

'How can someone do that to their own sister? I can't bear the thought of it.'

'It makes me grateful I'm an only child,' I said, walking around to stand behind my dad. 'And even more grateful I have the best dad, who never tires of listening to me and has the best advice in the business.'

'Second only to Agatha?' dad said.

'Your daughter is wilful, impetuous and disobedient,' Greg said, looking at me as he spoke.

'Good job she has such a wonderful husband then, to keep her in line,' dad said.

'Well said, Philip. Yes, she's lucky to have me,' said Greg, moving away from me as I went to poke him in the ribs. 'And, of course, the feeling is mutual. Now the case of the missing Zara Carpenter has been well and truly solved, my wife can concentrate on preparing to become a mother. She'll settle down into family life and I'll come home to proper home-cooked meals every night. Slippers warmed by the fire, clothes neatly pressed, packed lunch prepared on a daily basis and my morning cup of tea all waiting for me each morning.'

'Do you plan to divorce me and marry someone else then?'

'Greg's right though, Janie,' dad said. 'It's time to put your sleuthing notebook away now and get your knitting needles out. Motherhood is a precious thing and you want to be well rested and well prepared when the little one arrives.'

'Okay, you both win. I'll behave, at least for a while.'

I left it a couple of days before I rang Libby. She thanked me several times for the scoop. Her approach was professional and after the interview she promised I could see the article before it went to press. Of course, we had to be careful that whatever her paper printed wouldn't jeopardise the criminal case.

Her focus was the personal story behind the tragedy. Her editor showed his delight by promoting her. No longer was she consigned to cover weddings and local fetes; he promised she would be the first on the scene for any significant news stories.

'We'll make a good team, you and I,' she joked, when she called in to the library van to tell me her news.

'A good team?'

'Yes, you ferret out the stories and I'll report them.'

'Don't let Greg hear you say that.'

'You're a natural, you've a nose for it.'

'Sticking it into everyone's business, you mean?'

'Zara is grateful you did.'

'Maybe.'

Dad, Greg and Zara had praised me for solving the crime, but part of me felt I'd been lucky, stumbling on the truth, rather than seeking it out. In 'Styles' Hastings

251

challenges Miss Howard, asking her, *'if you were mixed up in a crime, say a murder, you'd be able to spot the murderer right off?'* She was confident she could, *'I'd feel it in my fingertips if he came near me,'* she told him.

Well, for all my antipathy towards Gabrielle, there was never a moment when I thought her capable of running down poor Joel. As devious and deceitful as he was, he didn't deserve to die like that.

A quiet Wednesday morning in the library van gave me a chance to do very little. I didn't want to read, I didn't even want to think too much and was hoping I didn't have to talk to customers. I contented myself with dusting and tidying and as I was finishing the final fiction shelf, I heard the door open.

'Good morning,' he said, approaching the counter with a purposeful stride.

'Mr Furness, hello there. How can I help? It's the non-fiction you like, isn't it? I'm afraid we don't have anything new at the moment. If you have a request I can put it forward to the central library. They're helpful like that.'

'It's not a book I'm after,' he said, putting a copy of the local paper down on the counter. 'This is you, isn't it?' he asked, pointing to Libby's article about Zara.

'Er, yes.'

'You did well, made a better job of it than the police.'

'I was just helping out a friend.' His fixed stare was making me uncomfortable. I waited, hoping he would move over to the book shelves.

'The luggage ticket,' he said.

'Pardon?'

'The luggage ticket you have in your lost property box.

It's mine.'

'I thought...when I asked you before...'

'I lied.'

I took the box out from under the counter and lifted out the envelope containing the ticket.

'There you go,' I said, handing it to him.

He shook his head and put the envelope back into the box.

'You'll need it.'

'Why would I need it?'

'If you help me, you'll need it. Will you help me?'

His expression was impassive, but his voice was faltering. I rifled through the filing cabinets in my mind; Bean, Greg and Zara. My search for Zara had taught me I could be more than just a good mum and wife. Janie Juke, solving mysteries. I like the sound of that.

'Yes, I'll help you,' I said.

Thank you

As part of my research for the book I contacted The Keep, which provides a wonderful archive of East Sussex records: **http://www.thekeep.info/collections/** They helped to ensure the details about Janie's library van was as accurate as possible. Sussex Police were able to confirm the back story for Janie's father, Philip, all made sense.

Most authors will agree that writing can be a lonely pursuit. So I consider myself very fortunate to have the encouragement and support of some wonderful people. Janie might have withered along the way if it were not for them. My brilliant writing buddies, Chris and Sarah, and my brother, David, continue to offer me not only invaluable critiques, but inspiration to keep going. Heartfelt thanks also go to family and friends too numerous to list here. I am grateful to you all.

And, in the words of one of my favourite songs, my love and thanks go to my husband Al, who is *'the wind beneath my wings'*.

If you enjoyed *The Tapestry Bag,* turn the
page to read an extract from Isabella Muir's
second Sussex crime novel

Lost Property

This case takes Janie Juke back in time to the
Second World War, where she learns about secret
missions and brave deeds.

Chapter 1

'What's your definition of a secret?' I am sitting in dad's kitchen, at the Formica-covered table that has been the site of many of our important chats over the years.

'Let's have a think,' he says. 'Well, I suppose it's information that is not to be shared?'

'And a lie?'

'In essence, it's the same thing. A lie might be the words that are spoken in place of the secret, or the words that are not spoken. A lie can be the silence.'

A month ago, I ended a search for a friend. A week ago, I was asked to begin another search. But this time for a stranger.

'What's this talk about secrets and lies? Is there something you don't want to tell Greg?' My dad can't see my face, but he has always been able to read my mind.

'Yes, I made a sort of promise.'

'When you married him?' dad smiles.

My hesitation in replying doesn't go unnoticed.

'Sorry, I shouldn't tease you,' he continues. 'You mean a few weeks ago, when you agreed to settle down and plan for the arrival of your baby. Has something happened to make you change your mind?'

'I've been approached by someone to track down a woman.'

'And you're wondering whether to tell Greg?'

'Yes, he worries so much. I know it's only because he cares, but even so…'

'Ah,' dad says and smiles, small creases appearing around the edges of his eyes that I haven't noticed before. 'Is that husband of yours still enjoying his new job?'

256

'He loves it. He's learning the building trade and I'm learning the vocabulary. I can now give you the low-down on the importance of unbridged cavities, while being able to spot efflorescence at a glance. It's fascinating. Mr Mowbray says Greg will be building a wall before Christmas. Fastest apprenticeship known to man.'

'And your apprenticeship?'

'Exactly. I have a sneaky feeling I could be good at this investigating business.'

Some may say investigating is an odd pastime for a librarian and perhaps pastime is the wrong word. The truth is, I appear to excel at sticking my nose into other people's business. Much of the blame can be laid at the door of Agatha Christie. From an early age her books filled my shelves at home and now I have even greater access to them, via the library. I've learned a lot from Poirot.

'It doesn't have to be a competition, princess. You both have a chance to learn a new trade. Although being a competent librarian is important in itself.'

'I know, you're right.'

'Maybe Greg needs more time, to get used to the idea?'

'I don't have more time. Bean will be here in a few months. This case needs to be well and truly solved long before then. If it's to be solved at all.'

In the first couple of months of my pregnancy I discovered my little embryo resembled a kidney bean. I told Greg and the name stuck. Heaven help the poor child when it's born if we forget the name is temporary, or if we haven't settled on a new one.

'Can you tell me anything about this new case?' dad asks.

'One of my library customers has asked for my help.'

On the days when I don't help dad, I run the local mobile library. I have a regular route and plenty of regular customers. Mr Furness was a newcomer to the library and it was on his third visit to investigate the non-fiction shelves when he approached me to do some investigating of a different kind.

'He wants your help to find a woman? Is that all you know? What else has he told you about her?'

'Very little. There appears to be a mystery regarding a left luggage ticket.'

'Intriguing.'

'Mm, maybe.'

'What's the ticket got to do with the missing woman? Has this man given you the ticket? Has he asked you to do something with it?'

'In a way, yes. You know the lost property box I keep in the van?'

Since I've been in charge of the library van, I've gathered some fascinating items of lost property. Customers arriving on wet days frequently become so immersed in their browsing that they leave with their minds full of new stories and their hands empty of their umbrella - or walking stick. You would think that, once outside, with the rain pelting down, they would hastily return to salvage their winter protection. But my collection of six umbrellas and three walking sticks appears to prove otherwise. I keep the smaller items of lost treasure in a cardboard box under the counter in the van. The box contains an assortment of spectacles, gloves and mittens, a silk scarf, a snuff box and my favourite item, a single pink ankle sock - an adult's one at that. Now and again I wonder whether its owner will be hanging their washing on the line one day and have a sudden recollection of the day when they called into the mobile library and left a sock behind. It's a fanciful thought though, as it has remained in my box for almost a year now.

Dad waits calmly for me to continue. 'Talk me through it, if you like. It might help to clarify your thoughts,' he says.

'Okay, I'll refresh our drinks first though, shall I?'

With drinks made and the plate of digestives topped up, I recount to dad as much as I know about Hugh Furness.

On his first visit to the library I guessed that Mr Furness was a stranger to Tamarisk Bay, or at least I hadn't seen him before. As he walked through the van doorway he dipped down slightly, the smart Trilby that was perched on his head just missing the frame. Once inside, he held himself upright, all six feet something and removed his hat. He reminded me of an actor. He kept his dark grey gaberdine mac fastened firmly around his muscular frame, the belt pulled in around his middle, like a neatly wrapped parcel. The deep red silk cravat around his neck reflected its colour on his chin, giving him a ruddy glow.   Perhaps in his younger days he could have been a Robert Mitchum, or Gregory Peck.

He had only been in the van a short while, when the comfortable silence was disturbed by the raucous sound of a coughing fit. Once Mr Furness started coughing it seemed he could not stop. He was distressed, I was distressed and the result was that, as soon as he could catch his breath, he put his Trilby back on his head and

259

left, embarrassed perhaps at the scene he had caused. A few minutes later I noticed he had dropped a left luggage ticket.

Reuniting the left luggage ticket with its rightful owner would appear to be the easiest thing in the world. However, when Mr Furness returned a few days later, I explained about the ticket and offered it to him, but he denied all knowledge of the little slip of paper.

We all know about the concept of 'third time lucky', although its origin is yet to be proved. Nevertheless, superstition, or folklore, notwithstanding, it was on the gentleman's third visit when I was able to establish the connection between the left luggage ticket and my enigmatic customer.

Dad has been listening intently. 'What did he say to you? Did he explain why he'd told you the ticket wasn't his?'

'Not really. He just said, *I lied.*'

'That brings us back to our conversation earlier, about secrets and lies.'

'Exactly.'

'I don't like the idea that this Mr Furness has started off his dealings with you by lying. It doesn't bode well.'

'Mm, good point. Well, I've asked him to call back next Monday. Hopefully I'll be able to pin him down and find out more.'

'Remember to read between the lines - that's where you'll find the clues.'

'Now you sound like Poirot,' I say, giving dad a hug.

On Monday morning, as I park the van in my usual place on Milburn Avenue, there is Hugh Furness, waiting.

'Good morning, Mrs Juke,' he says, stepping into the van and removing his hat. His hair is pure white. I've noticed it before, but now everything about him has added significance. He may be my first official client. He is old enough to be going grey, perhaps, but white? I make a mental note to write my observation in my notebook.

'Hello there, you're nice and prompt,' I say.

He smiles. It's the first time I've seen him smile and it surprises me how much it changes his demeanour.

'Thank you for agreeing to help me. Where shall we start?' he says. There's a briskness in his voice, an urgency; this is not a man to be messed with.

'One step at a time, Mr Furness. I haven't agreed to anything yet.'

The smile fades away, leaving an expression that could be irritation. Equally, I know so little about this man, my attempts at reading his body language are as tricky as an Eskimo trying to understand smoke signals.

'There's a lot I need to ask you and plenty you'll want to share with me, I'm sure?' I say.

I can't tell whether he agrees, or if he thinks I have already overstepped some imaginary line. 'Let's arrange a meeting, shall we? Somewhere quiet.'

He raises an eyebrow.

'I know, libraries are quiet, but this is my place of work. We would have to stop speaking every time someone walks in.'

As if on cue, the door opens. Mrs Latimer, one of my regulars, is returning a couple of books. She approaches the counter, seemingly unaware she is interrupting. She wants to chat about her son, who is recovering from a nasty cold.

261

'Of course, Bobby's asthma is worse than ever,' she says. 'I'll have to keep him off school again, but I'm worried he'll never catch up. That's why I thought I would borrow a couple more books. We do a few lessons at home, but he's not keen. Says he'd rather be watching television. I ask you. When I was a youngster there was just the wireless and that would only go on for the news.'

I smile and nod, trying not to encourage her too much. While I'm listening to her chatting, Mr Furness moves away to browse the bookshelves. Moments later, as Mrs Latimer transfers her attention to the children's book section, he returns to the counter.

'Case in point,' he says.

'Yes. Let's choose a meeting place. Do you know the town well?'

'Not very.'

'There are some gardens, in the Maze Road area of town. I can show you on a street map, if you like?'

I take out a map of Tamarisk Bay and spread it over the counter.

'Just here,' I point. 'There's a little café, well in truth it's more of a shack. But if the weather is bad we can sit inside, if not we can wander around the gardens and chat. Does that sound okay?'

An imaginary conversation is playing in my mind. Greg is glaring at me in horror as I tell him I'm going to be wandering around Tensing Gardens with a man I barely know. Fortunately, Greg won't have to worry because I won't be telling him, at least not yet.

'Tensing Gardens is fine,' Mr Furness says, bringing my attention back to the here and now.

'Tomorrow afternoon? 4pm?'

'Certainly. Thank you, my dear,' he holds his hand out to shake mine. It feels as though I am agreeing a formal contract with a man I know nothing about, to undertake a job I have little experience of. Greg would call me impetuous, dad might use the word impulsive. My reckoning is that I'm just a little crazy.

'This is just a preliminary chat, you do understand? I don't know if I'll be able to help you.'

'I have nothing to lose,' he says, looking directly at me. His voice is firm and yet there is a hesitancy about him.

'Tomorrow then,' I say.

He nods, takes his hat from the counter and leaves.

My only other customer returns to the counter with her books.

'Didn't the gentleman find what he was looking for?' she asks.

'I'm not sure,' I reply.

Lost Property
is available now from Amazon on Kindle or in paperback.

Lightning Source UK Ltd.
Milton Keynes UK
UKHW04f0702050918
328323UK00001B/11/P

9 781872 889122